The
Man Haters
Club

a Bobby Bain novel

By Lisa Leader

This book is entirely a work of fiction. References to real people, events, establishments, organizations, or locales are intended only to provide a sense of authenticity, and are used in a fictitious manner. All other characters, and all incidents and dialogue, are drawn from the author's imagination and are not to be construed as real, but purely coincidental.

The Man Haters Club

Copyright @ 2019 by Lisa Leader

ISBN 978-1-7923-1315-8

Printed in the United States of America

Library of Congress Cataloging-in-Publication Data is on file at the Library of Congress, Washington, D.C.

Cover art by Cody Vance
Cover design by Martha Singleton, Next Big Step
Interior text design by Martha Singleton, Next Big Step
Editing and publishing by Next Big Step Editing & Publishing
www.nextbigsteppublishing.com

Dedication

Dedicated to the best storyteller ever: William Henry Leader, Jr.

My dad only read non-fiction. He especially loved biographies. He said there were too many interesting true things to read about and he didn't think he would ever finish all of them to start on fiction. He never traveled out of the United States only because he hadn't seen all the things he wanted to see here yet.

After he was diagnosed with lung cancer, I would take him to most of his chemo visits. I was working on my book at the time. I would read it to him while we waited and he would smile and shake his head as if to say, "Whose kid are you?" I suspected he secretly liked it.

Before he died he told me, "You know, I'm going to make an exception and I'm going to read your book."

I already knew that….

Chapter 1

Bobby had been sitting there for a while, just quietly observing the two well-dressed and obviously well-bred women. There was nothing better for him to do at the time, so he just enjoyed the music. Alison Krauss was his absolute favorite. He savored his single malt Scotch and watched the two women, who appeared to be carrying on quite an animated conversation.

Bobby and Liz went way back. They were classmates in medical school, ending up in New Braunfels, Texas working together at the same hospital. He was not quite as familiar with Natalie, although he recognized her from pictures in the society pages of the local newspaper. He knew she was a lawyer – and he absolutely despised that particular type of "blood-sucking vermin." Bobby didn't exactly know what she specialized in, but he assumed it was divorces. Pretty much ALL the good-looking women attorneys specialized in divorce litigation. And these two women were certainly attractive. It wasn't just the Scotch talking this time.

This was not the first time Bobby had noticed them together at The OutPost. He was starting to get very curious about them. Liz never mentioned that she was meeting Natalie, and he found it peculiar that he had now seen them together not once, but twice. The thought finally dawned on him that maybe this was something more than a mere social meeting. Perhaps, this was business…

When curiosity finally got the best of him, Bobby decided to saunter over to their table.

"Hello Liz," he said. "Fancy seeing you here without Adam."

"Good evening, Bobby," Liz said, not bothering to try to hide her annoyance with him. She turned to Natalie and said, "Natalie, this is Bobby Bain. He is the anesthesiologist that I usually operate with. We also share office space." Barely looking at him, Liz then said, "Bobby, this is Natalie Brennand," truly wishing that he would just leave after the quick introduction.

"Glad to make your acquaintance," he lied. "Sooo… what brings you here, Liz? Is there trouble in paradise?" he asked, while trying to hide his hopeful tone. Bobby had been wishing for nearly twenty years that Liz's relationship with her husband, Adam, would implode. Bobby had been deeply infatuated with the tall, vivacious blonde from the moment he first set eyes on her during medical school orientation.

"Can't two friends meet for a drink without SOMEONE starting gossip?" Liz immediately scolded him.

"Well – I see you here talking to a lawyer, so I just thought maybe you and

Adam…" Bobby added optimistically.

"Dr. Bain, I specialize in real estate law – and we aren't talking shop," Natalie interjected. "We are just discussing a few things that we have in common."

"Such as?" Bobby asked, not wanting to change the subject.

"Seriously Bobby, why are you being so annoying? Not that it's any of your business, but Samantha is down the street getting her hair cut and dyed. Hopefully back to blond, not red. Natalie and I enjoy meeting for drinks whenever we can, which isn't often because of our kids. In fact, this is only the third time that we have been able to get together in months. Adam has even dubbed it the meeting of 'The Man Haters Club,' so you might want to just mosey along," Liz taunted her meddlesome best friend.

"The Man Haters Club? Really? This sounds intriguing! If the other club members are as good-looking as the two of you, I think I might be interested in joining!" Bobby promptly announced.

"You are looking at all of the members," Liz said with a laugh.

"Well, I like what I see!" Bobby said, lecherously.

"Well, you can't join. In case you haven't noticed when you are in the shower, you are of the wrong gender!" Liz retorted.

"Oh, come on, Liz. Let me in! You know you will be glad that you did. I can provide you with secret information from the enemy camp. I can even educate you on how men think."

"We weren't aware that they did," Liz said, interrupting Bobby.

"And in return, maybe I can even change one or two minds about the males of our species – at least for a night or two. Maybe even three."

"Are you serious? You want to join our club just so you can have a one-night stand?" Liz snapped.

"No, not at all – not one night. You didn't hear me… I said maybe even two or three nights!" Bobby said with a sly grin.

"You are disgusting, Bobby Bain!" Liz said – although she didn't really feel that way. He lived to push her buttons. The unlikely pair bonded in med school. It took Liz some time, but she eventually realized that Bobby was a good person with certain "idiosyncrasies" that set him apart from the norm. These idiosyncrasies had assured his single status -- probably permanently.

"So, what's on the agenda for my first meeting?" Bobby asked, totally ignoring any further objections from Liz or Natalie. "What pressing matters do we need to discuss? Do we have any old business that we need to finish? Do you want me to hold an office?

I don't think I would be comfortable being president at this point, but maybe vice-president…"

Natalie then reported, "Liz, I wanted to let you know that I had lunch with Brooke Allan just this week. I'm happy to report that she and Giselle Kruse really hit it off, just like I thought they would. Brooke retained Giselle as her attorney, and Giselle was able to get Brooke temporary custody of her kids, until they go to trial. It seems that the new girlfriend/nurse was not overly disappointed that Kevin lost temporary custody after having to take care of three sad kids for two long weeks. Now that his girlfriend has realized that the majority of Kevin's income will be going for child support and alimony, he is not at all the 'great catch' that she once thought he was.

She has already moved on to a single, never-been-married orthopedic surgeon who is new to town. She even called Brooke and told her that she was sorry that Kevin tricked her. She is going to give a deposition telling how Kevin lied to her about the situation with Brooke. Can you believe it? She is willing to help Brooke in any way that she can. Meanwhile, Kevin has been begging and pleading with Brooke to reconsider the divorce and to take him back, but she is loving just taking care of three kids, not four."

"So, our first 'community service project' was an overwhelming success. Bobby, I'm sure that you are now sufficiently bored with the idea of joining our club," Liz stated.

"Actually, I'm enjoying this immensely! More than you could possibly know! You have no idea how I do my best to avoid being in the operating room with Kevin. He is a narcissistic asshole, to say the least. His best quality is that he was smart enough to marry Brooke. If you ladies will be kind enough to allow me entrance into your highly selective club, in return, I will be happy to provide free flowing libations at each meeting."

"We may drink WAY more than you realize, Dr. Bain," Natalie informed him.

"My offer still stands! In fact, if either one of you has too much to drink, you can count on me to drive you safely home. I can even put you in your jammies and tuck you in!"

"Oh, brother!" Liz said, while rolling her eyes.

The two women gave each other a "this might be interesting" look, and quickly agreed to the arrangement before Bobby could change his mind -- or they came to their senses.

"I see the vote is unanimous," Bobby announced, as if he had somehow won a coveted election. He proceeded to flag down the waiter and ordered another round of drinks, so they could seal the deal with a toast.

When the drinks arrived, Liz decided it was a good time to tell Natalie about her initial encounter with Bobby Bain.

"I met Bobby in the first few weeks of med school. Our class was scheduled to assist with free physicals at an off-site, neighborhood clinic. Our instructor suggested that the students should carpool because parking was an issue – there wasn't enough and it wasn't at all safe. Once, one of the students came out to find their car sitting on cinder blocks minus tires, rims, and the battery. The school figured with fewer cars there, the fewer the problems there would be. Bobby, who I had never seen before, walked up to me and offered me a ride. I happily accepted, relieved not to be driving my car there. A couple of the other students overheard Bobby when he offered me a ride, so they did not hesitate to ask him for a ride. But he told them, 'I wish I had room, but I drive a 'Vette.' When we reached the parking lot, I quickly realized that his 'Vette' had four doors and four cylinders -- it turned out to be a Chevette. I asked him why he didn't let the others ride along. He said, 'look at the backseat.' You know, Natalie, it was full of all kinds of crap. There were old newspapers, magazines, fast food bags, clothes, and many other things that I couldn't even identify."

"Thanks Liz, for ratting me out."

"Anytime Bain," Liz answered back with a grin.

"Did Liz ever tell you what she was known for in school? Somehow, I bet she skipped that detail…" Bobby then asked Natalie.

"Don't you have somewhere to be, Bobby?" Liz said, while glaring at him.

"Actually, I'm free the entire evening," Bobby said, with a wry smile.

"I can't imagine why…" Liz remarked.

"Where was I??? Oh that's right, I remember… on the morning of our first anatomy test, guess who comes dragging into class after studying all night, with a black shoe on one foot and a brown shoe on the other? Yes, you are right! New Braunfels' finest eye surgeon, Dr. Liz Schaeffer!"

"I don't believe it for a minute!" Natalie emphatically told Bobby. The Liz that Natalie knew was always so impeccably put together – hair, make-up, and clothes.

"It's actually true," Liz laughed.

"I can't decide if you guys are like brother and sister, or an old married couple," Natalie said, to neither Bobby nor Liz's amusement.

"I will keep the rest of my Liz stories for the next meeting. Hey, how often do we actually meet?" Bobby asked his fellow members.

"Whenever a man irritates us," Natalie quickly said.

"That could be daily, just in case you didn't know, Bobby," Liz told him.

"I'm sure it is. You are married to Adam, after all!" Bobby replied, more than pleased with his witty comeback.

"That's enough, Bain!" Liz warned him.

"Dr. Bain, we meet whenever we are kid-free. Which isn't really often... It typically works out to be about every three or four weeks. This is only our third meeting," Natalie told Bobby.

"I don't mean to change the subject, but is Brooke still single? I mean, is she okay? Are you sure there isn't anything else that the club can do for her? I think I may just check in with her and make sure there isn't something else that she needs," Bobby said, trying his best to sound sincere and empathetic.

"Why don't you do that Bobby? That sounds right up your alley," Liz said, knowing Bobby didn't need any encouragement from her or anyone else. Nor could anything possibly dissuade him.

"Make sure you two let me know when the next meeting is. See ya," Bobby said, now more than eager to leave.

"That was really weird," Natalie said, as soon as Bobby had left and was out of earshot.

"You haven't seen anything yet," Liz muttered under her breath.

Chapter 2

The preposterous thought of Bobby worming his way into The Man Haters Club amused Liz the whole way home. Up to this point, the club had been a complete joke between the two women, but Liz was now secretly pleased that Brooke had actually been helped due to their efforts. She started to think back about the two prior times she had met with Natalie. She then remembered how she slid onto the open barstool next to Natalie only a few weeks ago and said, "Natalie, I have been thinking… we really should have a mission statement."

For a brief moment, Natalie deliberated on what Liz had just said. She hoped it was just Liz's dry sense of humor. On the other hand, Liz could at times be a very analytical person, so there was the possibility that she really meant it. Then again, maybe not.

Liz was pleased that Natalie had saved her a seat, since the bar area of the restaurant was almost filled to capacity. That particular evening, it was full of overweight attorneys reinventing their day in court over martinis, single malt scotches and premium bourbons. The bar's proximity to the courthouse had made it their favorite haunt at the end of the day.

Natalie was in charge of picking the location, since she had lived in New Braunfels longer than Liz. She picked a great spot, The OutPost, for their get-together. It was Liz's first time there and she had been anxious to try it. She had heard so much about it lately. The restaurant's building renovation had recently been featured in a prominent national architectural magazine. It was not an everyday occurrence for the small town to make it into such an important publication. The article described the transformation of the former post office into an upscale restaurant and bar. It was hard to imagine that the rich woods, gorgeous windows, and worn brick had ever been anything other than a beautiful restaurant.

Even though the article went into excruciating detail, it left out one interesting element: the bathrooms. The word MAIL was cleverly etched into the glass of the wood door entering the restrooms, so it read MAIL on the men's and FEMAIL on the women's. Liz had already decided that the get-together was a success, since she was finally going to see the inside of The OutPost. She has always loved architectural details and interior design.

Liz and Natalie had been friends for close to five years. Jackie introduced the two of them. Jackie happened to be Liz's friend, and her occasional tennis partner. She also worked for Natalie as her legal secretary. Natalie was a very successful real estate attorney in the San Antonio area. When the two women first met, they instantly liked each other and quickly found out that they had much in common.

Natalie was tall, willowy thin, with brunette shoulder length hair that could be worn either curly and wild, or sleek and smooth, as the occasion called for. She had absolutely no wrinkles, making it difficult for anyone to believe that she was over forty. Liz had never been sure whether this was attributable to Natalie's great DNA, or to Botox, or perhaps a combination of both. One of these days, Liz planned to get up the nerve to ask her. Liz had once even fixed Natalie up with a former friend of hers. He was naturally quite taken by Natalie, but there was one major problem. She loves cats, and he didn't. Enough said. Fortunately, Natalie had never held this against Liz.

"I'm actually really good at creating mission statements. I created one for the law firm. How about 'to boldly go where no woman has ever gone before – to develop such a high level of self-esteem, self-reliance, and self-sufficiency that she will never ever be dependent on the whims of any worthless, shiftless, good-for-nothing man'?" Natalie suggested, humoring Liz's request.

"I like it, but part of that sounds awfully familiar," Liz said, wondering where she could have possibly heard it before.

"Star Trek. My ex was a Trekkie. It was the first of many red flags that I somehow managed to ignore," Natalie confessed.

"No kidding. I cannot imagine you with someone that was into that. It's a great mission statement -- as long as you think that we won't get sued for the Star Trek part. I will have to defer to you for a legal opinion. You didn't actually watch Star Trek with him, did you?" Liz wondered. She couldn't imagine Natalie doing such a thing.

"No way," she said, with a laugh.

"Whew… That's good. I did not want to lose any of the respect I have for you. I tried to come up with a mission statement, but after my frazzled drive over here with a teenager trying to convince me to allow her to dye her hair red, I could only come up with a slogan good enough for t-shirts," Liz confessed.

"Okay -- I'm listening."

" 'Men and Teenagers: You can't shoot them… It's against the law!' I think the t-shirts could be a great fundraiser to offset our future cocktail expenses," Liz said, starting to think it might actually be a good idea.

"I agree," Natalie said, raising her glass in a mock toast.

Meeting Natalie at The OutPost was not only convenient, but it would also probably end up being the high point of Liz's day. Her day started innocently enough. She had lovingly made breakfast for Adam, her husband of seventeen years, and Samantha, the couple's fifteen year-old daughter. Her husband was a man who oscillated between being exceedingly charming and even twice as difficult.

When neither Sam, nor Adam would even touch the cheese omelets and fresh fruit that she got up thirty minutes early to prepare for them, Liz remained unruffled. She decided her culinary efforts would not go to waste. She knew there were two other members of the household who repeatedly held her cooking in the highest esteem. That would be Fritz, the family's Jack Russell/Wire-Haired terrier mix, and Butter, their massive golden retriever. Butter got his name when he was a pup and somehow got up on the dinner table and devoured an entire stick of butter. Both dogs were more than receptive to having leftover omelets for breakfast. In fact, they both licked and licked their metal dog bowls clean, chasing the bowls with their tongues all around the terrace, causing an ungodly racket of metal being scraped against concrete, further agitating both Adam and Sam. Neither Adam, nor Sam would ever be accused of being cheery or engaging first thing in the morning.

Liz then drove Sam and her best friend, Lexy, to the girls' high school. Unlike Sam, Lexy was always talkative and pleasant in the morning and Liz appreciated that. Like most mothers, Liz realized you find out the most reliable information by driving the carpool. She just silently listened and tried to keep all the kids' names straight. She decided there was a lot more intrigue nowadays than when she went to school. In fact, she couldn't remember anything remotely interesting happening back then at her high school.

Soon after dropping the girls off, Liz had a revelation. Usually, Sam and Liz sparred over Sam's choice of appropriate school attire. This morning, Liz only had to tell Sam to change one article of clothing. The norm on most days was three. The teen's make-up was even school appropriate. Some mornings, Sam looked like she expected to be dropped off at a strip club, instead of her high school. Liz then realized that Sam was preoccupied that morning. She wondered if Sam's attention was focused on her hair appointment that afternoon.

Liz, an ophthalmologist who specialized in oculoplastic surgery, then started thinking about work and the rest of her day. She had seven lid surgeries scheduled that morning and eight follow-up appointments in the afternoon. The majority of her patients were usually women, but that morning she had two men scheduled. She had noticed more men wanted to look younger these days. While she loved making people feel better about their tiny imperfections, her real joy was helping those who needed her services, but couldn't afford them. As a result, she volunteered her medical services for several worthy causes in her community at no cost to these patients.

Liz had purposely picked that day to meet Natalie since Sam's hair appointment was going to be only a couple of blocks away. It wouldn't be too long until Sam could drive herself, but until she turned sixteen, Liz was still her designated driver. Liz loved their hairdresser, Renay, and the trendy salon, but also hated waiting for Sam there. The salon was decorated in a sleek, modern, and minimalistic manner. That meant hard black benches with no backs and dim lighting. Not the place she wanted to wait for two hours!

That evening, on the drive over, Liz told Sam the story of how her dear Dad would carefully place 'Magic Tape' on her bangs and meticulously trim under the tape when she was in grade school. She told Sam that in the old days, you would only get a real haircut right before school started. That was also when she got a new pair of dressy school shoes and new tennis shoes. Liz told her that when she was little she always thought that she could run faster with her new tennis shoes. Then Liz went on to tell Sam that her Mom would pick her hairstyle — which was usually a pixie cut or a pageboy.

The teenager was completely unimpressed with the story and the hidden messages it contained and simply answered, "Whatever, Mom."

Liz then decided to try another subject – cartoons. "Did you know there were only three television channels when I was growing up? Cartoons were only on TV for one hour after school, and on Saturday mornings, and there was no special network that showed just cartoons," she told her, wondering what Sam's reaction to this revelation would be.

"I think you might be lying to me, Mom" was all Sam could say.

It was always better for everyone concerned that Liz drove Sam to the hair salon, rather than Adam. Adam was not known for his patience with Sam, or anyone else for that matter. He was the kind of man that is accustomed to having people listen to him. He sometimes forgot that he was no longer at work and tried unsuccessfully to boss Liz and Sam around. They both dealt with him in different ways. Liz was more passive, while Sam enjoyed the challenge of testing his limits.

Sam considered it a coup if she could get Adam to agree to something that she knew her mother would never allow. A great example is when Adam caved in to Sam's request for her beautiful, naturally blonde hair to be dyed black. For some unknown reason, Sam loved to see Adam and Liz at odds with each other.

Adam was thrilled to hear that Liz would be taking Sam to the hairdresser after the last debacle. He had no idea that it would be such an ordeal to get her hair back to blonde. How was he supposed to know that Sam's hair would probably fall out if it were to be bleached blonde again? Liz didn't say much when she saw Sam's dark locks. She just simply asked him, "Did you okay this?" When he said that he did, she quietly walked out of the room. She wished that he had asked her if the change in hair color would be a good idea, or not.

A lot of the couple's marital strife was unspoken. In Adam's mind, Liz had just yelled at him and berated him for not checking with her. But in actuality, Liz knew that what was done was done, and could not be easily undone. She was more concerned about why Sam would pull a stunt like that. She didn't like the way Sam tried pitting one parent against the other. Liz grew up in a home where if one parent said no, then you knew better than to ask the other one. Because Adam frequently lost his temper with Sam, he was more likely to give in to Sam's requests out of remorse.

Liz needed the two hours to catch up with Natalie. Adam actually liked Natalie and didn't mind a bit that Liz would meet up with her, but what he undeniably didn't care for was that Natalie had recommended her own divorce attorney to Liz. Of course, it is only logical that Liz would ask Natalie, who is an attorney, who she would recommend – especially given the circumstances Liz had recently endured.

"Natalie, did you know that Adam has dubbed our little get-together for drinks, 'The Man Haters Club'?" Liz informed her.

"Liz, if I wasn't so pissed off about what he put you through, I might even find that funny," Natalie replied.

The two women picked up their respective drinks – a dirty martini for Natalie and a gin and tonic for Liz -- and toasted to the first official meeting of the 'Man Haters Club.' Natalie raised her glass again, and decided that the first order of business should be a proclamation declaring their passionate dislike for all narcissistic men. Liz readily agreed. As an addendum, Liz added to the list "any man who even considers cheating with their plump receptionist, especially if she resembles Miss Piggy with a lisp."

Natalie ended up putting her drink down so quickly that a small amount sloshed over the edge onto the embossed cocktail napkin.

"Are you freaking kidding me?" Natalie asked, wondering how in the world anyone could consider doing this to Liz. Natalie always described her friend to others as "the total package"— funny, smart, outgoing, and beautiful. According to Natalie, Liz was also one of the best friends a person could have.

Liz slowly shook her head no. She was just getting ready to add that "Mrs. Piggy", as she had just renamed her to avoid any confusion with the beloved Muppet character, had small maroon colored bumps on the back of her flabby arms. She was ready to launch into a few more unflattering descriptors when the young, good-looking bartender butted in and asked Natalie, "Excuse me, but are you wearing Chanel No. 5?"

Natalie flirtatiously and instinctively smiled back. Liz looked at her friend like she had lost her mind. He then told Natalie, "A lot of extraordinary women have worn Chanel – my Mom, my wife, and Marilyn Monroe."

He got to Liz with the "my Mom" part. Liz joined the conversation at this point, telling him that her Mom also wore it.

He placed another drink in front of them. "On the house," he announced as he poured himself a drink and joined them. "To all the remarkable women who wear

Chanel No. 5," he said, as they all raised their glasses in unison.

Natalie and Liz then returned to their prior conversation, before the interruption.

"So, I guess we don't hate ALL men, do we? It should be on a case-by-case basis, because that bartender wasn't so bad!" Natalie pointed out.

"You're right, he wasn't!" Liz wholeheartedly agreed.

"Will we be adding any other members?" Natalie inquired.

She helped Liz realize that theoretically they could easily end up with several million members. Liz was scared that they could end up with so many of them that it would qualify them for a spot in the Guinness Book of World Records – "World's Largest Club." At this point, they decided that membership should be by invitation only.

At that moment Liz decided to ask Natalie more about her ex-husband, Tim – or as Natalie refered to him, Tim Moody. It always made Liz smile because of the way that Natalie always refered to him by his first and last names. Elizabeth Dole used to do the same when discussing her husband, Bob Dole, when he was running for president. Anyway, Natalie confided to Liz that she and Tim Moody were married for nineteen years. Liz remembered the words "narcissist" and "freak" coming up more than once in their conversation. Natalie explained that she really tried to stick it out for the sake of their only child, Dirk. Then one day Natalie realized if she stayed with Tim Moody, Dirk would grow up thinking it was okay to treat women the way Tim Moody treated her. She decided the best thing for Dirk would be for her to leave his dad, so one day she finally did.

"I kept hoping, while we were separated, that Tim Moody would blow himself up with Viagra, but it never happened," Natalie said, as she slowly shook her head.

"Wow! I know someone who tried putting extra butter in her husband's food hoping that would do him in," Liz countered.

"That's beyond brilliant! You can buy butter anywhere, it's not illegal like arsenic, and butter makes everything taste better! I can think of a thousand dishes where a little extra butter wouldn't be noticed. In fact, it might even make the dish better! Liz, I have to know, how did it work?" Natalie asked.

"It didn't – because it takes too long. If it worked, everyone would do it!"

"Isn't that the truth? I guess you are completely right about that. Still, it's a fascinating notion. I just remembered that you were telling me about this fat pig-woman who was after Adam," Natalie said, reminding Liz.

"First, let me say that I now realize, in retrospect, that some of this is my fault. I am way too trusting. I always think the best of people. Big mistake! I have great first instincts, and I should have listened to them. Sam and I both thought she seemed weird the first time we met her at his office.

"On the flip side, I know Adam can be a little hard to work for, so I have always made sure he buys his workers nice gifts for Christmas, and on their birthdays. I always wanted him to get them something that they would like and enjoy.

"I asked him what Mrs. Piggy liked to do when she wasn't at work -- and he had no clue. He didn't know a thing about her outside of the office – nor did he seem to care. So, I went ahead and asked one of the other ladies who worked for the company if she knew what Mrs. Piggy liked to do in her spare time and they told me that she liked to cook. This woman told me that Mrs. Piggy occasionally would even bake a cake and bring it in for the office.

"So, silly me – I bought her a cookbook: a collector's edition of 'Mastering the Art of French Cooking' by Julia Child, for Adam to give to her. You should have seen how I giftwrapped it. The giftwrap alone was a work of art. The stupid woman then thought she was in the movie 'Julie and Julia'. She proceeded to cook every recipe in the book and would bring it in and serve it to Adam for lunch almost every day. I'm talking things like Boeuf Bourguignon, Coq au Vin, and Chicken Fricassee. Routinely, Adam would come home from work when he was hungry for supper. But all of a sudden he started working later and later, because he was eating this huge French lunch, so he wasn't hungry in the evening – and he began to regularly miss dinner with Sam and I. He had never done that before.

"I also noticed, when I stopped by the office, that she was acting a little creepy – like a Stepford Wife. 'You're so funny, Adam. You're so smart, Adam. You're so handsome, Adam.' And then, she would just repeat the compliments over and over – like her computer malfunctioned and was stuck on some sort of endless, repetitive loop. But who would have ever considered her a threat? While she is a few years younger than me, she definitely doesn't look it. I thought she was about the most uninteresting person I ever met in my life and you know me, I find almost everyone fascinating on some level. She laughs like Wilma Flintstone and her hair honestly looks like rats have chewed on it. On top of everything else, she is married! I later found out that she is one of those women who always seem to have a little crush on whomever happens to be her boss—but I naively assumed her view of marriage and family would be the same as mine. I also thought at the time that Adam valued all that I did for him and Sam. And boy, was I wrong – on all counts!

"When I mentioned to Adam that I thought Mrs. Piggy had some boundary issues, he readily disagreed. Later, Mr. Miller, our marriage counselor, asked him if he ever grilled his boss a big old juicy rib eye and brought it to him at lunch. Adam emphatically said, 'No.' Then, he proceeded to ask him if he ever made his boss 'special occasion cupcakes.' 'Hell no!' Adam roared. 'E-x-a-c-t-l-y,' Mr. Miller said, knowing his point had been clearly made."

"Unbelievable!" was all Natalie could say.

"Natalie, I want to tell you something that I haven't shared with anyone. I have never had this feeling before," Liz said, hoping she wasn't making a mistake by confiding this secret to her friend.

"Liz, you know there isn't anything that you can't tell me!" Natalie said, hoping Liz wasn't going to tell her she was now thinking about "playing for the other team." In law school, one of her closest friends switched teams and wanted Natalie to be a member of "her new team." Natalie didn't currently have a significant other, but she liked the team she was on. However, she also didn't care what team anyone else played on, so she prepared herself for whatever Liz was going to say…

"I keep having these recurring images that I'm proudly holding a beautiful silver platter with Mrs. Piggy's head on it, her eyes completely glazed over, with an apple in her mouth and curly parsley carefully placed around the edge of the platter, just like Julia Child would garnish it," Liz confessed.

"Are you sure it's Julia Child, or could it be Meryl Streep playing Julia Child?" Natalie asked. She was relieved that this was the problem Liz was referring to.

"Natalie, you are completely missing the point. I'm starting to freak out. I really think this woman is OBSESSED!" Liz said, more than convinced of the fact.

"Are you talking about Meryl, Julia, Mrs. Piggy, or you?" Natalie said, hoping to give Liz a little perspective.

"Hilarious, Natalie. But… you know… you may have a point."

Chapter 3

Liz couldn't believe it had already been weeks since she had confided to Natalie about her little secret. She was really looking forward to catching up with Natalie again while Sam was getting her hair done.

When Liz picked Sam up from school, she had hoped to hear all about her daughter's day. Instead, she had to listen to Sam plead, beg, and barter to dye her hair red, changing from the black that she had tricked her father into allowing during her last hair appointment. This was why she absolutely dreaded taking Sam to get her hair done. The teen stopped just short of blackmail or extortion, by just a tad. Liz was beginning to lose count of how many different ways she could say no to red hair in a twenty-minute drive. Other than magically learning to speak a foreign language, Liz finally decided she had exhausted all possibilities.

Sam's fixation with having red hair probably had deep roots in her early childhood. It all began when Liz started reading her favorite childhood book, *Pippi Longstocking,* to the little girl. Liz had loved Pippi because it contrasted with her own parents' very by-the-book parenting style. Pippi lived on her own, had a monkey as a pet and even a horse who lived on the porch. Pippi was known for her trademark red hair that she wore in braids that stuck out to the side. One braid stood up and the other one pointed down.

Sam, like Liz, seemed to like that Pippi was so unconventional—she ate pancakes for any meal, mopped the floor by skating with scrub brushes on her feet, and brought her horse inside her house whenever she felt like it. Pippi slept upside down with her feet toward the headboard, which little Sam soon began to imitate.

One day Liz had the brilliant idea of braiding Sam's hair over a pipe cleaner to make her braids stick out like Pippi's. She even adjusted them so one pointed up and the other one pointed down. For a while this became their Saturday morning ritual —making pancakes for breakfast, braiding Sam's hair like Pippi's, and then the two would go to the stable. Liz would lead Sam around on her thoroughbred, Max. Sam would even place a little sock monkey that Adam's Mom had given her in the front of the saddle, pretending it was a real monkey. She made up her own Pippi song that she would sing over and over while Liz would lead her all over the grounds.

Liz suddenly realized how ludicrous it was to blame Pippi Longstocking for Sam's insistence for red hair. She had also read Green Eggs and Ham to her at least a hundred times, and had even dyed Sam's eggs green for breakfast a couple of times when she was a toddler. They didn't still eat green eggs. Sam was just going through another phase, like every other kid.

Instead, Liz started thinking about meeting Natalie and wondered if Natalie was such a persuasive arguer as a child. She would have to ask her as soon as she got to The OutPost. Maybe Sam was destined to be a hotshot lawyer. This last thought momentarily comforted her.

After what seemed like an eternity to both of them, Liz and Sam finally arrived at the salon. Liz felt the need to go in and make absolutely sure that Sam's hairdresser, Renay, fully understood that under no circumstance was Sam's hair to be dyed red, black or any unnatural hues like cotton candy pink, blue or burgundy. Also, that the goal was to move Sam back to her lovely natural golden blonde locks as soon as humanly possible. Only when Renay repeatedly assured Liz that she would not dye Sam's hair any color, except for blonde, did Liz leave the salon and get back in her car.

Liz then drove the two blocks to meet Natalie. Liz pulled into the parking lot of The OutPost, thankful that she was still early enough to get a decent parking space before the dinner crowd started to wander in.

It was easy to locate Natalie, since she was the only person in the bar not wearing a dark suit with Lucchese cowboy boots. Only in Texas do you see attorneys wearing tailored suits accessorized with cowboy boots and Stetson hats. Liz greeted a few familiar faces as she made her way over to Natalie's barstool. Natalie surprised her by immediately sliding a gin and tonic her way.

"I had the bartender make it when you said you had left the hair salon," Natalie explained.

"Thanks, now I know why you are my friend. I really needed this after debating with Sam the merits of blonde vs. red hair. She can go on and on and on... It is so hard not to explode!" Liz wearily explained.

"This is one of those moments when I'm glad that I have a boy," Natalie laughed.

"You know what has always puzzled me? She constantly tells me how badly I dress, but somehow I always find my clothes in her room. She also frequently 'borrows' my jewelry without permission. She is clueless about the difference between real and costume jewelry. No matter how many times I talk to her or punish her, she never stops taking my things."

"Well... Dirk has NEVER borrowed any of my clothes. At least not that I know of..." Natalie told Liz, tongue-in-cheek.

"That is probably a good thing! So... what's new?"

"Well, you will love this. I just found out from one of my girlfriends that Tim Moody tried to date the therapist that he started to see when I left him. Who does that?

Well I will tell you! Tim Moody… that's who. He always tried to get me to go see her. I didn't want to see her because I'm sure he told her all kinds of atrocities about me. Can you believe her name was Bambi? Only Tim Moody would pick a therapist using the criteria that they had to have a stripper name! According to him, she told him that because I was going through menopause, it was making me do unreasonable things -- like leave his sorry ass! Knowing Tim Moody as well as I do, I bet he totally made that up."

"Did Bambi ever go out with him?"

"No, she isn't crazy—he is. So how are things with your charming husband?" Natalie asked.

"Heaven help him! Deep down, I know he's trying to be a better person, but this is the perfect example of why he drives me nuts at times. A couple of nights ago, we were getting ready to make love, and I just wanted him to say something nice to me, you know, like any woman would! Something like … 'I am so glad you took me back because I can't imagine how empty my life would be without you.' So I told him, 'you know sex starts a little higher than where you are concentrating right now!' Adam stopped what he was doing, and grabbed one of my breasts, and then he looked at me like a kid who has the right answer in school and asked, 'the boobies?' I told him, 'you might want to try a little higher...' He looked at me thoroughly confused and said, 'you want me to rub your head?'"

"Liz, I have to know –is he still alive?" Natalie interrupted.

"Barely."

"I'm not sure that even the best therapy can fix that," Natalie stated rather seriously.

"We will see… Mr. Miller is pretty amazing. Of course, Adam's idea of foreplay is saying, 'Let's git nakkid.'"

"Poor Mr. Miller."

"Can you believe we are actually having our second 'Man Haters Club' meeting? What do you think about us doing a little 'community service' work?"

"Liz, I am telling you right now, I am not selling any cookie dough! Aren't we taking this excuse for drinks a little too seriously?" Natalie exclaimed.

"I didn't say fundraising!" Liz laughed.

"So, what do you have in mind?"

"Well, did you hear what happened to Brooke Allan?" Liz asked her.

"No. What happened?"

"Kevin took their three kids! It seems that he secretly rented a house just for him and the kids, and his operating room nurse/girlfriend, to live in. Then, he told Brooke that he wanted a divorce immediately, and that he would take care of all the details for her – like hiring the lawyer and filing all the necessary legal papers. That way she wouldn't have to worry her pretty little head about anything. He explained that she just had to sign the papers and they would be done. She was completely blindsided!"

"Please tell me that she didn't fall for that bullshit?" Natalie asked.

"No, she hasn't signed anything, yet. But I don't think she actually believes she has many other options."

"Wrong! She is actually in the driver's seat, and I bet that's where we come in. Am I right?" Natalie asked.

"Yes, you are! We must help this woman understand that even though he was the one bringing home the paycheck – in Texas, she is entitled to 50% of everything that they accumulated since they got married. She put him through med school. She did all of the cooking, cleaning, and raising the kids. She was always at all the kids' games. Have you ever even met this guy?? I wouldn't even know who he was if I didn't know him from the hospital! Brooke needs to know that she doesn't have to accept the lawyer that Kevin wants her to use. She needs to find her own lawyer, who will watch out for her and for the kids' best interests. And I figured you would be the perfect person to help her out with that. Who would you recommend?" Liz asked.

"I know the perfect person -- this colleague of mine who is known for being a real pit bull in custody cases," Natalie said.

"What's his name?"

"Who said it was a guy? 'His' name is Giselle Kruse and she's one of the best in town. Brooke will think she's hiring a fellow soccer mom, but holy crap, Giselle gets the opposing attorneys to agree to things you wouldn't believe. I don't know how she does it. She's very pretty, and she has this voice that sounds angelic and mesmerizing. I know this attorney that swears that she put him in a trance during the proceedings. He started wearing an I-Pod in court whenever he is up against her. Now, he loses because he can't hear what is going on, but she can't 'put a trance' on him."

"That is absolutely the most ridiculous thing I have ever heard of," Liz remarked.

"Giselle won't stop until those kids are safely back under Brooke's roof."

"Would you mind explaining all of this to Brooke?"

"Not at all."

"I didn't think that you would. I actually already asked her to meet us here.

"That sounds a lot better to me than selling cookie dough!" Natalie teased Liz.

Chapter 4

Liz was one of those people who try really hard to be on time, but never is. It's not because she was the type trying to make an entrance. She just ran a few minutes behind because she always had way too many things on her plate. She once read an article on the many reasons people are late, because it bothered her, and soon realized she fell into the category of "trying to get one more thing done before she walked out the door." She wasn't the type to waste a single minute.

Today, the stars were all aligned. She actually arrived for the fourth meeting at The OutPost when she had planned. It was exactly 5:25. Since Bobby had proclaimed himself a member of the club, Liz decided that it would be better if she secured a booth in the bar, rather than bar stools for their get together. She wasn't entirely sure that he would show up. You could never be completely sure with Bobby Bain. She carefully scanned the room for the most private booth, and was surprised to see that Dr. Bobby Bain was already occupying that particular booth. He had a smug look on his face that she knew all too well.

"Hello Liz, you seem a little surprised to see me. You shouldn't be – you know how Bobby Bain is once he sets his sights on something," Bobby said.

"That is indeed the question I have been asking myself over and over again – what is it exactly that Bobby Bain has his sights on this time?" Liz replied, already knowing the answer to the question. She knew Bobby was once again romantically unattached, and trying his best to change such status.

"You, better than anyone, know that I am a person of many and varied interests. I believe you could refer to me as a 'Renaissance Man'," Bobby said, sounding like he actually believed this himself.

"Those weren't the words that came to my mind... I believe the first word would be pervert -- and I believe the second one is opportunist. Do you want me to go on?" Liz said, enjoying the playful banter.

"Actually, let's change the subject, even though you may find it less interesting than talking about me. I was wondering... Is your friend Natalie dating anyone?" Bobby asked.

"Do you mean would she go out with you? She did once marry Tim Moody, so maybe she could take TOTAL leave of her senses one more time, but personally, I don't think that is going to happen. That reminds me -- what happened with Brooke?" Liz asked.

"I believe I will save that report for the 'old business' part of our meeting. There isn't any silly rule that club members can't date is there?" Bobby wondered.

"Since this is a club for women, I don't think we really anticipated that ever being a problem," Liz said, thinking to herself that only an idiot would join a 'Man Haters Club' as a way to meet women, and then wonder why they weren't the least bit interested in him.

"Good. I wouldn't want to be kicked out of the club," Bobby replied in earnest.

"Yes, that would be horrific. I think you may have forgotten the ONLY reason that we allowed you in. So… where is my gin and tonic?" Liz asked, reminding him of his obligation to provide the adult beverages for the meetings.

On cue, at that precise moment, a waiter appeared with a gin and tonic and a single malt scotch on a small black tray. He handed the gin and tonic to Liz and the scotch to Bobby. He then informed Bobby he would return shortly with the appetizers.

"Appetizers? Hmm, it looks like someone is trying really hard," Liz said, but not completely surprised. Bobby can be off-putting to some, with his bull in the china shop approach, but Liz was used to it by now.

Liz looked up just as Natalie was walking in and she raised her hand, so Natalie would see them.

The waiter again seemed to appear on cue with a dirty martini for Natalie. Then, he quickly returned with two-dozen oysters on the half shell.

"Hey guys, sorry I'm so late. Oh my God… I love oysters! Bobby, how did you know I wanted a dirty martini?" Natalie asked.

Bobby looked at Liz and raised his eyebrows and smiled a knowing smile. Liz seriously considered smacking him, but it would only make her look bad. If she waited long enough, Natalie would probably do it for her.

"Natalie, were you off today? You look so fresh and relaxed," Bobby said

Liz agreed with him. Natalie looked like she spent the day at a spa. Her hair was straight and shiny. Her outfit showed off her five foot nine inch tall figure to perfection. She had on stone colored slacks and a silk sweater of the same color with black silk threads woven into it. A black form-fitting jacket with extensive stone-colored topstitching showed off her fabulous figure. She looked casual, but very elegant at the same time.

"No, I am swamped at the office. I have several deals closing on the same day next week, but I was really looking forward to seeing my friends," Natalie replied.

"I was REALLY looking forward to seeing you too," Bobby remarked, while he gazed deep into her eyes.

Natalie looked at Liz, and even though they tried not to, they both burst out laughing simultaneously.

"Bobby, I meant my friends—vodka and vermouth!" Natalie explained.

"I knew that…" Bobby muttered. Then he quickly tried to save the situation by adding, "My friends are Jim and Jack!"

Suddenly, from completely out of nowhere, Marilyn appeared at the booth. Without a single word she wiggled her way into the seat right next to Bobby. Marilyn was certainly not known for being shy. So, they knew she would probably tell everyone why it is that she was there and how in the world that she knew they were going to meet. Marilyn doesn't look remotely like a computer genius, but that is exactly what she is. She actually has a degree in computer forensics, but there is little to no demand for that in New Braunfels, Texas. Marilyn has been supplementing her income by doing small computer jobs for a couple of the doctors and law firms in town. Liz was one of the first ones to hire her to update her computers in her office. In fact, Marilyn had been working in Liz and Bobby's office all week.

Some in town would say that Marilyn had a dark and somewhat shady history. She was more than just a little secretive about her past. She said she was a former Las Vegas showgirl -- but everyone suspected she did a bit more than simply "show" her assets. Rumor had it that she was working at Ms. Mona's Catty Shack as recently as 5 years ago, and not as a bartender. What was known about Marilyn, and what she readily admitted to, -- was that she had an uncanny ability to read men. She knew how they think, she knew how they act, and she knew how to predict their actions, past, present, and future. This kind of talent could come in handy if a woman knew what to do with it -- and Marilyn certainly gave the impression that she knew EXACTLY what to do with it.

Marilyn was not her real name. It was the stage name she took to conceal her real identity. Her given name was really Mary Lynn Knippe -- and she was born in Kokomo, Indiana. But she left her hometown years ago -- and all the problems associated with growing up in a crazy family. Her mother would fight constantly with her stepfather -- between trips to her psychiatrist. She never knew her real father because he was smart and got the hell outta Dodge three months after she was born. Her brother Earl was diagnosed as bipolar, along with ADHD, fibromyalgia, and Chronic Fatigue Syndrome. She has always suspected that the truth of the situation was that he just preferred sitting on his ass collecting those fat disability and unemployment checks from the ever-benevolent Federal government, as opposed to getting a job and actually working for a living. She would much rather be on her own -- fending for herself -- rather than collecting food stamps, unemployment, and disability, alongside the rest of her immediate family. She left all those problems behind in Indiana -- along with her name. Now she was just Marilyn.

"Can you please pass the oysters down this way, Bobby?" Marilyn said, as she reached for a small plate and the three-pronged fork that accompanied the order.

The waiter reappeared and Marilyn ordered a Cosmo.

Liz looked over at Natalie. Natalie, in turn, looked at Bobby. Bobby then looked at Liz and the collective body language indicated that none of them had a single clue why Marilyn was there, and how in the world she could have possibly known about their meeting.

After a few minutes, the waiter arrived with Marilyn's Cosmo. Liz, Natalie, and Bobby immediately requested another drink due to the sheer awkwardness of the situation. Marilyn continued to sip on her Cosmo and seemed oblivious. She occasionally would use her fork to spear another oyster. Marilyn was the only person in the group who didn't appear to be uncomfortable.

After the waiter delivered the second round of drinks, Marilyn cleared her throat and began talking: "First, I want to thank all three of you for having me at your meeting, uninvited. I know you are wondering how I even knew about this little get-together. Liz, when I was working on your computer this week I ACCIDENTLY saw the correspondence between the three of you. I've got to tell you, I really like what you all did to help out Brooke. Her ex-husband, Kevin, tried stiffing me on a computer job once. He is a real piece of work. He asked me, "How would you like to be paid in sausage?" He then leaned over, put his elbow inside his thigh and kept hitting the inside of his leg like he was hung like a horse. I told him to pay me the three hundred that he owed me and if I wanted 'sausage' then I could grab a 'little smokie' like his at the grocery store. He is one of those guys that think the rules don't apply to them. He would have completely screwed-over Brooke and those darling kids if you guys had not gotten involved.

"I realize that 'The Man Haters Club' started as a joke between Natalie and Liz. Bobby, I haven't completely figured out your place in all of this. I think I know, and it seems a little twisted – but I'm okay with that. I do know what he did for Brooke and the kids. Bobby, did you tell Natalie and Liz what you did? I bet you didn't!"

"If I did that, we couldn't call it altruism then could we?" he joked, totally ignoring her request.

"Bain, do I need to get out my Portuguese Nut Cracker to get you to talk?" Marilyn asked.

All eyes turned on Bobby. It seemed to Liz that Bobby's mouth went a little dry and he looked a little proptotic, or "bug-eyed".

"I'm going to give you a pass Bain, but only this one time," Marilyn stated, in a matter-of-fact manner.

Bobby smiled weakly and just nodded an acknowledgement.

"That asshole, Kevin, told his kids that Brooke had cancer and might die. He then explained to the kids that the only way their Mom was going to get better was if she could rest. He told them that he was going to take care of them, with help from the nurse at his office. She was even going to come live in the same house and take care of them. God only knows what excuse he used for the nurse sleeping in his bed. He conveyed to them that if they told anyone why they were living in a different house with the nurse, then their Mommy might die." Marilyn explained.

"Unbelievable – and outrageous! What lengths some people will go to not have to pay child support! He probably consulted with that idiot, Tim Moody on that one," Natalie added.

"Bobby gave them the use of a cabin on the Guadalupe River for two nights. Brooke and the kids spent the weekend floating down the river, cooking hot dogs and s'mores on a campfire, and sleeping in their new sleeping bags. Brooke thought they won it all through some contest," Marilyn explained.

"Bobby, that was so sweet of you! How very thoughtful!" Natalie cooed.

Bobby seemed to gain a little color back in his face with Natalie's compliment.

"I'm confused, how did she explain the cancer away?" Liz asked.

"She told the kids that sometimes, even doctors make mistakes," Marilyn said.

"How do you know all of this?" Bobby asked Marilyn. Bobby was starting to re-alize that nothing was safe on his computer with Marilyn around. He would entertain the thought of firing her, but his private parts and his computer would probably never "boot up" again. He couldn't wait to hear her explanation.

Nevertheless, he would have to wait, because Marilyn just ignored him. After a bit, she waved the waiter over and ordered another Cosmo.

"I don't know if you are accepting new members, but I want to join your club. So, what do I have to do?" Marilyn asked sincerely.

"Gee Marilyn, this has only come up once before and that was when Bobby wanted to join," Liz told her.

"We only let him join because he pays for the drinks," Natalie explained, momen-tarily forgetting that Bobby was sitting right across from her. When she realized that she had said that out loud she started gazing at the table and then took a big sip of her martini.

"Marilyn, could you give us a few moments alone so we can discuss this?" Liz asked her.

"Sure. I need to visit the ladies room anyway," Marilyn answered. She sashayed away from the table towards the MAIL rooms.

"So, what do you two think about Marilyn being a member?" Liz asked Bobby and Natalie.

"I am totally for it!" Bobby announced immediately.

Liz and Natalie couldn't help but laugh at his enthusiastic response.

"I'm sure you are. You don't want her to bring out the Turkish Testicle Twister, do you?" Natalie said pointing out the obvious.

"It was the Portuguese Nut Cracker," Liz corrected Natalie.

"Whatever, ladies…" Bobby said, clearly exasperated that this topic was even being discussed in front of him.

"Where does she come up with this stuff? She cracks me up, and scares me at the same time!" Natalie remarked.

"I vote for 'she scares me'!" Bobby said.

"So, what does she have to do to become a member?" Natalie asked.

"How about, she has to tell a funny story about why she hates men?" Liz suggested.

"That works for me!" Bobby said, again agreeing a little quickly.

"Me too! I bet Marilyn's story will be a good one!" Natalie said with a smile.

"Bobby, I have never seen a woman have this effect on you. I have to admit, I'm enjoying it immensely!" Liz said, with a laugh.

When Marilyn returned to the table, Liz informed her of the requirement for membership. Liz also asked her whether she needed some time to think of a story.

"Nah… I'm ready. Do I need to stand, because I would prefer not to. Our location is in enemy territory, you know," Marilyn said as she glanced around at the men hovering around the bar.

"I agree. You can stay right where you are," Natalie answered.

"Will anyone be offended by references to male body parts or colorful language?" Marilyn asked the group.

"Bobby might be if the male body parts are mutilated in any manner," Liz remarked, not missing an opportunity to rile Bobby a little.

"Obviously, you haven't spent much time around Liz, or you wouldn't have asked about the colorful language," Bobby said, trying to get a rise out of Liz.

"I do not use foul language!" Liz said, as if she herself believed it.

Marilyn leaned forward as if she was going to start talking, and then sat back taking another sip of her Cosmo and began:

"I used to be married to this Marine named Gil. He was six foot two and all muscle. Ladies, I will be the first to admit that it was lust at first sight. After a whirlwind courtship, he asked me to marry him before he had to ship off to Korea. We got married after dating only three weeks. As time went on, Gil's requests in the bedroom got kinkier and kinkier. After awhile, I noticed that all he wanted to talk about was his penis. How long it was, how big it was, how he had never been with a woman who hadn't liked it, etc. Needless to say, I wasn't too sad when he left for a year long unaccompanied tour to Korea. He had been gone about five weeks when I got sicker than I have ever been in my entire life. I woke up and realized a whole day of my life was missing. I had been running such a high fever that I must have slept through the entire previous day. I was still sitting there slightly bewildered when the phone rang, and it was Gil. He immediately began talking about the adventures of his penis, as usual. I snapped at him, "Do you know that I have lost a whole day of my life because I was so sick that I was unconscious?" He was quiet for about 15 seconds and then said, "Too bad I'm not there, or I would give you a shot of 'penis-cillin!'" Marilyn said and then stood up and took a bow.

"Yuck!" Natalie said, making a face.

Bobby said absolutely nothing.

"I would like to welcome you, Marilyn, as the newest member of the Man Haters Club," Liz proclaimed.

Bobby, Natalie, and Liz clapped quietly.

"So… what ever happened to Gil?" Bobby asked.

"He died in a training accident in a jeep. He was playing with himself and just drove off a bridge," Marilyn stated, very matter-of-factly.

"Are you serious?" Natalie asked.

Bobby was very quiet. He had heard from his grandmother when he was a child that you could go blind from doing this, but he had never fully contemplated that you could lose your life doing it -- until just now.

"Yep. So, I got his GI Bill money and decided to get a degree in computer forensics," Marilyn explained.

"Well, on that happy note, I am going to have to run," Liz said, while wondering to herself if anything Marilyn had said was true, or even close to the truth.

"Me, too!" Natalie added, following Liz out to the parking lot.

Chapter 5

"Do you have anywhere to be?" Marilyn asked Bobby immediately after the others left.

"Not particularly. Would you like another Cosmo?" Bobby asked politely.

"If you are having another one, I guess I will too," Marilyn replied.

"It wouldn't be right if I left a beautiful woman alone in a bar full of lecherous lawyers," Bobby answered.

Marilyn ignored the compliment. Instead she asked, "Bobby, do you understand why I wanted to join the Man Haters Club? It just seemed that you and Liz have been a little happier lately. I don't know whether it's because of this ridiculous club, or not. I do think when you help someone that it makes you not obsess on your own problems as much. Believe me, I have tried just about EVERYTHING to feel better about myself. Do you know that I once tried popping a rubber band on my wrist every time I had a sad thought? My hand damn near separated from my arm. I even tried eating only 'happy food' -- bananas, spinach, turkey and salmon."

"Hell, that's not 'happy food' -- that was 'healthy food'. 'Happy food' is cheesecake, pecan pie, ice cream and bacon. That was the problem," Bobby said, trying to lighten the mood.

"Bacon?" Marilyn asked.

"Everybody knows bacon is meat candy!" Bobby explained, using one of his favorite quotes.

"Don't forget chocolate! I ate so much chocolate that I couldn't sleep, I was so wired from the caffeine. Have you ever tried aromatherapy? That was total bullshit. I spent over $600 in candles! The only one who was happy was the owner of the candle shop," Marilyn mused.

"My colleagues told me that they thought my problem was that I worked too much, and that I needed a hobby. I took up photography. I was even asked to do a one-man exhibition at Gibbon's Art Gallery on Main Street. The review in the newspaper lauded my ability to capture the loneliness and desperation in my subjects. So, I scratched photography off my list," Bobby told her.

"Someone told me a pet would help. I rescued a Westie from the Animal Shelter. I never had a dog before. I love him to death, but he is actually a little depressing to own. No one told me terriers are just cats in dog costumes. He only comes when he wants something. I'm not going to elaborate, but let's just say he has a problem with wanting to mark his territory -- which may or may not include his owner. He also does a great "honey badger" imitation when disturbed from a nap. Keep in mind that the average dog naps 20 hours a day," Marilyn told Bobby, who was still laughing at the image of her dog marking Marilyn as his own.

"Hmmm… I was recently thinking about getting a Chihuahua. I guess I will scratch that one off my list," Bobby said.

"I think Golden Retrievers are a better option," Marilyn informed him.

"Depression is like a cockroach infestation – one day you have one problem, and the next day your problems have multiplied exponentially. Difficult to eradicate and it can come back at any time," Bobby philosophized, with the help of the Scotch.

"Liz was telling me that she never had depression before this stuff with Adam. You and I are evidently lifetime members of the depression club. Liz, on the other hand, can't even comprehend what has happened to her. She had two big misconceptions about depression. Number one was, she thought it couldn't happen to her. Number two was, when it did happen, she thought it was only a one-time thing. I had to explain it to her in terms she could understand. I told her…

"One day your doorbell rings and it's an aunt that you have heard of, but never met. You invite her in and get to know her. It is an interesting enough visit, so you tell her that the next time she is in town you should get together for dinner. The dinner goes great, and you invite her to visit at your house for a weekend sometime. Big mistake…

"She wakes you up at 4:30 AM making all kinds of racquet, and then she doesn't like what you made for breakfast. She asks if you can drive her across town to shop, and then conveniently forgets her purse. You had already planned a dinner party to introduce her to some of your friends, and she is downright obnoxious to everyone. You can't wait for Sunday to come because she is leaving right after lunch…

"Sunday finally rolls around and you get her out of your house. You tell yourself --never again!

"A month later you come home and she is sitting in your living room. Your daughter has left her in. She wants to know what's for dinner. After you get rid of her, you explain to your daughter to not let her in your house.

"She continues to show up when you least expect it. You are never ready for it. No matter how much you are on guard, someone else lets her in -- at home, at the office, or you run into her at the grocery store, or even at the mall.

"You can't control her…

"Meet my Aunt …Depression …" Marilyn gestured to the empty spot next to her in the booth. "She wasn't here when I came to this get together, but she just sat down and she is asking for a Whiskey Sour."

"Well, let me introduce her to my Uncle … Melancholy…." Bobby said, gesturing to the empty seat on his side of the booth. "He is asking me for a Screwdriver. I'm going to order them a drink, and we are going to let them sit at that vacant booth and get to know one another, because they seem to have a lot in common. There just isn't any room for them at this booth," Bobby told her.

Marilyn smiled and realized she was more optimistic than she had been in quite a long time.

Chapter 6

"Look who the cat drug in? I thought I was going to have to do both the surgery and the anesthesia today!" Liz teased Bobby, as soon as he walked into their office.

"That, I would like to see!" Bobby grumbled.

"How late did you stay at The OutPost with Marilyn?" Liz asked.

"I think a little too long…" Bobby mumbled.

"I don't believe I have ever heard you complain before about spending too much time with a beautiful woman -- especially if she is downing Cosmos like water!" Liz remarked.

"There has to be a first time for everything. Last night was definitely a night of firsts," Bobby said, with a sigh.

"There has to be more to that story. Do I need to call Marilyn and have her bring whatever it was that she was threatening you with last night? What was it, Turkish Testicular Tweezers?" Liz asked, bringing back yet another unpleasant memory from the prior evening.

The thoughts of Marilyn's contraption instantly made him weak again. "Okay. Okay. I kinda let Marilyn think that I may be gay," Bobby blurted out.

"Happy, lighthearted gay, or homosexual gay?" Liz asked.

"Which one do you think?" Bobby snapped back.

"That's hilarious! Obviously, she has no idea of what a pervert you are!" Liz remarked.

"I'm glad you find it so funny, Liz. Marilyn started telling me about her bouts with depression, and I felt so bad for her. She is the only person besides you that I have ever opened up to about my own battle with it. I guess she jumped to this conclusion because I was so openly expressing my feelings. I also inadvertently told her I had thought about getting a Chihuahua. Then, she told me that she had 'accidently' seen some correspondence between you and I about my lover not feeling the same about me anymore. For the life of me, I couldn't figure out what she was talking about. When I got home, even though I was exhausted, I looked at some of our last e-mails, and guess what you and I were talking about?"

"You just said, it was your boyfriend," Liz said, somehow keeping a straight face.

"I'm being serious Liz. You and I were discussing about how I thought that Sam doesn't think I'm so cool anymore. She thought Sam was my boyfriend – not your

"I would stop, if I could. I really can't help it. So… I'm really curious how this ended."

"In a nutshell, she told me that she really thinks that coming out of the closet might help me with my depression," Bobby explained.

"Gee, I'm sure simply telling Marilyn the truth never crossed your mind!"

"Momentarily…"

"Why would you pretend to be gay? Women like cowboys or guys with motorcycles."

"It seemed like a good idea at the time. Think how flattered she will be when she turns me 'straight'."

"Do you want me to talk to her? I can truthfully tell her that you are not gay, but that you are very odd. Also, that as far as I know, that you have never had a homosexual lover, at least since I have known you," Liz offered.

"What do you mean by saying 'since I have known you'?" Bobby snapped.

"I've just always heard that young boys experiment during puberty," Liz tried to explain.

"What exactly is your reference for that?" Bobby questioned Liz.

"I was only trying to help!"

"This is one of the moments when I wonder why we are friends, Liz!"

"I know what you mean, I have lots of those moments too," Liz said, thinking how the tables were usually turned.

"Actually, I have it under complete control," Bobby said, and then smiled a wry smile that Liz knew all too well.

"Bobby Bain! This might be an all time low -- even for you! I don't think pretending to be gay to spend time with a woman is your best seduction plan!" Liz shrieked.

"Liz. Liz. Liz. Why do you think the worst of me? I have given this some thought, and maybe I have suppressed my feelings because I'm worried about being outcast and shunned," Bobby mused.

"Being an outcast and shunned has never worried you before, Bain," Liz snapped back.

"Marilyn and I are going shopping later this afternoon, after you and I finish in the OR. She thinks I need to begin to express my true self: that part of me that I keep hidden," Bobby explained.

"I can't wait to see the new wardrobe," Liz said, trying her best to keep a straight face.

"My motto is simple—I will wear a pink shirt, if it means I will get lucky and get to remove a woman's skirt," Bobby said, unable to hide his annoying smirk.

"I'm sure this will work as well as your many other previous plans of seduction. We'd better head to the OR, so you can finish up and go shopping. I see an ascot and driving loafers in your future."

Sure enough, Marilyn was waiting for Bobby when he and Liz finished in the OR a few hours later. While she waited, she killed time by snooping through the computer in Liz's office. This was a computer, which up to now, Liz had incorrectly assumed was securely password protected.

"Hi, Bobby! Are you ready to go? I've got our day all planned out. Since you have been on your feet all morning, I thought we should start with a pedicure. Then, we will stop by Rupert's Atelier to see if you like what they carry. Cocktails and tapas at Ernesto's Cantina. My hairdresser told me all about it," Marilyn said very excitedly, as soon as she saw Bobby.

"Let me change out of these scrubs, and then we can go!"

"You two have fun!" Liz said, as she imagined Bobby having to pretend to really like shopping. She wished that tomorrow was another OR day because she never got tired of hearing how Bobby's hair-brained seduction plans went awry, as they always did.

After Bobby changed, he and Marilyn said good-bye to Liz, and walked out to the parking lot. "I'll drive since I know where we are going," Marilyn said, as they approached a bright red, late-model VW Bug convertible.

Bobby got in the car, and made himself comfortable by reclining the seat just a tad more. "I have never had a pedicure before. What does it entail?" Bobby asked curiously.

"Actually, I have never been to this place. It's new. Don't tell anyone, but they do fish pedicures in the back room. The government recently outlawed them. I am always up for new things, how about you, Bain? You like to try new things, don't you?" Marilyn said, in a deep sultry voice that made Bobby want to agree to anything she might possibly suggest.

Bobby had no clue what a fish pedicure was, but responded like a dog would to the tone of her voice. "Fish pedicures have always intrigued me," he said, while trying his best to sound suave and debonair.

Within a few minutes they arrived, and parked in one of the many open parking spaces in front of the new strip shopping center. The acetone fumes immediately overwhelmed Bobby as soon as they entered the nail shop. He looked over at Marilyn, and she seemed completely unfazed by the odor. A young woman led them into a private room in the back of the shop.

Marilyn leaned over and told him, "Just do what I do. Follow my lead."

She sank into a giant moss green futon in the center of the dimly lit room, and patted for him to sit on the cushion next to her. There was a large square table butted against the futon so Bobby was unsure what to do with his feet. He looked over at Marilyn for guidance and noticed that she had just removed her gold strappy sandals and had started to roll up her white denim jeans. He followed her lead, and did the very same. He removed his brown leather loafers. Next, he removed his socks and slowly rolled them up, and discretely placed them in the loafers. He placed the loafers next to him on the bamboo floor by the futon. He purposely moved slowly, so he didn't appear inexperienced. He then started to roll up his khaki dress slacks. He rested his feet on the top of the table just like he got a pedicure every week.

The young woman who brought them into the back room returned carrying a ceramic flask. She proceeded to pour the liquid from the flask into two small ceramic cups.

Marilyn leaned into Bobby, and whispered, "It's sake."

The young woman introduced herself as Mei. She handed them both a small ceramic cup that was decorated with cranes. She said something that Bobby did not fully understand, but noticed that Marilyn was lifting her cup and nodding. Bobby lifted his cup also. Then they both took a sip.

"Whoa! I thought that was going to taste like white wine. It's more like a dry vermouth, only drier, if that is possible," Bobby exclaimed.

"It's an acquired taste. What do you order to drink when you have Japanese food?" Marilyn asked.

"Usually Japanese beer," Bobby replied, not realizing there were other options.

Mei motioned for them to lift their feet slightly as she slid the solid top off of the table revealing hundreds, possibly thousands, of small fish.

Bobby didn't realize that a fish pedicure would actually involve fish. He has referred to himself in the past as suffering from ichthyophobia, the fear of fish. When Bobby was a first grader, he had a goldfish named Goldie who lived in a small clear bowl on top of his dresser. Unlike most kids with a goldfish, Bobby realized that owning goldfish was a test propagated by his parents. If he could successfully care for a goldfish then they would be more likely to allow him to get the pet he really wanted -- a Collie puppy that looked just like Lassie.

One morning, his alarm clock rang and he started his normal routine—put on his slippers, feed a pinch of fish food to Goldie, and hurry down the hall to the bathroom.

Except this morning, there was no goldfish in the bowl! He quickly looked all over his cold linoleum floor looking for the wayward fish. He searched high and low. Seeing his chance of getting a Collie puppy becoming more distant by the minute, he screamed for his parents. After a thorough search, it was determined that the little orange goldfish was nowhere to be found. Bobby's parents didn't seem to blame him, but he had no way of proving himself a deserving dog owner either. From this point on, Bobby could no longer bring himself to eat fish sticks, and he also started avoiding carrots since their orange color reminded him of his tragic loss. He wouldn't swim in lakes or rivers, only swimming pools. He didn't like eating in restaurants that had large, decorative fish tanks, or the ones that he could see fish being served in its natural state – with a fully attached head. Bobby's parents didn't ever seem to notice, nor make a connection to his strange way of dealing with Goldie's demise. Every once in a while, for years, they would ponder what could have ever happened to little Goldie.

Many more years later, when Bobby was in med school, this cold case was finally solved. One day, he was refinishing his childhood bedroom furniture into something a little more grown-up when he placed the furniture on end to sand it. Underneath a small ledge were the remains of little Goldie. Years of wondering and speculating could finally be put to rest—Goldie had decided that the little fish bowl on the dresser wasn't big enough and had jumped out onto the waterless linoleum floor. He probably flopped and jumped until exhausted. His little sticky body made one more valiant attempt at returning to his small bowl, but instead he remained stuck in a well-hidden ledge under the dresser for fifteen plus years. Bobby had been making slow progress with his fish phobia since the mystery of Goldie's disappearance had been solved, but now… he was supposed to put his feet in a tub with a gazillion of them?

He looked over at Marilyn, who had put her feet right in. The small fish were darting around her feet, and would occasionally take a tentative nibble. She smiled whenever that happened, completely to Bobby's amazement.

Without hesitation, Bobby grabbed the ceramic flask containing the sake. He took a giant gulp and then he plunged his feet into the soaking tub. The small fish immediately swarmed, and starting feeding off the dead skin on his feet like it was a prisoner's last supper. He wanted to squeal like a girl and giggle hysterically, but he knew that doing so would blow it with Marilyn.

"What kind of fish are they, Marilyn, baby piranhas?" Bobby asked, desperately hoping for a negative answer.

"They are doctor fish. They don't even have teeth, Bain!" Marilyn explained.

"Why are they all going crazy over me? I get the same response from mosquitos."

"You have way more dead skin than I do. I get a pedicure every two weeks, but from the looks of that feeding frenzy, this must be your very first one."

"That's kinda embarrassing," Bobby said, and then let out a huge giggle when the fish moved on to some previously undiscovered dead skin between his toes.

"What's really embarrassing is your womanly giggle, Bain!" Marilyn said, with a laugh.

Marilyn caught him downing the sake out of the serving flask and insisted that he share.

"Mango or raspberry?" Marilyn asked, for absolutely no apparent reason.

"Mango or raspberry what?" Bobby wondered.

"Just answer the question, Bain!" Marilyn barked.

"Mango," Bobby answered

Bobby was still pondering the significance of this line of questioning when Mei returned to the room and took Marilyn's feet out of the fish tub. She dried them with a pre-warmed towel. Bobby was hoping that he could soon remove his feet from the fish-infested waters also.

A petite Asian woman entered the room and introduced herself as Reiko. She then began to towel dry Bobby's feet. She then took a small wooden stick and began to push back Bobby's virgin cuticles with it. Bobby quickly decided it hurt like hell. He began to wonder where she might have learned this torture technique. Were her ancestors members of the Viet Cong? Marilyn seemed to be enjoying this ritual.

"Bain, she is just pushing your cuticles back," as if she could read his mind.

"I knew that," Bobby answered.

Reiko asked Bobby if he picked a polish. His blank look said it all.

Marilyn answered for him, "Let's do a transparent black on the toes."

Bobby had no clue to what it was that they were talking about. Marilyn showed Bobby a very dark candy apple red that she chose for her toes. He was glad Marilyn hadn't suggested that for him.

Bobby enjoyed the next part of the pedicure that involved a peppermint scrub rubbed vigorously on his feet, toes and lower legs. This was followed by a quick, cool rinse and towel dry. Reiko then took lotion and massaged his tortured feet and toes. She then wrapped his feet together in a very warm moist towel. Between the sake, massage and warm towel Bobby began to struggle to stay awake.

When the towel started to cool, she unwrapped his feet and dried them again. She took a bright yellow piece of foam and separated his toes. Then she slipped his feet into a lime green slipper made of very thin foam. They didn't look like they would hold up to walk across the room. She then started to paint his toes with a clear polish. When she was done she picked up a different bottle that he realized was the black polish. He looked admiringly at his feet. The black was very sheer and shiny and while he wouldn't admit it to any of his guy friends – it was actually kinda cool. She finished his toes with another coat of the clear.

She then picked up his brown loafers and moved him to the main part of the salon that was now filled with attractive women. Reiko motioned for him to sit and put his feet under a table that had a purplish light underneath it. Bobby had learned one important thing today, and that was to do as he was told. As he started to sit he heard, "Dr. Bain, what in the world are you doing here?" He looked up to see Brooke Allan's beautiful smiling face.

"Actually I'm getting my first pedicure, Brooke," he said, soon realizing that she probably didn't believe him.

He sat down, put his feet under the table and picked up one of the magazines lying there, and started to read. He was now even more embarrassed to realize that he had picked up the latest issue of O, the Oprah Magazine.

Marilyn came out from the back and immediately saw Brooke. The two began giggling and pointing at Bobby who saw his chances with either woman rapidly diminishing.

Reiko came back and sprayed a can of something on Bobby's toes. He imagined it was "frost bite in a can" from the feel of it. She set the can down and he picked it up when she walked away to see what it was. It was something to quickly dry his toenails. When he realized no one was looking at him, he sprayed it on his big toe until it turned white. Two seconds later, he was screaming inside. He hoped the frostbite feeling would go away quickly because everyone was now looking at him wiggling around. Marilyn was giving him a look that he translated to mean that she would not be going on another outing with him in the near future.

Bobby paid for the two of them, and tipped Reiko and Mei very generously. Marilyn thanked him and they walk out to her car. Bobby was having a tough time walking in the thin lime green foam slippers, so Marilyn walked ahead and picked him up in the convertible.

Chapter 7

When they pulled up in front of Rupert's Atelier, Bobby bent over in the car to put on his socks and brown loafers. Marilyn quickly stopped him. "You can't put socks on or wear shoes until tomorrow. It will screw up your pedicure," she revealed to the clueless Bobby.

He carefully walked into the shop in the flimsy green foam slippers. As he glanced around the store, he thought to himself how he had only seen clothes like this in his Maxim magazine. He subscribed to it so he could look at the hot girls featured in the magazine's pages, not for the clothes. He has always wondered who in the world bought this stuff.

"Welcome! I'm Rupert. This is your first time here, isn't it? Is there anything in particular that you are looking for?" the outgoing man asked.

"We are looking for some resort wear," Marilyn explained.

"We just got some fabulous pieces in," Rupert told them, as he walked them past the Italian suits to a corner where the shirts were all in sherbet and Popsicle colors.

"Do you have anything in mango?" Marilyn asked.

"Of course! It's this season's hottest color. The magazines are showing it this season paired with lemon denim, but we have to remember that this is New Braunfels, Texas. I would probably tone it down a tad, and wear this nice white twill with it instead," Rupert explained, as he handed Bobby a mango shirt and white twill jeans in his size.

Bobby whispered to Marilyn, "How did he do that? How in the world did he know my size?"

Bobby went into the dressing room to try on the colorful outfit. He eventually came out with the mango shirt tucked into the twill pants.

"Oh my goodness, no!" Rupert exclaimed, as he walked over and untucked the mango shirt. He picked up a pair of brown huaraches sandals made from Italian leather and handed them to Bobby.

"Wow! Turn around," Marilyn instructed Bobby.

"Oh, my! Those pants make your rear look really nice," Rupert said, a little too excitedly for Bobby's liking. Bobby decided for Marilyn's sake not to cold-cock Rupert.

"Could you remove the tags and let him wear that out of here?" Marilyn asked.

"Sure, let me steam the shirt again from where he tucked it in. Where are you two off to, if I may ask?" Rupert said.

"Ernesto's Cantina," Marilyn replied.

"Make sure you order a DosArita!" Rupert recommended.

Bobby put his new outfit back on. Later, when he looked at his American Express receipt he realized why he had never shopped at this store before. His shirt, jeans and sandals cost more than any suit he had ever owned.

"Thank you, sir! You look fabulous!" Rupert said whole-heartedly, as Marilyn and Bobby left.

"Remind me to never go in there alone," Bobby said to Marilyn when they got back into her car.

Within moments, they had arrived at the popular Ernesto's Cantina. Marilyn had to circle the parking lot several times until a parking spot finally opened up.

"Come on 'Mango'," Marilyn teased him, as they got out of her car and walked into the establishment. Ricky Martin was blaring loudly over the speakers. The restaurant seemed to have an over abundance of men who looked like they might shop at Rupert's. Bobby easily identified the pineapple sherbet, dreamsicle, and the raspberry sorbet colored shirts on the restaurant's patrons. The hostess seated them at a small turquoise painted wooden table that had a vantage view for people watching. A slim waiter, who was dressed all in white and identified himself as Julio, asked them what he could bring them from the bar.

"I would like an X-rated margarita – frozen, no salt," Marilyn replied.

"I will try your DosArita," Bobby told Julio.

Before he went to place their order, Julio warned them that the salsa he had brought them was extremely hot. He explained that this was a Yucatán restaurant, not a traditional Mexican restaurant, so the salsa was made from habaneros, instead of jalapeños.

He returned first with Marilyn's drink – a passion fruit margarita with splashes of red raspberry, blood red orange and mango liquors. It looked like a beautiful sunset. He explained he would be right back with Bobby's drink, as he needed both hands to carry it. He returned with one of the largest margarita glasses that Bobby had ever seen. In the margarita, upside down, was a Dos XX bottle of beer.

Bobby was unsure how to drink this unstable concoction. He decided to start sipping the margarita. As he drank the margarita, the upside down beer started to slowly fill the displaced margarita. He didn't think he would like this drink when it came, but he decided that Rupert was correct. It was quite tasty. He was also finding the salsa mouthwatering. The only problem was that when he quit eating it, his mouth would burn like crazy and he had to quickly resume eating more of it. He soon developed a pattern of margarita, chip with salsa and then more margarita to keep the burning under control.

Julio was surprised when he came back to check on them that both Bobby's DosArita and the salsa were almost finished. He was even more surprised when Bobby asked for another DosArita. He was shocked when Bobby teased him that the salsa was "for babies".

Julio returned with another DosArita for Bobby. He informed them that the chef was disappointed that Bobby was unhappy with the salsa, so he was making a special batch just for him and it would be out momentarily.

Julio followed the Mayan chef to Bobby and Marilyn's table where he proudly places the new salsa on the table. It was completely green in color. Marilyn surmised that this salsa was probably close to ninety-eight percent habanero. The chef nodded, spread his hands and said, "Espero que disfrute su comida (I hope you enjoy your meal)."

Bobby waited until the chef was out of hearing range and replied, "Mucho Poocho". This was the only "Spanish" he knew. He actually thought that it meant big dog.

Bobby placed a large amount of the habanero salsa on his tortilla chip. He could see some small black flecks where the peppers had been lightly grilled and he could also see numerous seeds in the green salsa. Whether it was Bobby's intoxicated state or his inexperience with habanero peppers, he quickly realized that he could feel the salsa inching its way from his mouth through his digestive track. It caused a flashback to his anatomy class in med school. He desperately grabbed the upside down Dos XX beer and found that it kept the fire at bay as long as he was constantly drinking it. When the beer ran out, he scanned the room for Julio who was now nowhere in site. He knew better, but felt like he had no choice except to drink the frozen margarita next.

"AUGH!!!" Bobby screamed and started holding his head like an aneurysm had burst in his frontal lobe.

"What's wrong?" Marilyn asked.

"Brain freeze."

Marilyn just shook her head. Julio returned and rushed over to their table. She asked him to bring them some butter and tortillas to calm the burn from the habanero salsa.

Bobby suddenly realized he was now drunk, and believed that it might be possible that he had permanently damaged his digestive tract. He also hoped that his eyes would stop watering and his nose would stop dripping like some snot-nose kid.

"Fernando," Marilyn motioned to a man who approached their table. He was dressed just like Bobby, with the exception of his shirt color. Fernando's shirt was the color of lime green sherbet.

Fernando sat down in the empty chair, next to Bobby. He motioned for Julio, and ordered another round of drinks for everyone. Bobby decided to stick with beer from now on.

Julio returned with their drinks and to take their dinner orders. He recommended

Sopa de Lima for Marilyn, which he explained was a chicken-based soup with slices of lime that he said was very light and refreshing. Fernando insisted on ordering his favorite - the Pollo Pibil chicken, which has been marinated in bitter orange and lime juices topped with achiote paste and then wrapped with tomatoes and onions in banana leaves and slowly cooked in coals until the meat was falling off the bones. It was served with homemade corn tortillas, black beans and yellow rice. Bobby wanted to order that, but Julio suggested that Bobby try the Cochinita Pibil, which was prepared just like Fernando's dish, but with one exception -- it was made with pork.

The food was delicious and unlike anything Bobby had ever had before. Bobby tried, in vain, to trick Fernando into trying the 'Chef's special' green salsa. Fernando roared with laughter when Bobby told him he had actually tried a chip full of the concoction.

"You will remember this evening again in the morning, my friend," Fernando said, as he grabbed Bobby's hand on the table for a brief moment.

When Julio returned Fernando whispered something to him and off he went. He returned with two wooden trays with four thick glasses filled with tequila.

"Mi amigo, tonight I will teach you many important things. Lesson one -- Lick, slam, and suck. With the tequila for now," Fernando teased.

This was the exact moment that a light went off in Bobby's inebriated head and he realized that Fernando might be his blind date. This made him extremely nervous and he quickly downed the first glass of the premium tequila. Fernando winked at Marilyn, and picked up his glass.

Forty-five minutes later, the four shots were history, and so were Bobby and Fernando.

"Time to go, Fernando. Come on, Bobby," Marilyn said as she tried to rouse the two groggy amigos. She gestured to Julio to help her get them out of the restaurant and into the backseat of her bug. Bobby put his arm around Julio and Fernando did the same. Bobby started singing the only Spanish song that he could think of which was, 'Feliz Navidad'. She silently cursed him because she knew that tomorrow this song would be playing over and over in her mind. Both of them were sound asleep before she even pulled out of the parking lot of Ernesto's.

Once she got them home, Marilyn couldn't decide what to do with them. They were too drunk to move and too heavy for her to carry. She decided to pull in the garage and just leave them there. So they wouldn't go anywhere, she removed both of their pants, and threw them high into the rafters of her garage.

"Buenas noches," she whispered, and turned the lights off as she walked from the garage into her house.

Chapter 8

Marilyn's head was a little achy upon awakening in the morning. She wondered if it was due to drinking margaritas after the sake, or perhaps she should have had a couple less of the X-rated margaritas. It was nothing a Motrin or Tylenol, and some extra fluids wouldn't fix she thought. Bobby, on the other hand, was in much worse shape. He had muttered something about the blinking of his eyes hurting his head, or some other such nonsense, when she dropped him back at his car this morning.

She was very glad that Liz didn't want her at her office until eleven o'clock. Liz had mentioned that she was going to take her horse out on the trails of The Preserve, where she lived. She was pleased that Liz was finally starting to take some time for herself.

Marilyn spent an extraordinary amount of time in Liz's office fixing her computers. Originally, Liz had wondered if she might have some weird magnetic field around her because her computers were always screwed up. Initially, Marilyn thought this was hogwash, but now she was beginning to think that this might be just as plausible an explanation as any. Poor Liz was so computer illiterate that Marilyn knew better than to try and do any trouble shooting with her over the phone. It was strange because Liz did so many other things really well. Liz used to joke that some of the things she liked best were the things that she wasn't good at – computers and dressage. Marilyn sincerely hoped that she was better at riding horses than operating computers, but she had to wonder.

Marilyn walked into Liz's private office unannounced, as she often did. She ended up scaring Liz half to death.

"I guess I'm a little jumpy today," Liz said, but her voice seemed uncharacteristically shaky to Marilyn.

"I should have knocked."

Liz just didn't seem like herself to Marilyn. For one thing, it was completely out of character for Liz to not immediately ask how the "outing" with Bobby had gone. Marilyn realized by her uncharacteristic silence that something was wrong.

"Liz, is something wrong?"

Liz tried her best to continue the ruse, hopeful that Marilyn would just drop the subject. Marilyn noticed tears starting to form in the corner of Liz's big blue eyes. Liz turned slightly away, and started to blink rapidly trying to make the tears evaporate faster.

Marilyn decided that she was going to have to force the issue.

"Liz, please, tell me what is wrong," Marilyn pleaded.

Liz grabbed a tissue and started to press it into her tear ducts. She was trying, in vain, to stop the flow of tears that were soon going to wreck her carefully applied make-up.

"Do you remember that I told you that I couldn't meet you any earlier than eleven because I was going to ride Max this morning? I was really looking forward to it because the weather was going to be perfect. I had it all planned out. I was going to get up at 6:15, put on my riding clothes, just put my hair up in a ponytail and pray that I wouldn't run into anyone I know without my make-up. Then, drop Sam off at school after going to get her favorite – an egg and cheese breakfast taco. That would put me at the stable by seven. It usually takes me about fifteen minutes to pick Max's hooves, groom him and tack him up. I wanted to be on the trail by seven fifteen. It takes about forty-five minutes to ride the trail that skirts the edge of the golf course. I figured that gave me plenty of time to untack Max and cool him down and still be out of there by nine. Plenty of time to drive home, shower, get ready and meet you by eleven. Everything was falling right into place. Max, Fritz and I were on the trail very close to seven fifteen," Liz said.

"I thought you fired Fritz? I never liked that pompous weirdo with his fake German accent. Who did he think he was fooling? I don't think I ever saw the guy without a drink in his hand," Marilyn replied.

"Fritz is my dog, not my old riding instructor. He is a Jack Russell terrier mix. The second we begin the trails, he will sprint off and then wait for Max and I at the half way point, on one of the benches before the eighth hole. That is The Preserve's signature hole on top of the bluff. I guess he likes the view.

Anyway, Max and I started off at a walk, and after a few moments began a posting trot. The workers were out, putting the finishing touches on the greens. I was feeling more relaxed than I have in a long time. The trail is lightly wooded then starts to open into the clearing by the bluff. When I looked ahead, I saw that Fritz was not on his bench. Then I glanced over by the trashcans to see if he might be rummaging through them. But he was nowhere in sight."

"No wonder you are upset. Do you think someone took him? Is this a picture of him?" Marilyn picked up a picture of Sam posing with a wiggling white dog with large brown-black spots who was trying his best to lick Sam's face, instead of posing for the picture.

"Yes, that's him but no one in their right mind would take him. When he is tired, he is grumpy. His run really tires him out. It would be like trying to pick up a live wolverine. Finally, I heard him barking like crazy from just inside the entrance to the woods. I was worried that maybe he had cornered some wild animal. The trail goes into heavy woods for about a half of a mile right at the clubhouse. It's the only part of the trail I'm not crazy about because Max gets spooky if we run into deer. I know this wasn't a deer because that would have run off."

"Do you think it might have been a bear, cougar or bobcat?" Marilyn asked, using animals that lived in her former home state of Indiana as a reference.

"I honestly didn't know what it was. I was scared that Max was going to dump me once we got in there. He was getting really tense, moving his ears back and forth, and blowing air out of his nostrils like he thought he was a stallion. I knew that unlike Fritz, he would bolt rather than fight if threatened -- completely forgetting I am on his back. I was hoping that the barking was due to a possum, or an armadillo, and not a skunk.

"What was it?" Marilyn asked.

"A woman. A woman that my dog sensed was not quite right."

"Why do you say that? Was she acting funny?" Marilyn asked.

"That is a loaded question. It was this creepy woman that worked for my husband. She does not live in The Preserve – not in the luxury condos, the golf course villas, nor the Estates. She had absolutely no business being on the horse trail, since she was not on a horse, or dressed in riding attire. She wasn't dressed like a golfer either, that somehow has hit their ball 300 feet up a bluff into the woods, or behind their head 100 feet. Unfortunately, the police do not agree with me."

"What did she do when she saw you?" Marilyn wondered.

"She just stared her usual vacant look. Thank goodness, Fritz came with Max and I right away. He seemed quite proud he had cornered such a large varmint. As soon as I safely could, I called the police. They arrived really fast, but of course, she had already disappeared.

I told them how I have seen her driving past my house, which is in a gated community. They said to call next time I see her. Then I told them that whenever I shop, she shows up at the grocery store a few minutes later. I am now in the habit of checking the parking lot to make sure that she isn't there when I go in. My parents live in the condos in The Preserve and I live in The Estates. We shop at the same grocery store. I run into my Dad maybe twice a year at the most, and he goes to the store for one item at a time, two or three times a day. I have seen her twice this week, and three times last week. The officer just looked at me funny and told me it is not against the law to go to the grocery store.

Then, they informed me that the woods by The Preserve is actually deeded a city park by the developer. Anyone who wants to walk in, or drive in, can. All they have to do is tell the guard that they wish to use the park facility, which consists of two picnic tables and Fritz's bench. Unbelievable!

Two of the officers wished me luck and got in their squad car and drove off. I have the feeling they will be laughing their asses off on the way to the Donut Ho. (The Donut Ho was a New Braunfels donut shop that was originally named The Donut Hole. The small shop's popularity rose when the 'le' fell off of the 'Hole' during a typical Texas thunderstorm, so the owners never fixed the sign. They found that the surrounding small towns would not allow a business named the Donut Ho to open in their towns, so only the original Donut Ho remained. Besides being popular with the locals, it had become pretty popular with the tourists who came to tube the river in the summer and buy their comical t-shirts.)

Suddenly I realized that there was an officer who was left behind. His nametag said 'Becker'. I remembered his name was Hans. Officer Becker's wife, Jan was a patient of mine. She had been mauled a couple of years ago by their neighbor's pit bull. Her neighbor was supposed to pay for her eyelid reconstruction surgery, but skipped town before the surgery. Bobby and I waived our fees. She and her sister owned the most wonderful bakery near the square across from The OutPost."

"I love the cheesecake from her place. Oh my goodness, have you had her cream puffs? Sometimes she dips them in chocolate. How crazy is that? They sell out before she can put them in the case. Oops sorry, finish your story," Marilyn said, after realizing that she might have gotten more excited about the cream puffs rather than what had just happened to Liz.

"Anyways, he asked me if she has tried contacting me in any other way. I told him about the phone calls that we had never received before, marked as PRIVATE CALL-ER on the caller ID. I told him I have stopped answering them. He asked me if I think that those calls might be from her. I told him that I'm pretty certain because PRIVATE CALLER came up on Adam's phone when she would try to call him. I also told him that she tries to disguise her voice, but I can still hear her distinctive lisp.

He wondered out loud what her motive is. I told him the truth. She is a nutcase who believes that if she has my husband, she will have my life. He assured me that he is going to take the case very seriously and would be in touch."

"Liz, do you realize that one of your shoes is brown and one is black?" Marilyn asked.

"Not again! At least they are the same shoe style," Liz said, trying to convince herself that this wasn't a sign of severe psychological distress.

"That's what I like about you, Liz. You can always see the positive in a situation," Marilyn said, with a laugh.

They both started laughing when Liz suddenly exclaimed, "Oh my gosh, what happened yesterday with Bobby? I can't believe I forgot to ask you. I have been so curious."

"Let's just say, I don't think Bobby Bain will try pretending to be anything he's not. What kind of desperate fool tries to spend time with a woman by letting her think that he might be gay?" Marilyn wondered out loud.

"Dr. Bobby Bain, that's who! So start from the beginning!"

"Well, as you know I picked him up, and we went to get a pedicure. He was hilarious! It was one of those fish pedicures where the fish nibble the dead skin off your feet. I had no idea that he's scared to death of fish, and he's so ticklish that it's embarrassing to be in the same room with him."

"I thought they outlawed those due to sanitary reasons?" Liz inquired.

"They have," Marilyn answered, without explaining why she would take Bobby for an illegal, unsafe pedicure, or have one also.

"I do know he is deathly afraid of fish. Something happened to him in childhood, I think. He must really like you if he stuck his feet in a tub of them."

"Then when we were leaving, he ran into Brooke, of all people. He was so embarrassed to be seen in there with his green foam sandals and black lacquered toes. He tried acting like he had never been there before, but I don't think she bought it. She acted like he had the plague."

"Bobby wanted polish?"

"I picked it for him. He might have had a little too much sake at that point."

"Then what happened?"

"Then we went to Rupert's Atelier. Rupert was so helpful. He was very complimentary of Bobby. He told him his butt was cute. You could tell Bobby wanted to punch him, but to his credit he didn't. He picked out a mango shirt, white jeans and huaraches sandals. I started calling Bobby, 'Mango' after that.

"I will have to remember that. M-A-N-G-O!"

"Then we went to Ernesto's Cantina where he drank way too many DosAritas, beers and tequilas. I introduced him to Fernando, my rather flamboyant hairdresser, who was in on the whole ruse. I think Fernando deviated from the original plan, which was to have a drink with us just to make Bobby uncomfortable. That backfired when they seemed to thoroughly enjoy each other's company. Next thing I knew they were having tequila shot samplers, and singing 'Feliz Navidad' at the top of their lungs. As soon as they got in the car, they both immediately fell asleep. I had to listen to their snoring the whole way home. I couldn't wake them up when we got back to my place. They were both too drunk to drive home, and too heavy for me to move. So, I left my garage door cracked about 4 inches, took their pants so they couldn't leave, and left them asleep in my car. I brought them a blanket a little later. They both snuggled up under it, and went right back to sleep.

When I woke up, I went to check on them. I had thrown their pants up high on the rafters on my garage ceiling so they couldn't leave last night. They had both retrieved them. Bobby sheepishly came in, and asked to use my bathroom. He came out looking wide-eyed. He was probably wondering what caused his butt to feel that way. I MIGHT reassure him in a day or two that it was the habanero peppers, and nothing else. Or maybe I won't!" Marilyn said smugly.

Liz realized that Bobby had finally met a worthy sparring partner in Marilyn. Liz was going to welcome the break.

Chapter 9

Bobby decided that one of the best things about being a physician was being able to start an IV on himself when he was hung over. Not that he had ever revealed that during his med school interviews. He hadn't had this much to drink in a long time, thank goodness. The more he tried to think, the more his head hurt. He decided it would be wise to take some Tylenol and some Motrin, too. He didn't want to take the Motrin on an empty stomach, so he rummaged through the break room in Liz's office for one of those low calorie, tasteless snacks that Liz and the other women seemed to survive on. He also found a Diet Coke in the refrigerator. The caffeine in the soda should be beneficial he remembered. In med school, they had learned that caffeine could increase the body's ability to absorb medicine. When he tried to remember why this occurred his head immediately began to throb again. He took the huge 800 mg Motrin tablet and the two smaller oblong 325 mg Tylenol with the Diet Coke. Within minutes, he had started his IV of 5% saline solution, and was almost asleep on the gurney in Liz's same day surgery suite.

The only thing that was keeping him awake was the nagging questions, "Why didn't he have his pants on when he woke up this morning in Marilyn's garage?" How did both his and Fernando's pants end up on the rafters? Did his ass feel like it was on fire because of the habaneros, or could there be another reason?? Surely not, he hoped.

Soon he was too tired to even care. He fell into a deep sleep.

Unexpectedly, his phone vibrating in his shirt pocket awakened him. He was so startled that he forgot he was on the gurney and when he reached for it, he unfortunately rolled off onto the floor. He felt a sharp sting in his left arm. He hadn't bothered to secure the IV. He noticed his head no longer hurt, but now his whole right side ached where he had landed.

He checked his phone to see who had awakened him from his deep sleep. It was Marilyn. He decided falling on the floor was worth missing that phone call. He was quite pleased with himself that he had dodged that bullet. He checked the time and it was 1:35 PM. He had been asleep for about two hours.

Suddenly the door opened and the lights were turned on.

"Bobby, what are you doing here? Are you okay?" Liz asked, as she rushed to his side.

He looked up at Liz from the floor and was alarmed to see Marilyn standing immediately behind her with the barrel of a gun pointed directly at him.

"Marilyn!" Bobby screamed at her.

Liz turned around and screamed even louder when she saw Marilyn was aiming a gun at her friend. Liz piercing scream caused Marilyn to jump, and the gun accidently went off knocking a ceiling tile squarely onto Bobby's head. Now, he thought his headache would be back with a vengeance.

Without a single word, Liz quickly snatched the gun from Marilyn and took the other bullet out of the gun. Liz and Bobby both stared at Marilyn for a while, speechless.

"I always wondered who would buy a pearl-handle .22 derringer? Next time, throw the gun at the perp. It's more effective. Thank God, this office is on the top floor or someone could have gotten hurt," Liz said, as she handed the empty gun back to Marilyn.

"What do you mean, 'could have got hurt'? I got hurt. Thank God, she is a crappy shot," Bobby added.

"Liz, I thought it was your stalker," Marilyn tried to explain.

"What stalker?" Bobby asked.

"Bobby, we can talk about it tomorrow. I need to go pick up Sam or I will be late," Liz said coolly, and left.

"Be careful!" Marilyn called after her.

"What the hell is wrong with you?" Bobby snapped at Marilyn, as soon as Liz left.

"I don't know what to say, but I'm truly sorry," Marilyn said sincerely.

"What exactly is it that you are sorry about Marilyn?"

"Well for starters. I'm sorry about yesterday."

"Which part, Marilyn? The part where the baby piranhas nibbled on my feet? Or Rupert telling me my butt was cute, so that I would buy a $275 shirt from him? Or, was it the part where you had me thinking that something happened with Fernando in the back of your bug?"

"All of it. Even though it was pretty shitty of you to try to trick me into spending time with you," Marilyn replied.

"It seemed the only way at the time," Bobby said.

"That doesn't make it right. It made me mad. I'm just as smart as you – just in different ways."

"You are right. You obviously had me going with the whole Fernando thing. I ALMOST thought for a moment that something had happened. I just can't figure out one thing -- how did my pants end up on the rafters?" Bobby asked.

"What are you talking about?" Marilyn looked at him quizzically.

The color drained out of Bobby's face.

"Why didn't you answer your phone?" Marilyn asked, changing the subject.

"I was trying to when I fell off the gurney. What did you want Marilyn? Did you want to invite me to get my chest waxed, or something?" Bobby asked.

"Look, I said I was sorry. I was trying to get in touch with you because I think Liz needs our help. What she told me today really has me worried!" Marilyn explained.

"So, she really has a stalker? I thought you were making that up so I would be side-tracked from the fact that the bullet from your gun caused my head to be cracked open."

"Yes, she really does. The police are even involved. Your head is not cracked open!"

"I'm not waiting until tomorrow to find out what is going on. Help me up off this floor," Bobby told her.

Marilyn extended her right hand to him, and when he was almost upright she lost her balance. She was now sprawled on top of Bobby.

"My patience is starting to wear thin, Marilyn," Bobby groaned.

"Try doing what I just did in a high heel sandal. Might I add, that if you were in better shape you wouldn't need my help!" Marilyn taunted him.

Bobby's instinct was to answer back with a snappy response, but Marilyn suddenly looked so vulnerable and enticing. She was slightly out of breath. His mind immediately went to the romance novels that Liz had started him reading. Marilyn was so close, and he was so aware of her beautiful, ample breasts. She didn't seem to mind when his gaze lingered longer than it should. She just smiled and took a deep breath. She looked so alluring. She moved closer. Should he just have his way with the wench? Maybe he should put his hand behind her dark tousled hair and slowly pull her to him. Her eyes were just begging for him to kiss her...

"Bobby, Bobby are you okay? I think you may have just fainted," Marilyn said, as she continued to slap the left side of his face like he was a CPR dummy.

"Huh?!?"

"You were mad at me, and then all of a sudden your eyes glazed over and you started calling me, Wen or Gwen or something," Marilyn explained.

Bobby realized that maybe he was not so unlucky after all! He shook his head wondering which would have been worse -- calling Marilyn a wench to her face or stealing a kiss.

"Let me help you up. We will do this a little slower this time. I'm going to take you home and put you to bed where I can keep my eyes on you. You might have a concussion. I will take real good care of you. As soon as you are feeling better, I will fill you in on Liz's situation, I promise."

"Marilyn, I'm sure I can manage on my own," Bobby told her, as stood up holding onto the side of the gurney.

"Please, let me make this up to you, Bobby!" Marilyn pleaded.

Bobby thought about her breasts again and simply said, "Okay."

Marilyn put her arm around Bobby's waist to help support him.   They turned off the lights, locked the door, and made their way to the parking lot where Marilyn's Bug was parked.

Bobby was already thinking that this would be a very interesting evening. He thought it had to be better than last night's sleepover at Marilyn's. At least tonight she had promised that he could sleep in a bed.

When they arrived at Marilyn's, Bobby seemed markedly weaker to Marilyn.

"Maybe we should call Liz, or I should take you to the ER."

"I am only thinking of you, Marilyn, my dear. The police can really jump to the wrong conclusions sometimes. I guess as long as you have a clean record, we can go to the ER. I will tell them it was an accident, you shooting the gun at me and all."

"I guess it's just the long drive back to my house. I am going to get your bath ready. You are quite the mess, Bobby Bain, between the IV solution, blood and ceiling tile pieces."

"Whatever you think is best, Marilyn. I just don't want you to somehow end up in police custody for something as silly as not having a license for your gun, or for attempted murder, or anything else like that. I sure could go for my grandmother's chicken and dumplings. That always made me feel better when I was a child."

"I can go pick some up for you. That does sound good. Where does your Grandma live?" Marilyn asked.

"I like to think that she is in heaven. A stray bullet from a drive-by shooter killed her while she was volunteering at an elementary school in the barrio. A senseless killing, that's what it was!" Bobby said, as he gazed up towards heaven for additional effect to his entirely bogus story.

"Tell you what, why don't you get your bath while I make dinner? I will make you some of my grandma's chicken and dumplings. I'm sure they won't be as good as your grandma's, but it always makes me feel better also. Let me get you a robe, and I will wash your clothes while you soak and relax in the tub. I will even let you have some of my lavender bath salts. That will relax you. Just put your dirty clothes outside the door, so I can start washing them."

Bobby slowly got up and limped on his left side into the bathroom, forgetting that it was his right side that he had landed so hard on. After a few moments, Bobby opened the door slightly, and placed his soiled clothes outside the door.

Marilyn quickly went to her pantry where she thankfully found three large cans of Progresso Chicken and Dumplings. She opened the cans, and poured the contents into her flame colored Le Creuset soup pot. She added two cups of water and placed the burner on medium-low. Marilyn then gathered up the cans and placed in her trash receptacle in her garage. She buried them under some trash for good measure. She was confident that that she would win another round against Bobby Bain. After all, she had won round one last night.

Back in her kitchen she chopped up a small piece of celery, a carrot, and left the pieces on her chopping block. She added a little white pepper and a dash of cayenne to the simmering mixture. Next, she took out a small clear glass bowl and mixed a few tablespoons of flour and water. She admired her work. It sure looked like she had made the dumplings from scratch. Her grandmother used to add butter to everything she made. Which may be why she was no longer around, or it may have been her chain smoking, or her bottle of gin a day habit. She added two generous tablespoons of butter to the now fragrant mixture.

"Marilyn! Do you have something I could wear while my clothes are washing?" Bobby yelled from the bathroom.

"I sure do! I will bring you something in just a minute. Let me run out to my garden real quick. I sure hope you are hungry."

"Yes, getting shot at really does something for the appetite!" Bobby yelled back.

Marilyn gathered some fresh basil and two Beefsteak tomatoes from her garden and came back in. She found a pale pink terry towel wrap with elaborate eyelet trim. She also grabbed the matching bathrobe that she bought at the same time. It was made from the same soft pink terry with an eyelet ruffle around the edge. She knocked on the door.

"Yes?" Bobby asked.

"I put a wrap and a robe by the door for you. You can see which one works better for you," Marilyn said, ever so sweetly.

She went back into the kitchen where she sliced the tomatoes and chopped the basil. She added the basil to the chicken and dumplings. She set the table just like her Grandmother had taught her, with the knife on the right and the fork on the left. The soupspoon was placed next to the knife. The napkin was carefully folded and placed to the left of the fork.

The door made a slight squeak as it opened and out came Bobby Bain wearing the pink towel wrap around his middle and the pink robe over it. The pink robe would not close due to the size of his chest. The eyelet ran vertically up and down the opening.

Marilyn had to quickly turn away, so she wouldn't burst out laughing.

After she was composed, Marilyn said, "I'm sorry, but all I had was pink. I bet you are starving. Sit down and I will get you some dinner."

"Marilyn, why is the table set for three?" Bobby asked, hoping that Fernando or anyone that he knew would not be joining them.

Before she could answer the doorbell rang. Marilyn just smiled and went to the door.

"Bobby, I didn't have a chance to tell you, but I thought Natalie should know what is going on with Liz also," Marilyn said.

"I am so glad you called, Marilyn!" Natalie said. She stopped dead in her tracks when she saw Bobby sitting at the table in a sea of pink, eyelet and curly chest hair.

"I better put Bobby's clothes in the dryer. I'll be back in just a moment," Marilyn said. She barely made it to the laundry room before she burst out laughing thinking of Bobby struggling to pull on the edges of the eyelet to cover more of his chest. She transferred his clothes to the dryer and put the dryer on delicate, the lowest dryer setting possible. She then went to join Bobby and Natalie in the dining room.

"Natalie, what is the normal sentence for attempted murder in Texas? I am just curious," Bobby asked, as soon as Marilyn walked back into the room.

"Time to eat," Marilyn announced, trying to act oblivious to Bobby's question. She placed the decorative soup pot in the middle of the table along with the platter of sliced homegrown tomatoes.

"This smells delicious," Natalie said, about the doctored-up Progresso Chicken and Dumplings.

"It's my Grandma's recipe," Marilyn said truthfully. Marilyn's Grandma never made a home cooked meal in her life. But she was a pro at doctoring-up anything that came out of a can or a box.

"You will have to give me the recipe. There is nothing in the world as comforting as Grandma's Chicken and Dumplings," Natalie said, trying not to glance Bobby's way.

Everyone seemed to be enjoying the doctored Progresso. Marilyn was glad that she opened all three cans, because Bobby helped himself to seconds.

Finally, after hearing about what had happened to Liz, Natalie asked Bobby and Marilyn, " What can we do about Liz's stalker? Do you guys have any ideas?"

"Marilyn could shoot her," Bobby said, volunteering Marilyn's services.

"I'm serious, Bobby," Natalie replied.

"Actually I did think of a plan," Bobby told them.

"Are you going to tell us?" Marilyn wondered.

"I think we should stalk the stalker," Bobby told them simply.

"I like the sound of that. Count me in," Natalie told Bobby.

"Me too!" Marilyn responded.

Chapter 10

"Have you ever done this before?" Natalie asked Bobby. She turned toward the driver's seat and seductively crossed her right leg over her left leg at the ankle, which now positioned her in the exact opposite direction of her previous vantage point, which had a view of Mrs. Piggy's teenie-weenie house.

"So, are you asking me if I have ever sat in my car alone with a beautiful woman wearing black leather pants that she could have borrowed from Cat Woman? No, I can honestly say that this is a first for me. It is also my first time to stalk a stalker," Bobby stated in a very matter-of-fact manner.

"You can be such the charmer when you want, Dr. Bain. I was referring to stalking the stalker."

"I don't recall ever doing this before. At least that is the story I am going to stick with," Bobby said, and then smiled.

"I brought a few items along that I thought might come in handy for a stake-out—doughnuts from the Donut Ho, Diet Coke and wet wipes. Marilyn told me that you had a really nice car, so I didn't want to get it all sticky. Is this another Chevette?" Natalie said teasing him. She remembered the story that Liz had told her, about Bobby trying to pass his Chevette off as a Corvette in medical school, the night that Natalie had been introduced to him at The OutPost.

"I have now graduated to a real "Vette". Actually it's a Corvette ZR1. 638 horse-power."

"It's very cute," Natalie told him.

"Gee, thanks. That's the exact image I was going after. Cute!" Bobby said, wondering if all the trouble he spent trying to impress Natalie would ever pay off.

"This is one ugly-ass house we are watching! I believe that the garage is bigger than the house. Who chooses to paint their white rock house, light beige? Did you know that Tim Moody lives in an ugly-ass rock house, too? " Natalie said like she believed that Mrs. Piggy and her ex-husband somehow match a special FBI profile—"freaks who live in ugly-ass rock houses."

"I'm sure it's the closest house that Mrs. Piggy could afford by Liz and Adam's house. If you cut across the schoolyard, it really isn't that far away. You could easily walk it," Natalie said.

"Which she does on a regular basis. I'm sure that was the majority of the attraction."

"Are you packing?" Natalie asked, suddenly changing the topic from the previous discussion of ugly-ass houses.

"I'm not going anywhere anytime soon. I have been mulling over the idea of going to Bermuda for some continuing medical education though. Never been there. I heard it's really nice."

"I was talking about packing heat?" Natalie clarified to the clueless Bobby.

"Oh, right! I have a Desert Eagle 44 Magnum, and I also picked up two NVGs for us."

"I think I will stick with the donuts," Natalie naively replied.

"Huh?!..."

"I just never have been a fan of freeze-dried food," Natalie explained.

"Not MREs—Meals Ready to Eat! NVGs are Night Vision Goggles. You use them so you can see well in the dark. I bought them off of E-Bay long ago. I guess I knew they would come in handy one day."

"What time is it?" Natalie asked.

"20:58"

"Try that again, but this time speak English."

"8:58"

"Look, the front room light just went off," Natalie said, pointing at the now dark house.

"Finally some activity besides this old woman whose house we are parked in front of peering through her Venetian blinds every two minutes. I guess I should have brought a less conspicuous car. I just thought the black color would be good," Bobby said.

"Yes it is, but your car costs more than the houses in this neighborhood. Now, what time is it?"

"9:02"

"I never knew it would be such hard work just sitting here doing nothing," Natalie said, stating the obvious.

"Did you ever spy on your ex?"

"No, I could care less what that freak is up to. I am an admitted Internet stalker. I always check people out before I do any business with them. I check out where they live. For example, I wouldn't want my financial advisor to live out of his means, but I wouldn't want to find that he lives in a shitty little house like this either."

"How did you get her address?"

"I looked it up on the county property appraisal sites and got lucky."

"What else do you know about her?"

"I know all of her family members' names, including her parents and husband, where she went to school and where she works. She put she was 'in a relationship' on a social networking site. So, from that I know she is delusional. She has a Master's degree from one of those on-line schools that advertises on television. I always wondered what kind of person signed up for that. I have a feeling her self-esteem is low, so that explains why she has spent most of her life working in an office, not utilizing her education. My guess would be that something bad happened to her in childhood - a rape, incest, or maybe she was horribly bullied. Who knows? I don't really care, there is no good excuse for someone to chase after someone else's husband."

"How in the world did you come up with that from the internet?" Bobby asked.

"I just filled in the blanks from the facts that I gathered. I came up with a profile. Just so you know, I'm never wrong on these kind of things," Natalie said, meaning it.

"I have a feeling you aren't," Bobby said, clearly convinced.

Natalie looked over at Bobby and without saying a word leaned in towards him. He started to move away, but when he did she put her right hand on the nape of his neck, and pulled him gently closer. Before he knew what the heck was going on, she started to gently kiss him. She stopped for a moment, then smiled at him, and pulled him close again. This time her kisses were more fervent, she even nibbled on his bottom lip. Bobby wondered if there could have been something in her Diet Coke? He had NEVER had a sober woman kiss him like that. Actually Bobby couldn't remember any woman - sober or drunk - kissing him like this.

Bobby decided he needed to act before Natalie changed her mind. His mind was racing trying to figure out how to logistically take this to the next level. The Corvette seat only reclined minimally and the center console was a huge impediment.

BANG! BANG! BANG!

"License, registration and insurance card," a big voice boomed at Bobby.

Bobby looked out of his window to see one of New Braunfels finest standing there. To say that the officer was not looking particularly happy was an understatement.

Bobby pushed the button that lowered the driver's side window.

"Good evening, officer."

"Stay in the car, sir. Keep your hands were I can see them. Good evening, ma'am are you okay?"

"Yes, officer. Everything is fine," Natalie calmly replied, and smiled convincingly.

Bobby opened his glove box, and found his insurance card and car's registration. For modesty's sake, he was thankful he did not have to stand and get out of the car at this moment. He took his wallet out of the car's middle console, and removed his driver's license. He handed all three of the requested items to the stern officer.

The officer took the items from Bobby without saying a single word. He walked back to his squad car and inputted Bobby's information. When he returned, he handed the items back and said, "I'm not going to ask you two why in the world you are sitting here making out like teenagers when you, Dr. Bain, live less than two miles from here. I hate being lied to." The officer handed everything back to Bobby and walked away without as much as a good night.

In his confusion, Bobby turned to Natalie as the officer drove off. He quickly did a mental calculation. The officer was correct. He could be at his house in minutes. Peeling Natalie out of her tight leather "stake-out" outfit would take even less. He could only imagine her long legs wrapped around him, kissing him passionately and begging him for more. His thoughts were abruptly interrupted by Natalie's apology.

"Sorry about that, Bobby. Your lower lip is bleeding. I think I accidently bit you when he rapped on the window so loudly. I honestly didn't know what else to do when I saw him pull up behind us."

"It's okay. Just don't let it happen again!" Bobby said, trying to not sound disappointed. He grabbed a wet wipe to check his lip. Sure enough, Natalie did bite his lower lip. There was a small amount of blood on the wipe.

"I could have sworn I felt your tongue when we were trying to act like we were making out," Natalie said, in a very accusatory tone.

"It's called acting, my dear," Bobby replied, trying to pretend that he was in on the plan.

"Look!" Natalie said, as she pointed to a figure dressed all in black exiting Mrs. Piggy's house.

"Is that her?" Bobby asked.

"I can't tell for sure. The figure is her height and build, but they have a black hood on like a ninja, so I can't tell if it's a man or woman. The person is completely dressed in black, but I would say that they move like a woman."

Bobby started his car and they slowly followed the character in black. The shrouded figure eventually cut across the schoolyard and headed in the general direction of Liz and Adam's neighborhood. Bobby decided this would be a good place to stop the car. He reached into the satchel by Natalie's feet and pulled out one of the two NVG's.

"Natalie, just look through these just like you would a pair of binoculars. Try to keep her in your sight. I will have my phone on vibrate. Call me, if you need anything. I'm going to try to follow her on foot. Here is the key fob to the 'Vette," Bobby told her, and then he quietly exited the car.

Natalie nodded in agreement, and gave him a thumb up.

Bobby quickly walked out of the illuminating light of the deserted schoolyard. He stayed in the dimmer outer perimeter until he reached the path, which led into The Estates of The Preserves, where Liz and Adam live. Even though Mrs. Piggy disappeared from his view long ago, he had an idea of where her best vantage point was going to be, so he instinctively headed in that direction. Liz and Adam's house was on the highest point in The Estates. Their backyard was on a commanding bluff high above the Guadalupe River. The Guadalupe River is a very picturesque river, which flows through limestone banks lined by bald cypress and an occasional pecan tree. That part of the river is frequented in the summer by tubers, kayakers and canoeists. Since the Guadalupe River can rise very rapidly, Liz insisted that they live on a high point, due to the river's tendency to rise above its banks and flood.

When Bobby reached Liz's house, he noticed that the light in her kitchen was on, as well as the light in her and Adam's bedroom. He rationally decided that the stalker would place themselves where they could peer into those windows. That would place them on the left side of the house. He deduced that would put the stalker in the yard of Walter and Ethel Landry, a fastidious retired military man and his charming wife. Liz adored the older couple because they keep a vigilant watch on the happenings of the street, but without being too nosy or obtrusive. They also took great pride in the landscaping of their yard. Bobby hid in the natural foliage of the neighbor's yard across from the Landry's. He took the NVGs from around his neck and started using the scanning techniques that came in the NVG brochure to see if he could locate the stalker.

Bobby heard Fritz begin to bark. When Bobby looked in the direction of Fritz's barking, he was able to quickly locate the dark figure. She was peeking out from behind a large rock trying to see into Liz's kitchen window. Fritz's barking became more intense and persistent by the minute. He was surprised that no one in Liz's family has come outside to check on the barking dog.

Bobby's instinct was to dial 911, but then he thought better of it. He was worried that he would end up with the same officer who knocked on his car window a few minutes ago. Bobby figured he had a high probability of ending up in jail if he explained that he was watching over his partner's home when he noticed a ninja looking in her window. He decided the best course of action was to call Liz instead.

"Hello," Liz cheerfully answered.

"Liz, do not panic, but Mrs. Piggy is outside your kitchen window wearing a ninja get-up. That is why Fritz is barking like crazy. Keep the same lights on, but go to your media room where there are no windows. I will stay here and call you when she has left. I have a gun, and will use it if I need to. Tomorrow you will be having motion lights with monitored cameras installed around the perimeter of your house. Carefully open the breakfast door, and let Butter out also. His barking and size should scare her off. I will be in touch," Bobby whispered.

The light by the breakfast door came on and out flew the huge golden retriever. He eagerly joined Fritz in the barking frenzy. The racquet prompted the Landry's to turn on their outside lights. Soon the Landry's house was lit up like an airport runway. The Ninja Pig decided it was time to leave and started to run back in the direction of the elementary school.

When Bobby realized she was out of the area, he called Liz right back. "She is gone. Keep all your outside lights on tonight. I'll see you in the morning," Bobby said. He hung up, so he could call Natalie.

"Natalie, it's Bobby. She is coming back your way. Start driving around her block. Call me when she is back inside her house."

"Where will you be?" Natalie asked.

"I will be following her back on foot."

"OK. Be careful."

"I didn't know you cared," Bobby said, wishing it were true.

"Whatever, Bain," Natalie told him.

Natalie took the Corvette out of park, and eased it out of the parking lot making sure she didn't bottom it out. She used to own a Maserati before her son was born, so she knew she had to be very careful getting used to the car's acceleration. The car had almost 200 hp more than a regular Corvette or her old car. She decided Bobby should be impressed with her driving prowess as she worked her way back to Mrs. Piggy's neighborhood. She found it hard to look for her, and drive. Mrs. Piggy's subdivision had lots of cars parked in the narrow street.

On her second circle of Mrs. Piggy's block, Natalie spotted her. She had now taken the black hood off, and her bleached blonde hair made it much easier to recognize her. Even though she was pretty confident that the ninja and Mrs. Piggy were one and the same, she was glad now that she could positively ID her. Natalie watched her walk back into her house and turn a light on inside the house.

She headed back towards the school to pick up Bobby. He flagged her down when she turned the corner. He opened the passenger door and climbed in.

"It was definitely her. She took the hood off right before she walked in her house," Natalie informed him.

"I watched her look in Liz's window."

"Poor Liz. She is a prisoner in her own home."

"That is one sick bitch," Bobby declared.

"Yep."

Chapter 11

Bobby knew he would find Liz pacing back and forth in her office. When Liz is upset she could pace a hole right through the carpet. He guessed that she probably hadn't eaten either, so he made sure he picked up her favorite breakfast tacos on the way over this morning. Potato, bacon, egg and cheese tacos seemed to have a very therapeutic effect on Liz.

"You know me too well, Bobby," Liz said, and smiled gratefully at him as she took the small brown paper bag containing the taco from him.

"Liz, seriously, you need to eat. You are looking even thinner than you normally look. You have to remember that you aren't in this alone. Natalie, Marilyn and I are going to help you. I already talked to Hans Becker about what we will need to do to get a restraining order against this maladjusted wench."

"So, what did he say? What will it take?"

"I don't think you are going to like this part. The judge told Hans he would be glad to grant a restraining order, once we have ten documented cases of her harassment."

"We have two, only eight more to go!" Liz said, wearily.

"Actually, we have none according to Hans. The horseback trails don't count because the spot where she was waiting for you is considered a public park. She has to be on private land. Unfortunately, we weren't able to get documentation of her looking into your windows. The new security system will solve that problem though."

"Who are the police protecting? Mrs. Piggy? It sure seems like the wrong person! What am I paying all these taxes for?"

"Liz, you are getting no argument from me!"

"This is why people become vigilantes! Maybe they will protect me, if I act crazy."

"I don't think we need to go in that direction at this point," Bobby said, hoping Liz was just being dramatic for emphasis. He couldn't exactly see Liz with a gun on each hip, but then again, he had never before seen Liz's family being threatened.

"I just want you to know that I am not going on vacation under these new circumstances!" Liz stated rather emphatically.

"Yes, you are. I have never seen you so excited about going somewhere. It's all I have heard from you for months is Mérida, México this and Mérida, México that. Should I remind you –friendly people, cenotes, haciendas, colonial houses, pasta tile floors and Yucatán food? I already called the security company, and they will be installing motion detector lights all around the perimeter of your property this morning. They will also be adding eight cameras that will be monitored internally and externally. By the way, I told them my name was Adam when I called. I think I should watch Sam instead of your in-laws while you are gone. Sam likes me way better anyways," Bobby told Liz.

"How can I possibly leave knowing she is lurking around? What if something happened?"

"Hans assured me that they would be patrolling more frequently. They will be looking for her vehicle. They now know to look for her on foot, because I told them about her Ninja get-up. The gate guards have been notified. They know to call Officer Becker if there is anything even slightly amiss. And don't forget about your guard dogs -- Fritz and Butter. They never miss anything. Fritz hates her, and barked the second she got near your house last night. Butter's size alone is intimidating. You may have forgotten my prowess with a firearm. I am an excellent shot and I am also smart enough to drag her sorry ass onto your property if I do shoot her. This is the great state of Texas after all!" Bobby said, as if it was all decided.

"Don't forget my new security cameras will pick you up dragging her sorry ass back onto my property and we will both end up in jail. Actually Texas' Castle Doctrine allows deadly force against even fleeing intruders. So make sure the body is facing in the proper direction."

"Gee, Liz you are way smarter than you look. I keep forgetting you are only a blonde by bottle, not a true, natural blonde."

"Did you call Hans last night when you saw her outside my house?" Liz asked.

"I called him a little after. Natalie and I had a little run-in with the law a few minutes before, so I thought it was in our best interests to handle it by ourselves."

"What exactly is a 'little run-in'?" Liz asked.

"We were momentarily detained in front of our surveillance spot."

"What does 'momentarily detained' mean?"

"An officer caught us making out at our observation area," Bobby explained.

"And you wonder why I hesitate to leave my only child with you...?"

"It was called a diversion. Natalie was trying to distract the officer from what we were really doing. She started kissing me when she saw a cop pull up behind us, while we were waiting."

"Let me guess, this was a Bobby Bain idea?"

"Actually, I only wish I could take the credit."

"Knowing you as well as I do, you probably called the cop yourself."

"I can't believe you would accuse me of that!" Bobby said, secretly hoping he might have an opportunity to use that trick in the future.

"What was your 'role' in this?"

"My role was to thoroughly enjoy a beautiful woman in skin-tight black leather pants throw herself at me. And trust me, I was enjoying myself until the cop rudely interrupted us by banging on the window demanding to see my ID. That's why I didn't call the police last night. I figured he would arrest me if he saw me again."

"Good thinking."

"I thought that was pretty smart of Natalie," Bobby said.

"I'm sure you do. Seriously, how do you get yourself in these situations with my friends?" Liz laughed.

"I don't know, but I kinda enjoyed it."

Bobby took the foil-wrapped breakfast taco out of the crumpled brown paper bag that Liz had placed on her desk. He removed two plastic condiment containers. In one was the pico de gallo, and in the other a green salsa. Liz's face lit up as he unwrapped the taco and she saw the melted cheddar cheese. Bobby dumped the entire contents of the green salsa container on the taco and slowly slid the taco toward Liz. Liz picked up the taco and took a slow bite out of it.

"I didn't realize how hungry I was," she told him.

"Liz, I think we need to all put our heads together, and come up with a well thought-out plan. Two doctors, an attorney and a computer forensic expert should have no problem outsmarting her. "

"You forget one important thing. You are counting on her acting logically, but she is bat-shit crazy."

"This is where Marilyn will be of use to us," Bobby said, with a smile.

"I won't tell her that you said that."

"Probably best not to! You would be short a valuable member of your operating team!"

"At least this time you are including me in your plans... It seems like you forget that it is my family that this lunatic is stalking! Why didn't you just tell me what you and Natalie were up to?"

"When Marilyn told me the whole story about what happened on the horse trails, I got concerned. Marilyn called Natalie and filled her in. Natalie volunteered her help. Everything quickly mushroomed from there," Bobby explained

"Except no one told me," Liz pointed out again.

"Well... now you know!"

Chapter 12

"I'm kinda glad we let Bobby join after all," Natalie said to no one in particular as they waited for the emergency meeting of The Man Haters Club to begin.

"Most of the time, he's not so bad. He has kinda grown on me too -- like a fungus," Marilyn said, cracking herself up in the process.

"Liz, I have to ask, why didn't you marry Bobby?" Natalie innocently inquired.

"WHAT!?! Are you kidding me?" Liz shrieked.

"No, I'm serious. You guys seem to get along really well, for the most part. You spend more time together than most married couples. You share an office and even hang out in your spare time. I like the way that he takes charge. He knows how to get things done," Natalie said.

"He did get The OutPost to put us in their meeting room at no charge. And he ordered all of us their famous chicken-fried rib eyes, mashed potatoes with country gravy, and broccoli with Hollandaise sauce. I bet we will even get a dessert!" Marilyn added.

"Speaking of the 'perfect man'... Where is he? Its 5:40," Liz said, purposely not answering Natalie's question.

After looking around, the ladies noticed that Bobby was talking to a tall, well-dressed man at the entrance to the restaurant. The two men were carrying on a very animated conversation. Bobby then looked at his watch, patted the gentleman on the back, and walked over to join the ladies in the meeting room. He immediately winked at Liz, and walked over to give Natalie a kiss on the cheek, and he very cautiously gave Marilyn a hug.

"What in the world are we waiting on? Let's get this meeting started!" Bobby said, trying to distract the ladies from his tardiness.

The women all looked at each other and rolled their eyes.

"As you know, we are all gathered to work on a plan, so we can keep Liz and her family safe from Mrs. Piggy. But before we work out our plan, I think we should add one more member to our exclusive club. I know this fellow who could really help us with the logistics of our operation. I want to make sure we don't miss a single detail," Bobby said.

"Another man? This is getting weird, isn't it?" Liz said, interrupting Bobby.

"If it's that good-looking guy you were just talking to, then I'm definitely in!" Natalie decided.

"Did you remember to tell him the part about it being a Man Haters Club? Somehow I have a feeling you might have left that part out so that you wouldn't be the only guy in this club," Marilyn said in an accusatory manner.

"Do you really think he's that good-looking?" Bobby asked, realizing what a predicament he might be creating for himself. He never thought of Nick as being good-looking, but obviously Natalie and possibly Marilyn thought so.

"Duh..." the women all answered in perfect unison.

"Anyways, Nick is my former roommate from Texas A&M. He was there on an Army ROTC scholarship, but he is now retired from the Army. Logistics support for the Special Operations community was his specialty and I think he could help us immensely. He can make sure we don't miss any details of our operation," Bobby explained.

"He sure does have options... He could easily join either our Man Haters Club, or you and him could form a Woman Haters Club. I'm just saying..." Marilyn pointed out of the blue.

"I vote YES!" Natalie enthusiastically said to everyone's surprise, especially since no one asked for a vote to be tallied, yet.

"I've always liked your friend, Nick," Liz told Bobby.

"Marilyn?" Bobby asked, not sure which way Marilyn was swinging today after her last comment.

"Are you kidding me? That guy is sex on a stick!"

"I'm confused, does that mean yes or no?" a perplexed Bobby asked Marilyn.

"That means yes," Liz clarified Marilyn's response for Bobby.

"So, it's unanimous. I will be right back. Let me go get Nick," Bobby said.

He promptly returned to the meeting room with the young looking, retired, "full-bird" Colonel. Nick waved at Liz and then spent a few moments getting to know Natalie and Marilyn. Bobby wondered if he should have brought smelling salts with him. The two women now looked dazed.

"Nick, I'm going to let you take the lead. As you know, I have encouraged Liz to go on her vacation to Mérida and leave Sam with me. However, that's only if I could prove to her that we would be able to keep Sam safe and know what Mrs. Piggy is up to at all times."

Nick stood up and said, "I agree with you, Bobby. The first order of business is to give this operation a name, so we can refer to it "secretly" in further communications. I'm thinking 'Operation Luau' since I understand that behind her back, she was called Mrs. Piggy at work."

"That's perfect! Liz, do you remember how you imagined Mrs. Piggy roasted with an apple in her mouth?" Natalie said. She had obviously forgotten that she swore to Liz that she would not reveal this secret to anyone.

Liz smiled a forced smile to the group.

Nick then explained how proper planning was the key to any successful operation. Without warning, Bobby and Nick looked at each other and started chanting together, "Proper Planning and Preparation Prevents Piss Poor Performance!"

"Remember that ladies! The Seven P's!" Bobby said enthusiastically about the military adage.

The three women glanced at each other nervously.

"Sorry, we got a little carried away. The primary goal of Operation Luau is to keep Liz and Sam safe from Mrs. Piggy. Our second goal is to document Mrs. Piggy's stalking behavior, so a restraining order can be obtained. Bobby has informed me that Officer Becker met with a judge to find out what it would take to obtain a restraining order against her. The judge will grant the order once ten documented incidents have occurred. So far, we are certain that she has shown up on the horse trails and then looking in the windows of Liz's house at night, but sorry to say, these were not verified by the police for one reason or the other as an incident."

"Which is total bullshit!" Marilyn yelled, interrupting Nick's speech.

Nick continued by saying, "What do we know about this woman? Bobby told me that she holds a delusional belief that Adam is deeply in love with her. Frankly if this were true, it seems to me, Adam would be with her. He would have divorced Liz to start a new life with Mrs. Piggy. Maybe even have a piglet or two with her. I assume she cannot process that Adam welcomed the attention, but that did not mean that he wanted her. I further assume, she now thinks by having unexpected appearances in his life that he will realize the error of his ways, and return to her. Bobby said that Adam has now realized what a colossal mistake he made by letting this crazy woman worm her way into his personal life. He does not ever want to see her again. I understand from Bobby that Officer Becker advised Adam to send her an email, so it is documented that he wants nothing to do with her. He sent her an email that stated, "Do not have contact with me in any form." Now any unwanted intrusions into their lives will be documented and accepted as such by the courts."

"Bobby filled me in that a few days ago, monitored security cameras and motion lights were installed around the perimeter of Liz's house. Liz and Adam's offices already had monitored security cameras. We know that she has a new job in downtown San Antonio. Natalie, I understand that you can fill us in on that," Nick said as he now sat down, and gave the floor to Natalie.

"She was hired at the law firm of Tate & Tate. They are a personal injury firm. I'm sure you have all seen their advertisements on television. Pamela Tate and I went to law school together. Pamela was my maid of honor when I married that idiot, Tim Moody. Pamela is also married to an idiot, so we still have a lot in common. Pamela said Mrs. Piggy is an okay worker, but Pamela is Team Liz all the way. She said when her ninety-day probationary period was over that she would not be given a raise no matter how great a job she does. Karma is a bitch. She will notify me immediately if she ever misses work or leaves at lunch. So five days a week from nine to five Mrs. Piggy will be accounted for. Her telephone records are printed out every day. They are also monitoring her computer. Pamela is personally scrutinizing the records making sure none of Adam, Liz, or Sam's numbers, or anything slightly suspicious, ever comes up," Natalie said, as she relinquished the floor back to Nick.

"Strong work!" Marilyn yelled. She had heard that saying from her late Marine husband and his Marine Corps buddies. It seemed to Marilyn to be an appropriate response at a time like this and she thought Nick, because of his prior military background, might like it.

"So, we need to just cover the varmint's whereabouts in the evening. Bobby is going to be solely responsible for Sam's well being. Natalie will be Bobby's back up, if he needs any additional help. So Natalie, Marilyn, and I will cover the evening hog hunts, as we will refer to them. Liz flies out Saturday morning and will be back the following Saturday afternoon. So we have seven days to cover," Nick informed the group.

"Actually I should have said this earlier, but Mrs. Piggy's employer is having their annual party on Friday night, so we have six nights to cover. Pamela said they encourage all their employees to take the limousine service that is provided. We can count on Pamela to keep us informed that night," Natalie added.

"Sam will be attending a journalism workshop hosted by UT Austin on Wednesday and Thursday and returning to school on Friday. I think Bobby, Fritz and Butter can hold down the fort on those nights," Liz added.

"UT?!? What the heck!" Bobby said. It was like someone stabbed him in the back, or maybe even kicked him in a sensitive area. University of Texas at Austin and Texas A&M have one of the most intense rivalries in collegiate sports.

Nick and Bobby looked at each other and sadly shook their heads.

"Bobby and Nick, I have two words for you – Walter Cronkite." Liz told the two men who were offended that Sam's daughter was attending the workshop at their rival university. The name of the UT journalism department's most distinguished student made them both silent for a brief moment.

"I just looked it up on my phone, and guess what? There is journalism at Texas A&M. Sam could be the first famous graduate of the program," Bobby told Liz.

"When the time comes for Sam to pick a school, I can't imagine that A&M

wouldn't be on her short list, Bobby," Liz said, knowing that you don't EVER tease Bobby Bain about the merits of Texas A&M. Liz and Bobby both knew there were lines you just didn't cross.

"So keeping Sam's journalism workshop in mind, we will need to schedule hog hunts for Saturday through Tuesday. Natalie, if you are free on Saturday I thought since you did the last surveillance with Bobby, that you could show me the ropes?" Nick asked Natalie.

"Natalie is a seasoned pro. In fact, Natalie is the 'Queen of The Diversion'," Bobby said, as he looked her way.

Natalie's face turned beet red. Liz shifted uncomfortably in her chair. Marilyn immediately realized that she was missing out on something and decided to make it her mission to figure out what it might be.

"Natalie, can you teach me what you know about diversions?" Marilyn asked, in what the others believed to be a very sincere manner.

Bobby had just taken a sip of his single malt scotch when the image of Marilyn and Natalie wildly making out begin playing in his mind. The thought of this girl-on-girl action made him so distracted that he momentarily forgot his purpose of being in the meeting. He was snapped back to reality when Natalie spoke up.

"I'll let Bobby teach you. I taught it to him," the unflappable Natalie told Marilyn.

"Sounds good," Marilyn said, determined that she would eventually figure out the true story behind 'the diversion'.

Liz just rolled her eyes.

"So that leaves Sunday for Marilyn and I," Nick explained.

"Works for me, and then we can have Natalie and Nick on Monday, and Nick and I on Tuesday," Marilyn volunteered.

Nick and Natalie both agreed.

"Natalie, can you debrief the group on what you think went well last Saturday night, and what you would recommend that we do differently?" Nick asked.

"Well, for starters, it may be obvious, but I made sure that I wore dark clothes. I also brought snacks and drinks, in case we got hungry. Next time, I probably would bring something less sticky than doughnuts. I bet police cars are one sticky mess.

I think that we should have used a less conspicuous car. Bobby's car costs more than any house in her neighborhood. I think that's why we got our 'surprise' visit from the police. I'm not sure if we looked like drug dealers, or pimps," Natalie said.

"Bobby as your pimp! Or maybe you were Bobby's pimp!" Marilyn piped up.

Again, everyone ignored her.

"Bobby, what would you do differently?" Nick asked.

"I agree that dark clothes are a must. Natalie's black leather pants were a nice touch. Natalie, I enjoyed the Donut Ho's donuts. I think my NVGs were a big help, but I think I would practice with them first. They took some getting used to. I think all parties should wear a watch, so they aren't asking the time every single minute. I think it's important to have a diversion planned ahead that can be immediately implemented if needed. I applaud Natalie for thinking ahead," Bobby said, and looked right at Natalie, and then sat down.

"Sounds like it was a successful mission. I would agree wearing dark clothes is smart, and certainly I have no objections if the women want to wear black leather pants. Don't forget a watch. Refreshments were a nice touch. Marilyn and Natalie, we will make sure that you both get some practice with the NVGs. And yes, Bobby, having a contingency plan is important," Nick replied.

"The car is a problem, and I do have a suggestion. I think we should park a car at the school. I think we could walk the street adjacent to her house and be able to keep her house in view and see when she enters the path. We will just act like we are a married couple out for a stroll," Nick further explained.

"What a great idea! If we hold hands it would seem more believable," Natalie suggested.

"Then he is going to look like a bigamist the next night with me!" Marilyn remarked.

"I was going to change my appearance," Nick said.

"I kinda go for the biker type. Tight jeans, motorcycle boots, Harley t-shirt, leather jacket, bandana…" Marilyn informed Nick.

"I like you just as you are," Natalie told Nick.

"Just don't get us mixed up!" Marilyn warned.

"I really don't think there would be a problem with that," Bobby said, with a smirk.

Chapter 13

"Sam, how in the world can you be a vegetarian when you don't like vegetables? Try explaining that one to your Uncle Bobby."

"That's not true! I like broccoli, corn and asparagus!" Sam clarified, as if there were no other vegetables.

"But sweetie, your body needs protein. How do you get your protein? Do you eat beans? How about nuts? Have you ever tried tofu?" Bobby asked, already knowing what the answer to these questions would be.

"Yuck!" Sam said, as she started to walk out of the kitchen.

"What do you want for dinner? Would you like to go out tonight?" Bobby asked, still continuing the conversation. He knew this answer also, as they had eaten pasta with asparagus and a smidge of cheese for the last two nights. If it weren't for the Blue Bell ice cream they had every evening for a nighttime snack, he would be wasting away, and so would Sam. He had to keep her alive until Liz returned from her trip.

"How about asparagus with pasta, instead of pasta with asparagus tonight? Call me when it's ready!" Sam yelled, from half way up the stairs.

"Will do, Peach!" Bobby said, using one of Liz's nicknames for the teenager.

He decided to make a trip to the liquor cabinet first. He poured himself a single malt scotch and then took a slow swig. He decided that he was flattered that she liked the dish he created for her so much that she wanted to eat it every day.

Bobby then walked back into Liz's beautifully appointed kitchen and located the stockpot. He put in on the stove and slowly turned the pot-filler handle. When the pot was almost two-thirds filled with water, he turned it off. Then Bobby drizzled a small amount of olive oil into the water and turned the burner to high. Next, he found the skillet and placed it on top of the stove. He pulled the last bunch of fresh asparagus out of the refrigerator, put it in the colander and rinsed it thoroughly. Then, he sliced it diagonally into about one and a half inch pieces. He put another small amount of olive oil followed by a dash of cayenne pepper into the skillet and then turned the burner to medium. He then added a little fresh garlic. He quickly stir-fried the asparagus and set it aside. The water in the stockpot was now coming to a full boil, so he broke the angel hair pasta in half and added all of it to the water. He reduced the heat to medium-low and stirred the pasta, so it wouldn't clump together and set the timer for four minutes and went to finish his drink.

He was undeniably becoming a pro at fixing this dish. Each night, the preparation went smoother and quicker. Before he knew it, the timer went off. He carefully drained the pasta and then put it back into the empty stockpot. He added the stir-fried asparagus and approximately three tablespoons of butter, stirring it all over medium heat. Then, he proceeded to add the Parmesan cheese and white pepper to the sauce. He located two "Tuscan-colored bowls" for the pasta. Finally, he garnished the pasta with a little fresh ground Mediterranean pepper and a pinch of grated Parmesan cheese.

The first night, he made the "colossal" mistake of serving the pasta on some dishes that looked like the china was covered in red bandanas and blue denim. Sam promptly informed him those were only to be used for BBQ, hamburgers or hotdogs. "Little Liz", he thought to himself!

"Princess, your dinner is served!" Bobby shouted, above the blaring music.

Sam scampered down the stairs and sat down in front of the pasta.

"Have you heard from your mother?" Bobby asked her.

"Yep," Sam replied.

"Well, did she say if they are having a good time?"

"Yep."

"Are they still flying back on Saturday afternoon?" Bobby said, beginning to become exasperated with trying to have a conversation with the teenager.

"I don't know. I can take care of myself, you know!" Sam stated.

"I'm sure you can, but I need you to take care of me while your Mom is gone. I might do something crazy like… maybe… I don't know… eat something different every night! I might have a salad the first night, maybe some tofu stir fry the next…" Bobby teased.

He knew Sam would roll her eyes at this, so he looked over at her. She looked very different from when she went upstairs. It took him a moment to realize what was different. Her hair had been wavy and almost to her waist when he started the pasta. But now, it was barely chin length!

What in the world was he going to tell Liz? Bobby thought kids only cut their own hair when they were four or five years old, not fifteen. Liz had explicitly warned him before she left that Sam wanted red hair, but nothing about her wanting to cut her hair off. He wondered if he fed Sam some mega dose of B vitamins or something, if it could grow back enough that Liz might not notice. He wanted to ask Natalie or Marilyn what to do, but they might call Liz in Mexico and that would be disastrous.

He looked at his scotch and could see no other solution at the moment, but to finish his drink in one big gulp.

"Sweetie, what happened to your hair?" Bobby said, while trying his best to remain calm.

"I don't know," Sam answered.

"Let me try this again. Your hair was long when your Mom left on her trip and now it's a little shorter," Bobby said through clenched teeth, losing his battle to stay calm.

"Hmmm. Can we have this pasta again tomorrow night?" Sam said, as she dumped her empty dish in the sink and darted up the stairs.

Bobby was so tempted to return to the liquor cabinet and pour himself another scotch. He truly felt baffled. What would Liz do? Probably not have another scotch.

He looked at his half eaten bowl of asparagus pasta and realized he no longer had an appetite. He picked the bowl up, opened the door to the backyard where an eager Fritz and Butter were waiting instinctively, like only dogs can. Butter ate his pasta without tasting any of the nuances of the seasonings. Fritz picked out the asparagus. Obviously, it was not prepared to his liking.

"My Mom is going to be mad that you gave the dogs table scraps!" Sam said, reappearing at the back door.

Bobby looked up and Sam's hair was now long and wavy again! He immediately decided the hell with his self-imposed two-drink limit and headed back inside the house to the liquor cabinet. He poured himself a drink and took a sip. Sam walked over and took the tumbler of scotch from his hand and poured it down the sink in the kitchen.

"They are called hair extensions, Uncle Bobby!" she said, as she unclipped them.

At this point, she led him by the hand to a chair and made him sit down. She then clipped them into Bobby's hair. He now had beautiful flowing blonde hair.

"When is your Mom returning?" Bobby wearily asked, as he tossed the blonde hair behind his back.

"I'll take these out now. We need to go to the stable. We are supposed to exercise Max for Mom," Sam said, as she unsnapped the clips holding the extensions into Bobby's 'follically challenged' hair.

"Great," Bobby said unenthusiastically. He hated horses and couldn't think of a more perfect end to this dreadful evening.

"We can get some pie on the way home, even though you didn't eat your dinner," she scolded him.

She headed back upstairs to change into her riding breeches and boots. When she came back downstairs, she went to the refrigerator to put some baby carrots in a plastic bag for Max.

"I'll drive. I won't tell Mom that you were drinking while you were watching me.

I'm learning, you know," Sam told Bobby just as she snatched the keys to his new silver colored Jaguar XF out of his hands.

Bobby was feeling nauseous from the short two to three mile chauffeured drive to the stable. He wasn't sure if his symptoms were from Sam's erratic driving or the stench emitting from Fritz. According to Sam, Fritz never missed a trip to the stable. The pasta obviously didn't sit well with the dog because he passed noxious gas during the entire trip. Bobby would bet that this might be the reason Liz did not normally feed her dogs table scraps. Thank goodness, Bobby thought, that the dog had picked the asparagus out of the pasta, or it might have been even worse. Regardless of the gas chamber torture, Bobby thought taking Fritz to the stable was still a good idea. Fritz seemed to have a sixth sense concerning Mrs. Piggy's whereabouts.

Once at the barn, Sam introduced him to an extremely attractive young woman with blonde hair named Lacy, who managed the stable. Lacy seemed much more interested in his Jaguar than in him, but Bobby would take whatever attention he could get at this point. He was pleasantly surprised when Lacy accompanied him to the outside arena while they waited for Sam.

Eventually, Sam reappeared carrying a six-foot long whip and a woven leash that looked about twenty feet long. Sam clipped the leash onto the bit of the horse's bridle and started letting some of the leash out. As she stood on the ground, the horse started to walk in a big circle around her. Without doing anything more than pointing the whip towards his tail, the horse started to move faster. After a few laps, she raised the whip higher, which made the horse go even faster. Bobby noticed that when she moved the whip to a lower position the horse would move slower. Unexpectedly, the horse started to buck like crazy and run like he was at the Kentucky Derby.

Bobby looked helplessly at Lacy, hoping she would do something.

"It's okay. She is just lunging Max. He was in yesterday because he got new shoes. He is just a little stir-crazy. Once he gets this out of him, he will be just fine," Lacy reassured Bobby.

"Are you sure? My short-term goal is to keep Sam alive until her mother returns from her trip."

"She has been riding Max in one form or fashion since she was two. She's absolutely fine."

"Do you also ride?" Bobby asked Lacy.

"I started doing hunters when I was Sam's age. Now, I do stadium jumping," Lacy said.

Bobby realized that something was probably lost in translation, but Lacy was so attractive that he began to imagine her laying in a hayloft on her back, her blond hair tousled around her, with himself standing over her in full hunting attire. He soon realized that it was his turn to say something. He decided the best way to impress her was to say something horsey.

"He sure likes those carrots, doesn't he?" Bobby said, immediately realizing how truly idiotic he sounded, especially since the horse wasn't eating a carrot at that moment. He had never been able to carry on a sexual fantasy in his mind, while continuing to carry on a rational conversation with an attractive woman, all at the same time. It sure looked like today would be no exception.

Lacy looked at him strangely. They both turned their attention back to the arena. Sam had taken the lunge line off of Max and put it and the lunge whip outside of the riding arena. Max just stood there quietly now, as if the whole process bored him.

"What are the little stairs for?" Bobby asked, referring to the molded plastic steps that Sam was moving to left side of Max.

"It's called a mounting block. Sam is too short to get on him without it."

Bobby's warped and sex-deprived mind went into overdrive with that comment. He stepped on his own foot hard, so he would stop thinking about Lacy and the mounting block. When he turned back toward Lacy, he noticed she was mindlessly running her hand up and down the shaft of the whip that she was holding for Sam. He then found it necessary to step on his other foot.

"Are you okay? I noticed that you keep stepping on your feet. Sometimes horses will do that when they are in pain."

Bobby knew he didn't have a plausible response, so he just leaned on top of the arena rail and watched Sam take the big bay thoroughbred over two three-foot jumps in a row. Next, she jumped a large obstacle that was painted to look like a brick wall. Max cleared the wall like it was five feet tall, instead of just three.

"I had no idea she could do this!" Bobby told Lacy.

"She's a very talented rider, and Max is taking good care of her. He's never jumped this high before with Sam. That's why he over-jumped the wall. It was real nice meeting you," Lacy said, as she turned and walked away.

He couldn't help but stare at her athletic body as she walked away. He loved the way that women's butts looked in their riding pants. They left nothing to the imagination. He started to imagine Lacy telling him he had been a naughty boy, while she hit her palm with her riding crop. Suddenly, he jumped because he felt something wet on his leg. He looked down to see that Fritz, the farting dog, had returned and had decided to use him as a fire hydrant. Luckily for Bobby, Fritz had spent the last hour re-marking his territory at the stable, and he was almost on "empty". Bobby then reached down and picked up the twelve-pound wiggling dog.

"We are both very lucky that Liz decided to put up with us, you know," he told Fritz.

Bobby and Fritz watched Sam cool Max down by walking him around the arena on a loose rein. Bobby's felt his phone begin to vibrate in his shirt pocket. The display let him know that it was Nick. He looked around to see where Sam was because he didn't want her to overhear him.

"Hey, Nick!" Bobby answered.

"Just wanted to let you know, Operation Luau was a success tonight. The Ninja Pig was caught looking in the kitchen window at 8:36. I immediately notified the security company. They sent a car right over, but she didn't stick around. She looked in the kitchen window and then headed straight home. They pulled the appropriate footage off of the surveillance cameras. According to them, they have clear, distinguishable pictures of her. The disc will be available tomorrow for you to pick up. I called Officer Becker and told him you would be in touch tomorrow," Nick reported.

"Finally! Hey, listen, Sam's walking back this way, so I need to go!" Bobby said quietly and turned off his phone.

Sam and Bobby walked Max back to the tack room where she unbuckled his girth, so she could remove his saddle and saddle pad. She handed Bobby a brush and instructed him to brush Max in the direction that his hair grows. She removed Max's bridle while Bobby was busy grooming.

"Look, he is making his cute face, Uncle Bobby! He wants to be sure I don't forget to give him his carrots!" Sam explained to Bobby.

Next thing you know, Bobby was being taught how to give Max baby carrots without losing a finger.

"He really takes them gently. It almost tickles," Bobby told Sam.

"I believe you like the stable more than you thought, Uncle Bobby," Sam noticed.

"It's a smidge better than a root canal," Bobby teased her.

"You know, Lacy just broke up with her boyfriend. I bet she would like to have pie with us," Sam said, trying to play matchmaker, just like her mother would.

"Maybe next time, when you don't have to get up early for school, and my car doesn't smell like farts, and my right leg doesn't have urine dripping down it," Bobby explained to her.

"You peed on your leg?!?!" Sam shrieked.

"No, your dog did!" he told Sam.

Sam laughed hysterically for about a minute, without being able to stop.

"The thing that you have to remember is that Fritz ONLY does that if he likes you. He's peed on me TWICE! The lady from the rescue said that Fritz was just marking his territory. I guess he thinks we belong to him now. I heard Dad once tell Mom that that was total bullshit, and that the rescue made that story up to get rid of him because he was probably pissing all over the rescue family's home," Sam said, in a very grown-up voice.

"I don't think 'bullshit' and 'piss' are in your vocabulary, Missy," Bobby told her.

"It was a quote. So, it's allowed," Sam explained believably.

"I will have to check with your Mom on that one. Let's put this beast up and get some pie."

"Uncle Bobby, will you try the French Silk Pie? My Mom had me try it. I swear I could eat it every day."

"Every day? I can't imagine!" Bobby said, thoroughly believing her.

Chapter 14

Bobby had been sitting in front of Sam's school for a few minutes, watching Sam texting on her phone. He finally realized she was probably never going to look for him, so he sent her a text reminding her that he was to pick her up. She looked up, grabbed her backpack and said good-bye to the weird-looking boy sitting with her. She then walked to the driver's side of the Corvette and opened the door.

"I'll drive," Sam said confidently, as she swung Bobby's Corvette door open further.

"I don't think so, Miss Pooh," Bobby said, as he pretended to close the door on her. She walked dejected to the passenger side and got in.

"Where's the Jaguar?" she immediately asked.

"Getting detailed. It smelled like dog farts," he said, with a laugh.

"Still? That sucks. Would you let me drive your truck?" she asked, looking at him with puppy dog eyes.

"When did you get your permit? I just realized your mom didn't say anything about it and that sure isn't like her!" Bobby said, now realizing that even the youngest members of the fairer sex were able to easily pull the wool over his eyes.

"I SURE do have a lot of homework tonight," Sam answered quickly, hoping Bobby wouldn't notice that she didn't answer his question.

"So… when was it?" he tried again, still following his gut instinct.

"Did you hear from Liz today?" she asked, trying a different tactic to change the subject.

"Liz?!? Do you mean your mother?" he asked.

"She lets me call her that sometimes," Sam informed him.

"I'll bet she does," he answered, wondering how in the hell Liz could put up with this shit, day in and day out, without downing a bottle of scotch, swallowing a handful of pills, or taking a long drive off a short pier.

"Could we get some ice cream on the way to Renay's? You look really hungry," she told him.

"Sure. When we get to the ice cream place, you can show me your learner's permit," he insisted.

"You know, Uncle Bobby, you are my favorite of all of my mom's friends," she declared, and then smiled the sweetest smile at him. That smile reminded him of Liz. The half-truths reminded him of Adam.

After an awkward stop for some ice cream, that did not include seeing the elusive learner's permit, they pulled up in front of the salon. Sam seemed to be in a hurry to get out of the car. Bobby may have won this battle, but he knew the war was far from over.

"Hi, I'm Renay," a beautiful brunette with an infectious smile greeted Bobby and Sam as soon as they had walked in.

"Nice to meet you, Renay. I'm Bobby Bain. I am this illegal-driving child's god-father," he said, as he took Renay's hand to shake it, while smiling warmly at her. Sam looked mortified as Bobby followed her back to Renay's station. Sam was now officially horrified that Renay told Bobby that he was welcome to sit at the next station, because that hairdresser was gone for the day.

"Sam, you have told me about your Uncle Bobby, but you never told me he was so funny," Renay said loud enough, so that Bobby could overhear.

"That's because he's not," Sam muttered.

"So, what are we doing today?" Renay asked Sam, as she began to inspect Sam's hair.

"I was thinking…" Sam started to say, but was interrupted by Bobby.

"How about keeping it the same? Doesn't it look great?" Bobby interjected.

"Bobby, I have the feeling that you are worried that Sam may leave with a hairstyle or color that Liz won't like. She called me from Mexico this morning to remind me — no red hair. I forgot to tell her that one of Liz's friends came in yesterday and she wanted Liz's exact hairstyle. I didn't know how Liz would feel about that, so I modified it quite a bit," Renay rambled on.

"Do you cut men's hair also?" Bobby asked.

"I sure do. My next appointment just cancelled. Do you need a cut, Bobby?" Renay asked him.

"That would be great! I will even let you two ladies decide on my new look," Bobby told the two.

Renay gave Bobby two large books with lots of men's hairstyles in it. He didn't know there were so many options. He nodded off looking at the first book.

He was abruptly awakened by laughter. He saw a girl that looked just like Sam, but with bright red hair, the color of Raggedy Ann's.

"Sam, he looks like he is going to have a heart attack."

"It's okay, I know CPR. My mom taught it to me," Sam informed Renay.

"Look Uncle Bobby, it's just a wig. It is so cool!" Sam said, twirling around.

"Until I babysat Sam, I didn't know about all this stuff. Did she tell you about the scare that she gave me with her hair extensions?" Bobby asked Renay.

"I told Renay while you were snoring. I think she said, "What a dork, your Uncle Bobby must be!" Sam said, clearly embellishing the conversation to Renay's complete embarrassment.

"It's okay, Renay. Sam only has a few more days to live, after her Mom finds out she was driving without a license," Bobby calmly stated.

"Uncle Bobby, I know you aren't going to tell on me because you love me too much," Sam said, again giving him the look that she copied from Liz.

"Bobby, why don't you and Red change chairs," Renay said, as she began to sweep Sam's hair clippings into a pile.

"I'm going to go check out the new lip glosses. This lip gloss is too boring for red hair," Sam informed them, as she worked her way to a counter where a young lady looked eager to sell her a lip gloss.

"Renay, Liz has always said that you do a terrific job. Just keep me handsome," Bobby said, in a flirtatious manner.

"I always enjoy everyone that Liz sends my way," Renay said sincerely.

"You said one of her friends came in yesterday and wanted her hair just like Liz's. Is that common?" Bobby inquired, trying to keep the conversation going.

"No, usually they have a picture of a model or an actress from a magazine. She had a clipping of Liz from a picture in the newspaper," Renay explained.

"Did she look like Liz when you had done your magic?" Bobby asked.

"Not really. Liz has really healthy, shiny hair. This lady colored her hair at home and it was really over processed. I did dye it the same color though. She looked better when she left. It was almost white blond before. A color that we in the industry refer to as stripper-blonde."

At this moment, Bobby started to panic and broke into a cold sweat. He realized that the new client sounded a little too much like Mrs. Piggy. He composed himself after realizing that would be insane.

"Was she tall like Liz?" Bobby asked, hoping that the answer would be yes.

"Actually, she was very short. Don't tell Liz I said this, but she was also a little pudgy," Renay confided to Bobby.

Bobby hurriedly moved the plastic cape that was protecting his clothes to the side, so that he could access his cell phone in his shirt pocket. He searched through the pictures in his phone and then handed it to Renay.

"Is that her?" Bobby asked, secretly praying for a negative answer.

"Yes, that's her. So, she is also a friend of yours?" Renay asked.

Bobby wanted to make sure that Sam could not hear any of their conversation, so he looked around the room. Sam was still jabbering away with the make-up girl.

"This woman used to work with Adam. She was fired and has been stalking the family ever since. Would you mind talking to the police officer that is handling the case? I'm afraid it is more than coincidental that she showed up here with that request," Bobby confessed to Renay.

"I knew it! There was no way that she could be Liz's friend. Liz's friends are funny and this lady was just weird. You know, she also wanted to get every product that Liz uses. I told her that some of the other products would be better for her hair because it was so damaged, but she only wanted the ones that Liz used," Renay explained.

"Would you be willing to talk to Officer Becker, Renay?" Bobby asked her, again.

"Yes, of course. Gosh, I just can't stop shaking," Renay told him.

Bobby pulled his business card out of his wallet. He scribbled his cell phone on the back. He then handed her his card. "Renay, please call me if she comes in again. You can call me at any hour, if you need to talk, or anything. I mean that," Bobby said genuinely.

"I might take you up on that. I'm really freaked out. Thank goodness, I didn't give her Liz's hairstyle. That would be the only thing that could make me feel any worse at the moment," Renay said, trying to find something humorous in the situation.

"Renay, you didn't do anything wrong!" Bobby reassured her.

"Bobby, could we please reschedule your haircut? I think it would be in your best interest," Renay said, with a smile.

"Of course! How about if I take your last appointment someday next week and then we can do an early dinner at the Gruene Door?" Bobby asked.

"That is my favorite restaurant!" Renay exclaimed.

"That's my Mom's favorite restaurant, too. Do you want her to come along?" Sam asked innocently, noiselessly rejoining Bobby and Renay.

"I'm sure your Mom is going to want to spend time with you next week. Knowing your Mom, she is missing you terribly. I bet she will want to take you driving, or horseback riding, Pumpkin," Bobby told her.

"I thought you were going to have Renay cut your hair, Uncle Bobby? It looks the same," Sam said, as she scrutinized his head.

"My new hairstyle is very complex and Renay said she needs more time, so we are going to reschedule it for next week," Bobby said, making up an excuse to cover the real reason that Renay hadn't cut his hair.

Sam took the red wig off very reluctantly, knowing they were leaving. Bobby took it from her hand and placed it back on her head. She looked at him quizzically.

"Uncle Bobby, I have to put it back," Sam explained to him.

"I think your Uncle Bobby can buy his favorite illegal-driving goddaughter a red wig, so she will stop pestering her mother for red hair," Bobby said, as he put his arm around her.

"Really! I can't wait to show it to Lexy!" Sam said, bouncing up and down.

Renay and Bobby decided on next Tuesday evening for Bobby's haircut, after consulting her appointment calendar. Sam could not have been happier with her new red wig. Sam couldn't believe her luck, when Bobby said she could also get the new lipstick. He didn't tell Sam, but the real reason was that he felt sorry for the girl, who was obviously on commission, selling the lipstick.

Renay hugged both Bobby and Sam goodbye.

"Uncle Bobby, can we go out for dinner tonight, instead of having pasta?" Sam asked, as they walked out to the Corvette.

"There is a God!" Bobby muttered, under his breath.

"Huh?"

"You bet, but I'm driving!" Bobby said.

Chapter 15

When Bobby told Nick that he liked his plan, Nick mistakenly thought that it was because of the plan's level of intricacy. But what Bobby really thought was that any plan that involved spending that much time with Natalie, was ingenious. Nick had swiftly come up with this plan after Bobby had informed him that Mrs. Piggy was now sporting a different hair color and hair cut, trying to look more like Liz and less like herself. The two men had decided that maybe it was time to observe her mental state, up close and in person.

So far, Mrs. Piggy had been staying put in the evenings, with the exception of the sighting on the first night of their watch. Nick's plan was brilliant -- Natalie and Nick would both separately attend Mrs. Piggy's work function on Friday night for a prolonged surveillance. Nick would try to charm her, and Natalie would try to engage her in girl talk. Bobby just wished he were the one attending the function with Natalie. He could imagine her tall, shapely frame in an elegant cocktail dress with strappy high heels. He couldn't stop his mind from wandering to her seductively stepping out of the dress. Too bad Nick would be the one there with her, not him.

Pamela quickly approved Nick being invited to the function. It sure didn't hurt when Natalie described him using Marilyn's description of "sex on a stick". In fact, when Pamela got off the phone with Natalie, the first thing that she did was call her personal shopper at Nordstrom's. She wanted to make sure she had a fabulous – and sexy -- dress. For the first time, she was now looking forward to hosting the party.

Pamela and Natalie had decided that Nick's alias for the evening would be Nicholas Solomon, an intellectual property attorney that the firm did some business with. Since all the attorneys attending the party were University of Texas alumni, Nick would pose as a graduate of Southern Methodist University's Dedman School of Law. Pamela graciously volunteered to meet with Nick before the big day and give him some pointers about posing as an attorney.

Natalie had business cards made up with Nick's pseudonym, which included a phone number that would be professionally answered by an online service. Nick, Natalie and Pamela had tried to go over every possible scenario that could take place that evening and decided they were fully prepared to pull off the ruse.

Nick and Natalie both arrived within moments of each other at the well-known San Antonio steakhouse that had been reserved for the firm's celebration. The invitation stated that the cocktail hour would start at seven and that dinner would be served at eight. They both decided that if they arrived around seven fifty, they could say hi to Pamela, but avoid most of the small talk with the other attorneys, which might blow their cover.

Pamela took full advantage of her position and arranged for Nick to sit right beside her. Natalie, Mrs. Piggy, and two male paralegals would also be at that table. Pamela had told her philandering husband, whom she found annoying, that it was very important for him to mingle. She used this as an excuse to place him at a different table on the opposite side of the room.

Nick arrived a few minutes before Natalie and confidently entered the restaurant. He was wearing a custom-tailored, dark gray suit that showed his toned physique to absolute perfection. He had on a light gray shirt with a dark fuchsia silk tie. Few men could pull off this look, except for Nick or a Calvin Klein model.

Nick saw Pamela as soon as he entered. She had on a light gray, raw silk cocktail dress with an especially daring low back. Her long legs looked even longer in her strappy high heel sandals. She looked very professional and business-like from the front, but the only business anyone was thinking about when she turned around, was monkey business. He walked over and greeted her with a handshake and a warm smile. She, in turn, introduced him to the three junior attorneys that were unsuccessfully trying their best to impress her.

Nick had realized long ago, that most people loved nothing better than talking about themselves. He figured as long as he capitalized on this important principle, the evening would go off without a hitch.

At exactly eight o'clock, a large man wearing a well tailored suit with a flashy, expensive looking watch walked over and put his arm around Pamela. When she immediately stiffened, Nick realized this was the other half of Tate & Tate. He then grabbed her hand and led her into the center of the room. The small crowd became instantly silent as he started to speak. He was a talented speaker and he made it sound like the firm had done some really important work over the last year, equal to finding a cure for cancer, instead of suing automobile insurance companies while hoping to score the big one. If one didn't know better, you would think that Tate & Tate really did care about its employees. Everyone then clapped and hugged like a long awaited engagement had been announced. The group then dutifully went to find their assigned places in the dining room.

Nick finally spotted his prey. Liz's description was incredibly accurate—short, plump, and he could actually see the small maroon bumps on the back of her arms. He wondered if they were contagious and sincerely hoped that they were not. She had on an ill-fitting dress, with fluttery cap sleeves that made her arms look even heavier. Her hair did not look anything like Liz's. He had to take a sip of his drink so he wouldn't laugh out loud. It was in some form of an up-do from the sixties. It was very lacquered and fussy-looking. This woman would have to be delusional to think that Liz's husband would be interested in her. He then started to realize that in just a few moments, he would have to pretend that this woman was not only beautiful, but also fascinating. This would be a far more difficult evening than he thought.

Nick felt a hand rest on his shoulder and when he turned around he saw that it was Natalie. He was relieved to see her. She had on an emerald green wrap dress that fit her perfectly. There was only one word that came to Nick's mind and that was, stunning.

"Nick Solomon! What a surprise! What are you doing here?" Natalie said, as she gave him a little wink.

"Natalie! How long has it been?" Nick exclaimed, in a completely believable manner.

The supposed long lost acquaintances walked around together to find their seats. The pig had already found her place at the table. Nick and Natalie walked around pretending to look for their chairs. When Natalie approached the table, she pretended that she had no idea that she and Nick were seated at the same table. "Nick, you are at my table!" Natalie exclaimed.

Nick and Natalie sat down. Natalie looked over at the pig and introduced herself. She then introduced the pig to Nick.

"What kind of attorney are you?" Nick asked Mrs. Piggy, trying his best to flatter her.

"I'm not an attorney," Mrs. Piggy replied.

"What firm do you work for?" Natalie asked her.

"Tate & Tate," she told Natalie.

"I was in Pamela's wedding," Natalie told her, thinking that Mrs. Piggy might become more engaged in the conversation after realizing that she was a close friend of Pamela's.

Mrs. Piggy just nodded. Natalie could normally hold a conversation with anyone, but she was momentarily not feeling up to the challenge. Thank goodness, Nick sensed this and took over the stalled conversation.

"Have you ever dined here before?" Nick asked, joining the conversation.

"Nope," she flatly answered.

"I just moved here. What are the best restaurants in the Riverwalk area?" Nick asked, starting to try to make eye connection.

"I don't know," she replied.

"I bet that is because you are a terrific cook. Am I right?" Nick asked, all while giving her a thousand-watt smile.

"I like to cook," she replied.

"Me, too! I love making intricate dishes that you can't get at a restaurant. Have you ever cooked any of Julia Child's recipes?" Nick asked, already knowing the answer. Natalie had already told him during the stakeout the entire story about Liz giving Mrs. Piggy the Julia Child cookbook and how she then "coincidentally" proceeded to cook lunch for Adam each day. Natalie also confided that the usually sane Liz had imagined Mrs. Piggy's head on a silver platter with garnishes surrounding it. She made Nick promise not to mention this to Liz. To date, Liz could not get over the fact that she had had such a disturbing thought. Natalie, on the other hand, thought it was utterly ridiculous because Liz was the most levelheaded person that she knew.

"Yes," Mrs. Piggy answered in her monotone voice.

"That's incredible! What were your favorites?" Nick asked. He was so thankful that he had researched Julia Child on the Internet. He had vague memories of her being on TV as a child. He remembered being mesmerized by Julia's distinctive voice. He made sure he knew what she was famous for cooking, her life story and looked at several of her more famous recipes.

"I like all of them," she answered.

Nick was so thankful for the interruption as Pamela and two of the firm's paralegals approached the table. He turned to Pamela and greeted her. He was hoping that Mrs. Piggy would try a little harder to communicate with him or Natalie when she realized that not only were they colleagues, but also friends of Pamela. He wasn't sure that she was that astute.

"I have been having the most fascinating conversation with your paralegal. We share a love of fine French cooking," Nick gushed about the hog to Pamela.

"I'm not a paralegal," Mrs. Piggy replied.

"Have you ever been to France?" Natalie asked the pig, trying to take this boring conversation in another direction besides French cooking.

"No," she answered yet again in her monotone voice.

"You should go sometime, you would love it. I think you would like Italy, too!" Natalie said, trying her best to help Nick keep the conversation going.

Mrs. Piggy didn't even acknowledge the conversation. Pamela, Nick and Natalie were drowning... For a moment, Nick looked over at the two paralegals sitting at the end of the table. They were engaged in an intense conversation about fantasy football -- lucky them. This hopefully meant that they weren't feeling slighted that no one had asked them about what they like to cook, or even offered them travel advice.

"Do you have any children?" Natalie asked, knowing this was a loaded question. Even a person as socially inept as Mrs. Piggy, would have to know that she shouldn't tell strangers whether or not she walked out on a child. This was going to be interesting.

She just stared at Natalie. No answer.

At this point Nick wanted to run away. How could a person be so boring? How in the hell could Liz's husband found anything fascinating about this dimwit?

"I have a 16 year-old son. He just got his driver's license. It's hard to sleep when he is out," Natalie told her.

Nothing. She said nothing. She doesn't even seem to be fazed that she should now be saying something. Nick then decided she must have been raised by a pack of wolves.

"Are you married?" one of the paralegals asked her. Pamela, Natalie and Nick can't even look at each other because they would burst out laughing. Nick hoped Pamela would give this guy a raise.

"Yes," she answered.

"Is he here?" the other paralegal asked.

"No," she answered. She started to fidget.

"Why not?" he quickly responded.

"We are separated," she announced just as the food arrived.

Mrs. Piggy seemed relieved that everyone forgot about asking her any more questions and instead the group concentrated on the variety of appetizers that were being served. The silence continued except for small comments about how succulent the steak was, and how perfectly it was prepared.

Pamela and Natalie excused themselves from the table after finishing the main course. Nick seized the opportunity.

"I'm sorry everyone has been asking you so many questions. I'm sure this is a painful time in your life," Nick said, in a very sincere manner.

"Yes, it's a sad time" she said, but Nick was aware that it was not for the reason it should be. He thought she was sad because Mrs. Piggy could not understand why Adam had not left Liz and Sam for her.

"Let me give you my card. If you ever need someone to talk to, I'm a great listener," he said, as he reached for the business card that Natalie had made for him.

"Thanks" was all that she said. She placed it on top of her evening bag.

Natalie returned to the table. She tapped Nick under the table with the prearranged signal.

"If you will excuse me, ladies," Nick said, as he rose

Natalie waited until Nick was gone. She picked up the business card on top of Mrs.

Piggy's evening bag. "Oh my… I see Nick gave you his card. He seems quite taken with you. He's a great guy. I shouldn't tell you this, but I think I will anyway. I may have had one too many martinis. Anyway, his wife died about three years ago -- a car accident. It was tragic, she was pregnant with their first child," Natalie whispered in the sow's ear.

Natalie realized that she should not have done this because she started to choke from smelling the pig's coiffure at such close range. She swore that it reeked of Aqua Net, Jheri Curl, gardenias and roses.

"You should go out with him," Natalie urged her. This time Natalie was being careful not to lean in so close.

"I don't think so," the pig said.

"Are you still hoping to reconcile with your husband?"

"No."

Natalie was thrilled to see Pamela approaching. Natalie thought to herself that she could keep a conversation with a rock going much easier than she could with this crazy woman. Pamela rolled her eyes behind the pig's back just as she joined the two.

"Sorry, I keep getting pulled in a million different directions. Did Natalie tell you she was in my wedding? We go back, forever. Where did our handsome dining companion go?" Pamela said to both Natalie and Mrs. Piggy.

"I'll go look for him. I know Nick wouldn't want to miss the dessert and coffee," Natalie offered.

Natalie found Nick by the bar. She quietly walked up behind him and whispered in his ear. He spun around and looked white as a sheet.

"Natalie, that wasn't funny. Not one bit. And for the record, no, I'm not interested. I knew all along that it was you pretending to be her. Her hair stinks and yours doesn't," said Nick, in response to Natalie's impersonating Mrs. Piggy suggesting a night of wild passion with Nick.

"It looks kinda crunchy," Natalie agreed.

"I just called Bobby and told him we may have missed our shot with the pig for the luau," Nick informed Natalie, referencing the code name for the operation.

"I don't know why, but it really turns me on when you talk Army talk," Natalie said, as she teasingly licked the chocolate off the edge of her martini glass.

Nick suddenly found it much harder to breathe. "Really?"

"Of course not. I just wanted to show you that I'm better at seducing someone than you are," Natalie teased.

Pamela then walked up and joined them at the bar. "What's so funny?" she asked.

Natalie whispered what had just occurred in Pamela's ear and soon both women were having a grand time at his expense.

"I think I'm going to head back to the table where my 'desserts' await me," Nick answered.

This comment made both women laugh hysterically.

When Nick returned to the table, he found the business card he had given to Mrs. Piggy just laying on the table near where she had been sitting. The two paralegals informed him that she had recently left.

"Are you sure?" he asked.

"Look under her chair, maybe she left her glass slipper behind," the now tipsy paralegal sarcastically suggested while the other one snickered.

When Pamela and Natalie finally walked back to the table, Pamela informed Nick that the limousine driver was already en route to Mrs. Piggy's house to return her home. Natalie and Nick decided to call it a night. They both thanked Pamela for everything.

As Nick and Natalie walked into the parking garage, Nick noticed that Natalie seemed really agitated now that the evening had come to an end. Nick wondered why because they certainly accomplished what they set out to do. He was almost positive that he did nothing wrong.

"Did I do something to offend you, Natalie?" he asked.

"What? Oh, no! Why are you asking me that?" she questioned.

"You seem really mad," he explained.

"You got that right. Can you imagine how Liz must feel? She is probably so confused, thinking that Adam was spending time with that weirdo rather than with her and Sam. I wonder if people even realize that when they act this way, that they are also cheating on their kids too, not just their husband or wife. God, I cannot think of one single quality that she has over Liz! Well, except that she takes up more space!"

"You won't get an argument from me," Nick said, as he puts his arm protectively around Natalie's shoulder and drew her closer to him. He had never shared with many people about how his marriage ended, because these days so many people thought of marriages as disposable. Now, he knew that Natalie would understand how he felt.

Chapter 16

Liz loved every moment that she spent in Mérida, but it was no surprise to anyone that she missed and worried about Sam the entire trip, much to Adam's dismay. She tried to keep in touch with Sam by using her preferred method of communication—texting. Liz sent Sam a text every time she saw something she thought Sam might find interesting. Not that it was unexpected, but she received very infrequent, short and nondescript texts in return. She knew by now not to take it personally. Bobby, on the other hand, knew that Liz would be on the first plane back to Texas if he didn't send her a reassuring text every few hours.

When Liz and Adam returned home from their trip, Liz was flabbergasted when Sam asked if the whole family, to include Uncle Bobby, could spend the next Spring Break in Mérida. That meant Sam was reading her texts and actually looking at the pictures that her mom was sending after all.

"Mom, tell me about the hotel. Was it super nice?" Sam asked. Liz was known for finding the nicest hotels and resorts at bargain basement prices. So, on the family's travels, Sam was used to staying in some of the finest hotels in the world.

"I think you will like it."

"Uncle Bobby and I looked it up. They have a free liquor cart when you walk in. I think I would like that," Sam informed them.

"The legal drinking age in Mexico is 18, not 15 and a half!"

"I bet they think we all look alike, so I'm sure they won't card me," Sam said, using a racial stereotype she had heard from Adam's parents.

"Right…" Liz replied, not wanting to argue with her willful daughter on the first day back.

"Uncle Bobby and I also looked at the underground river you were going to swim in. It looked spooky."

"It's called a cenote. Your dad and I had to climb down a real shaky ladder to get to it. I bet we climbed down 40 to 50 feet. It's like a cave with a crystal clear swimming pool at the bottom that was the perfect temperature. The trees above send their roots down to the water, so the roots actually hang from the ceiling of the cave. I took a ton of pictures."

"Did you go see the flamingos?"

"Yes, there were thousands of them and we also saw a huge alligator! When I took its picture, it opened its mouth really wide and posed! We also went to the ancient Mayan pyramids at Uxmal."

"What was your most favorite thing?"

"When we went to lunch at the Hacienda Ochil with Jorge."

"Who's Jorge?"

"He's my new friend. He's from Canada."

"Actually his name was George, but your Mom felt like she had to call him Jorge the whole time because we were in Mexico. Trust me, that wasn't the least bit annoying. You know your mom, she makes friends everywhere she goes," Adam chipped in, sounding a little envious.

"It could be worse. What if she gave them a home like Butter and Fritz?" Bobby pointed out.

"Or Bobby," Adam said almost inaudibly.

"What kind of lotions did they have in the hotel?" Sam asked, completely changing the direction of the conversation. Sam always thoroughly tested every single solitary product provided in the luxury accommodations where she usually stayed. This included not only the shampoo and conditioner, but also the exotic and fragrant soaps, lotions, shower caps, mouthwash, sewing kits, shoe polishing cloths, pens, tiny notepads, robes, slippers and those little eye masks to block out the lights.

"Nada," Liz answered, using one of the few Spanish words that she knew which didn't pertain to food.

"Nothing!?!?" What was the thread count of the sheets?" Sam asked, trying to act like she might die if she stayed in this establishment.

"What the Hell difference does it make?" Adam snapped, thoroughly exasperated with his entitled child.

"Let me show you what I brought back for you!" Liz said, changing the subject. Liz had agonized about what to bring Sam back from the trip. As anyone knows, buying a gift for a teenager can often be more miss, than hit. Liz finally picked out a large, colorful, cloth purse from a Mayan woman who was selling purses, scarves and belts on the street. The purse was eye-catching and "happy-looking" with its embroidery and colorful fabric. Liz had decided that if Sam didn't like it, then she would use it on the weekends. Sam surprised Liz because she ended up loving it as much as Liz had.

One of the gifts she brought back for Bobby was a bottle of Xtabentún, an anise-flavored liquor, fermented with honey, and then mixed with rum. "I found out that the Mayans used a similar liquor to achieve visionary and trance-like effects," Liz told Bobby, as she handed the bottle to him.

"I can't wait to try it!" an intrigued Bobby told Liz.

"The Mayans achieved this greatly enhanced effect by having the liquor quickly introduced into their bloodstreams -- by making an enema out of it!" Liz told a now longer interested Bobby.

"My dad will try it!" Sam innocently said, volunteering Adam to be the first to try the uniquely administered liquor.

"My ass!" Adam promptly answered, without a hint of irony.

Liz also added to Bobby's extensive guayabera shirt collection by purchasing him a Yucatán shirt made with fibers from the henequén plant. The linen-colored shirt had the characteristic four front pockets and two rows of vertical pleating, with overlaying intricate embroidery.

Sam and Bobby both listened with interest when Liz told them that a lot of the Mayans still sleep in hammocks. She explained that it wasn't unusual for the whole family to sleep in one giant hammock.

"How big are their families?" Sam asked. She had always been curious about family size, probably because she was an only child.

"Our waiter told us he had four girls. So, that meant six people in one hammock. Don't you feel a teeny weeny bit spoiled now?" Adam promptly asked Sam.

"Not really," she answered truthfully.

Adam turned to Bobby and told him in a lower voice, "The same waiter told Liz and I that they practice 'hammock sutra'. He was hilarious."

"That's like that book you brought home and gave to Mom. I still remember her whispering to you not to bring that in the house 'because I'm a snoop and would find it'. Lexy and I looked and looked for it until we finally found it. It was gross. They were doing it like clams and dogs…" Sam told the embarrassed grownups.

"Samantha! That is more than enough. That isn't something we talk about when Uncle Bobby is here -- or ever!" Liz tried to silence her as quickly as possible, which had never been an easy feat.

"Mom, it might help Uncle Bobby. You always say he can't keep a girlfriend long. I'm just trying to help him keep a girlfriend," the teen explained.

"I don't think that is the problem, Sam. Again, this isn't the kind of thing we should talk about in public," Liz tried one more time, in vain, to explain to the naive teenager.

"So, if that isn't the problem, Liz. What is it? I need to know," Bobby said in a mocking tone, trying to stir the pot.

Fortunately or unfortunately, depending on who looked at it, Sam herself ended up being the one to change the subject away from Bobby's dating practices.

"I don't think I want to sleep in a family hammock. Dad farts too much. I wouldn't be able to sleep," Sam enlightened everyone but Liz, who unfortunately already knew this to be true.

To Adam's relief, it was now Bobby who interrupted Sam and told the couple about Fritz farting all over the interior of his Jaguar. Bobby certainly had a knack for telling a story, and he even had Sam laughing about it all over again, as if she had never been there.

Sam seemed, for the most part, happy to have her parents back home. Completely out of character, Sam confessed to conning Uncle Bobby into letting her drive. Liz decided to go a little easier on Sam's punishment as a result of her heartfelt confession. Sam reluctantly accepted her punishment of having to wait one extra month before getting her learner's permit, with minimal grumbling.

Liz was relieved that it appeared that everything had gone smoothly with Sam and Bobby. But just to be sure, before she left, she had carefully measured how much Scotch was in their liquor cabinet. She figured this would be an accurate reflection of the state of affairs. She was thrilled to see that there was still a very respectable amount remaining.

As much as she would have liked to stay on vacation mode, Liz began to have some anxiety thinking about Monday. Not only did she have a full schedule of patients, but she had also committed to giving an evening lecture to the local plastic surgery society. Luckily for her, she could just recycle a lecture that she had presented at a meeting in Atlanta a few months ago. She would have rather gone to the stable with Sam so they could ride, but she quickly realized that the stable would have to wait until Tuesday.

Monday flew by and before she even knew it, it was time to head over to The OutPost for the continuing education meeting. Liz has always hated to talk in front of a group, let alone a group of plastic surgeons. She could imagine them scrutinizing her wrinkles, whether her thighs needed liposuction, or if she would even benefit from breast augmentation, rather than listening to the particulars of her lecture.

Liz could no longer hide her nervousness. She asked herself over and over again, "Why did I agree to do this?" She silently prayed that no one would ask any questions that she couldn't answer. After a quick double-check of her make-up in the car's vanity mirror, she hoped that the lights would be dim during her presentation. She tried to reassure herself that no one should fall asleep, since they would be eating during her lecture. This would also mean that probably no one would be listening simply because they would be too busy eating. This was completely fine with her.

Liz got out of her car and decided to just go in and get it over with. She was surprised when she spotted Bobby. He smiled a very devious smile as he walked over to greet her.

"You let me go on and on all day about how nervous I was and you never said you were presenting also!" Liz scolded him. She was correctly assuming that was the only reason why the anesthesiologist would be at a lecture for plastic surgeons.

"Surprise! Surprise! Surprise!" he said, while doing his best imitation of Gomer Pyle.

"You have the tougher act to follow – right after they eat and I bore them to death," Liz said, obviously looking for a little reassurance.

"I think I might already I have a question or two for you!" he said, hoping the friendly banter would distract her.

"You might want to reconsider that, Bain," she warned him as she made her way to the podium.

Once Liz began speaking, she started to relax. She immediately apologized that some of her pictures might be a little unappetizing for mealtime. One of the doctors piped up and remarked that it was nothing compared to watching lipo. Liz did not argue with that.

Now that she wasn't as nervous, Liz started to glance around the room and was overjoyed when she realized that everyone was still awake. But most importantly, she was able to answer all the questions that her colleagues asked, no matter how off-the-wall they were. Occasionally, she peeked over at Bobby who would pretend to be asleep or he would start to raise his hand like he actually had a question. Bobby seemed to forget that he would be the next speaker at the podium.

By the time Bobby walked up to the podium, everyone seemed anxious to go home. Especially since they had already finished their dinner. He wondered if he had chosen the best topic – a new kind of anesthesia with a different mechanism of action, which result-ed in a faster recovery time. Too late now, he thought to himself.

Once the lecture started, the group seemed attentive and genuinely interested to learn about this new anesthesia agent, with its fewer side effects. As much as Liz loved to poke fun at him, Bobby had always been an incredible lecturer. In fact, he was so good that she decided from now on she would volunteer his services any time someone asked her to speak. She patiently waited for him to answer all the questions that the surgeons posed. When it was over, Bobby walked Liz out to her car.

"Please remind me to 'just say no' the next time anyone asks me to give a lecture," Liz told Bobby, using the anti-drug slogan from the 1980's.

"What do you mean? You have never had a problem saying no to me, Liz!" Bobby said with his usual brashness. And with that thought, he closed her car door.

Before she knew it, Liz was pulling into her driveway. She noticed something sitting on her front porch. She presumed that this was Fritz and Butter's doing. The dogs must have brought one of their "treasures" onto the porch.

As she neared the doorway, she was relieved to see that it was a gift basket, not a dead squirrel to bury after a long day of work. It was a large metal basket filled with shredded lime-green crinkle paper. Nestled in the paper, were two large bottles of Liz's favorite shampoo and conditioner, another bottle containing bath soak and a fragrant candle. The entire basket was wrapped with hot pink netting and topped with a pink and lime-green striped bow. The pink and green polka dot gift card read, "Thanks so much! Renée."

Liz thought to herself, talk about perfect timing. She had noticed, just this morning, that she was starting to run low on conditioner. But Liz could have sworn that Renay didn't spell her name that way.

Liz brought the pretty basket into the house and decided to refill her smaller conditioner bottle before she forgot and was standing naked and wet in the middle of the shower. She brought the almost empty bottle of conditioner into the kitchen. Liz knew that the larger bottles were more cost effective, but they just didn't fit on her shower shelves and she thought that they looked ugly sitting on the floor of the shower. As she started to squirt the liquid from the larger bottle into the smaller bottle, she noticed that it smelled different than usual. In fact, instead of having its usual mango fragrance, it smelled REALLY BAD. She wished she could recall what the smell reminded her of. The aroma was very familiar. Then, it came to her in a flash. Depilatory cream?!?!?!

At that exact moment, Fritz walked into the kitchen to make sure Liz was not dropping any crumbs or handing out any samples. He quickly exited with his tail tucked between his legs. Fritz somehow knew what thought had just popped into Liz's head when she saw his abundant furry coat. The doctor in Liz fortunately came to her senses recalling that the FDA wouldn't allow testing on an animal under these circumstances.

She took another whiff of the foul-smelling cream. Liz was now even more convinced that this was hair removal cream. She couldn't decide whether it was the "regular" or the "bikini" formula. Throwing caution to the wind, she dabbed a bit on the fine hair of her forearm. She decided to wait four minutes, assuming this was the fast-acting formula. She set the kitchen timer and waited. Sure enough, after four minutes she wiped the cream away -- along with her hair.

Liz could only think of one possible suspect – Mrs. Piggy! That explained why Renay's name was spelled incorrectly. Adam used to complain constantly that Mrs. Piggy had poor attention to detail.

A wave of calmness came over Liz, similar to when she was in the operating room. She didn't panic, she just picked up her phone and called Bobby, and then she called

Officer Becker. Hans was adamant about her not handling the basket and contents any further, possibly destroying any possible fingerprints. He would make the proper arrangements for the evidence to be picked up.

Liz had the funniest thought – Mrs. Piggy had recently attempted to copy her hairstyle and color. Would Mrs. Piggy have also copied her bald look, if Liz had actually used the conditioner?

Chapter 17

Liz suddenly realized Adam's birthday was only two weeks away. It had completely snuck up on her this year, with all that had been going on. She always tried to do something really special for his birthday. That was because she had a sneaking suspicion that his childhood was less than idyllic, even though he wouldn't ever talk about it.

"Your Dad's birthday is only two weeks away! What are we going to do this year?" Liz asked Sam.

"We could do an Elvis party!!! Dad loves Elvis. We can get an Elvis impersonator and turn the garage into a diner. We can all wear stuff from the fifties from when you guys went to high school. When Elvis shows up, Dad will completely freak out. He can scream and go crazy! Just like on that Elvis DVD you showed me when I was little," Sam said.

"First, Samantha Schaeffer, your Dad and I did not go to high school in the fifties! Second, on the DVD, the women were hysterically screaming, not the men… And last of all, that was Michael Jackson, not Elvis…" Liz explained to the historically confused teen.

"Maybe… if we got a Michael Jackson impersonator, they could teach Dad to Moonwalk. I bet he would like that…"

"Which Dad are you talking about?" Liz wondered out loud. Liz thought the only Michael Jackson impersonation she ever saw Adam try involved him grabbing his crotch and she surely didn't want to discuss that with Sam.

"Well, then we could have a party at the Greek restaurant instead. They have parties there, you know. I have seen the pictures on the wall of people partying in togas. Dad really likes that one girl that belly dances there. I heard him tell Uncle Bobby that she looks like somebody famous, but with way bigger boobs."

"Hmmm… I was thinking about something a little more low key this year…" Liz told Sam. The idea of both Adam and Bobby, ogling a woman's boobs all night didn't truly appeal to Liz - whether it was for a birthday party, or not.

"Yeah…it's not like Dad was really good this year, anyway…" Sam said referring to how her parents had almost gotten divorced.

"Your Dad is trying to be a better father, Sam."

"If you say so, Mom…" Sam promptly remarked. Sam wondered what her Mom saw that no one else did.

"I do…"

"I want to help you plan it this time!" Sam said excitedly.

"I would love your help. You always have really good ideas."

"Do you know what Dad would really like?"

"What?" Liz answered, wondering what Sam was going to come up with next.

" A party at his favorite Tex-Mex restaurant!!!" Sam revealed.

"That's true. Whenever he is out of town for a couple of days, he always stops for take-out on the way home to get his fix."

"I'm going to get it all planned! I just came up with this great idea!" Sam told Liz.

"Are you going to tell me what it is?" Liz asked her.

"Nope!"

"Who are we going to invite?" Liz asked.

"Me! You! Lexy!" Sam told Liz.

"I didn't know that Lexy and your Dad were that tight," Liz said wondering what excuse Sam was going to come up with, so she could invite her best friend to the party.

"Dad just acts like he doesn't like her. He actually thinks she is pretty cool.

"Dad is a good actor, I guess."

"Yep… Who else?" Liz asked.

"Grandma and Grandpa, Uncle Bobby and a special guest!"

"Grandma and Grandpa will be on their trip."

"I forgot Dad!!!" Sam said breaking into a hysterical laugh. Sam was cracking herself up that she almost forgot to invite the person whose birthday it was.

"Okay, I will make reservations for six – Dad, you and me, Lexy, Uncle Bobby and a special guest."

"Can we have that lady that makes those cool cakes make one for Dad?"

"Do you mean Toni?" Liz asked.

"Is that the lady who made that teacup cake for Grandma?"

"Yes. I already thought of a great idea. What does your Dad like more than any-thing?" Liz asked Sam thinking she would have no problem answering this.

"That's easy… I have heard him tell you this a jillion times when you tell him he should get a hobby or something. He always tells you that he has hobbies – sex and beer! Did I guess right?"

Liz took a deep calming breath, and answered: "Kinda… I saw a cake that looked like a beer can pouring into a beer mug. They wrote, 'CHEERS! Happy Birthday!' in icing on the mug," she answered, ignoring the sex part of Adam's hobbies list.

"Ok, Mom, you make the reservations for 7:00 PM on Dad's birthday, and order the cake, and I will take care of the rest!" Sam said confidently.

"Okay, but you let me know if you need help with anything," Liz told Sam.

Two weeks later, on the morning of the party, Sam asked if Liz could drop Lexy and her off at the mall to get a present for her Dad. She told Liz that Lexy's Mom would pick them up from the mall and get them to the restaurant in time for the party.

"Don't be late!" Liz warned Sam.

"I'm going to put the stuff for the party in your trunk, so I don't have to take it to the mall. Don't open it until you get there!"

"I promise!"

"Make sure you get there before Dad!" Liz warned Sam.

"Mom, you already told me that…"

Liz was counting on Bobby getting Adam to the party. Bobby wasn't very thrilled with having to spend any one-on-one time with Adam, but he always did whatever Liz asked him to do. Too bad, he thought that she had forgotten to mention that he should be civil to Adam.

Bobby picked Adam up at the appointed hour with the excuse that he wanted Adam to check out a car that he was thinking about buying. Their love for cars was one of the few things that the men had in common. Adam got into Bobby's Corvette, and off they went.

Liz drove to the restaurant by herself, worrying the whole way if Sam would be on time… if Bobby could keep his snarky comments about Adam to himself… and if Adam could refrain from drinking too much… When Liz arrived at the restaurant, she removed a large lawn garbage bag that Sam had placed in the back of her car, and took it inside.

Bobby had asked one of his buddies to pretend like he was selling a rare Shelby Cobra. What he hadn't counted on was how little Adam would converse with the owner. Adam wasn't much for small talk. They ended up finishing within minutes of arriving. Bobby knew that he needed to occupy Adam's time for another thirty-five minutes. Liz had reserved the smaller of the two party rooms at the restaurant. The establishment was divided into a bar and a restaurant. Bobby decided to park on the bar side and buy the 'Birthday Boy' a shot or two of tequila before the party began.

"Let's properly celebrate your birthday! I hear that they have some of the finest Añejo and Reposado tequilas. My treat." Bobby said.

"I heard that also, but you are going to have one, too!" Adam told Bobby, knowing that would ensure that Bobby couldn't rat him out to Liz for drinking.

"Of course!"

Bobby spotted a table that looked in the direction of the entrance of the bar area, not the restaurant. This way Adam wouldn't notice Sam or Liz when they arrived.

"Where are your wife and daughter today?" the waitress asked Adam. Even though the restaurant was huge, his family always seemed to have the same waitress serve them.

"My wife is picking her up from something," Adam told her, either not wanting to go into detail about where Sam was, not remembering or not caring.

"Do you want your usual?" she asked referring to a large Dos Equis draft beer, with a slice of lime.

"No, not today…" Bobby interrupted. "We want a shot of your best tequila. It's Mr. Schaeffer's birthday!" Bobby announced loudly to the waitress, purposely trying to embarrass Adam.

Adam scowled at Bobby after the waitress walked away.

She returned with two small glass tumblers of the finest Reposado tequila that the bar had.

"Could I trouble you for a glass of water, also?" Bobby asked.

"I'll get one for both of you," she pleasantly said.

She returned with two glasses of water. Bobby thanked her, and took several large sips.

Bobby picked up the glass and said, "Adam, I hope this is a birthday you will always remember -- surrounded by your lovely family."

"Thanks, Bobby but we aren't going to celebrate it until next weekend," Adam informed him.

"Well, in that case, Salute!" Bobby said. Adam picked up the glass, tilted his head back, closed his eyes, and finished the golden liquor in one gulp. Bobby quickly poured his drink into the glass of water he had been sipping from. Adam was distracted and didn't suspect a thing.

"Man, that was smooth!" Bobby said convincingly, delivering an Academy Award winning performance.

The waitress returned, and mentioned to the men a new premium tequila they had just added to the menu.

"I would like to try it. Adam, are you game?" Bobby asked.

"Sure," he said, since Bobby was going to have another.

A minute later, she returned with two more glasses filled with the golden liquor.

Again, when Adam downed his shot, Bobby quickly dumped his drink into his water tumbler.

"I liked that one the best," Adam told Bobby.

"I actually think I like Añejo tequilas better." Bobby told Adam, referring to a type of tequila that is aged even longer.

"I have to agree with your friend," the waitress said when she returned, joining their conversation.

"We have a great one that I bet you both will like," she told them.

"Well, don't just tell us about it!" Bobby teased her.

She shortly returned with two more shots. This time the liquor was darker, almost amber in color.

"Would you mind getting me a different glass of water? I saw a little gnat in the ice cube," Bobby told her.

"I have seen you eat the worm in a bottle of Mezcal, but you won't drink a gnat!" Adam remarked, referring to another imported liquor from Mexico.

"I will be right back," she told the two men.

She returned with a fresh glass for Bobby. He took a long drink.

"Adam, you never told me if you liked the car, or not," Bobby said remembering he forgot to ask Adam's opinion.

"It was pretty nice, but I bet that even if you buy it, you still won't be able to get a date," Adam said throwing one of his typical barbs at Bobby.

Bobby ignored Adam's jab. He raised his tumbler, and Adam did the same. As soon as Adam put his head back, he once again dumped his shot into his water.

The owner of the restaurant, who Adam knew from Liz always chatting with him, walked up to the men with three tumblers filled with a mahogany colored liquor. He put the tumblers down, and greeted Adam with a hearty handshake. Adam introduced him to Bobby.

"Mr. Schaeffer, this round is on me. I heard it's your birthday! This is Extra Añejo tequila. Instead of being aged one year, it is aged three! It's from my special stock," the owner explained.

"Thank you, so much," Adam said, as he reached for the tumbler.

"I have heard about this, I can't wait to try it. Gracias!" Bobby said.

"Feliz Cumpleaños!" the owner said, toasting Adam.

This time, the men all slowly sipped the aged spirit. Bobby took a small sip. After awhile, he excused himself so that he could check on Liz while Adam was distracted.

"That's why I don't drink the water. Then, I don't have to get up like a girl every few minutes to take a leak," the now wasted and unfiltered Adam remarked when Bobby informed them that he would be back momentarily.

Bobby pretended like he was going to the men's bathroom, but instead he slipped over to the party room to see Liz. Liz was just sitting in the party room all by herself wearing the largest sombrero on that he had ever seen.

"Hola, Liz!" Bobby said as he entered the room.

Liz spun around to see who just entered.

"Augh!!! When did you grow a moustache?" Bobby shrieked.

"Funny, Bobby!" Liz said, as she peeled off the fake Pancho Villa moustache, and removed the sombrero.

"Adam, is at the bar talking to the manager. He brought him a drink to celebrate his birthday."

"That is awfully nice of him. Look, Sam has name tags for us all to wear besides these crazy moustaches," Liz said, proud that Sam had thought of such clever decorations.

"Let me guess, this one is mine," Bobby said, pointing to a Tío Bobby nametag.

"You haven't seen Sam, have you?" Liz asked.

"Don't worry she will be here. I better get back to the birthday boy," Bobby said.

"Don't let him drink too much!"

"Anything else?" Bobby said, mocking Liz.

"Be nice to him, it's his birthday!" Liz said.

"Don't worry, I have been real nice…" Bobby mumbled.

"What?" Liz wondered.

"Yes, dear!" Bobby said, with a grin and walked back to the bar area.

As he entered the bar area, he immediately noticed that all eyes were turned towards two young women walking across the room -- a tall, thin beautiful blonde and an exotic-looking brunette. The blonde had on red high heels that looked like Mary Janes, with ivory thigh-high socks. Her dress looked like it could have been a private school uniform. It was a conservative gray plaid material, suitable for a man's sport coat. What distinguished it from a school uniform was its short length -- it barely covered the young women's behind and its tight fit on her perfect proportioned body. Her friend had on the same red shoes and thigh-high socks, but had on an extremely short pair of navy blue shorts with a double row of brass buttons, a boat-necked three quarter length sleeved red striped shirt and a sailor hat perched on top of her long curly auburn hair. The two women walked right up to him, as if they wish to speak to him. Bobby moved to the side figuring he had just walked in front of whomever the two stunners wanted to talk to.

"Hey, Uncle Bobby!" the tall blonde said.

Bobby was at an uncharacteristic loss for words. Finally he said, "Your Mom is waiting for you on the other side."

"Uncle Bobby, could you get Lexy and me a margarita, pretty please?" Sam asked, knowing it was a rhetorical question as far as Bobby was concerned.

"Good luck!" Bobby said, knowing Liz was going to have a fit at how inappropriately Lexy and Sam were dressed for the occasion.

"Huh?"

"Never mind…" he said.

Bobby looked over at Adam who along with the manager was ogling the girls.

"What did you have to pay them to talk to you?" Adam said, not realizing the two women were actually his fifteen-year-old daughter and her best friend.

Bobby ignored him.

"Is that those girls again?" Bobby said.

When Adam turned to look, Bobby poured the remaining liquor into Adam's tumbler.

"No, that's two old ladies. Geez, no wonder you have problems getting a woman," Adam remarked.

"Nothing like what you are going to have…" Bobby said in a low enough voice Adam couldn't understand.

"What?" Adam asked.

"Let me settle up this tab, and then I'll introduce you to those girls. So finish up your drink. The blonde is a daughter of one of my friends," Bobby told the unsuspecting Adam.

"Really? She was pretty hot!" Adam said and gulped the remainder of his drink down.

"You should see her Mom. She is beyond hot!" Bobby remarked truthfully. He didn't know which would make Liz hotter -- seeing how inappropriately Sam was dressed, or watching Adam try to pick up his own daughter.

Bobby paid the tab and left a generous tip for the waitress. Adam and Bobby walked toward the party room where the girls were. Bobby let Adam walk in first.

"Surprise! Happy Birthday!" Liz, Sam and Lexy yelled in unison.

Adam looked truly surprised. He then turned to Bobby and said, "You got me this time, Bain."

"Honey, I have never seen you look more surprised!" Liz said as she walked over to greet him with a kiss.

"Dad, here is your name tag – El Jefe. It means 'the boss'," Sam said as she slapped the sticky nametag on his shirt.

Lexy then put the giant sombrero on his head. Sam was waiting with a huge Pancho Villa adhesive moustache that she had bought at the party store.

"Adam, you are one lucky man!" Bobby said.

Adam just glared even harder at Bobby, but somehow with the Pancho Villa moustache and oversize sombrero, it wasn't effective.

They all found a seat around the banquet table.

"Dad, you smell kinda funny…" Sam said as she drew attention to Adam's inebriated state.

Liz leaned in to Adam and gave him her version of the Breathalyzer. She took a deep whiff as she moved in for the final test – a kiss.

"I only had two drinks…" he answered. Liz had lost count of the number of times that a clearly drunk Adam had only had "two drinks" or "had a drink on an empty stomach".

Before Liz could answer otherwise, a pale figure entered the room with blue-black hair, heavy black smudged eyeliner, a gray paper-thin cardigan sweater with a white V-neck t-shirt, several long chains, black trousers and combat-style boots.

Sam and Lexy yelled, "Sasha!"

"Hey!" Sasha answered back in a monotone voice.

"Is this our surprise guest?" Liz asked Sam.

"Yes! Are you surprised, Dad?"

Adam looked surprised all right.

"Dad, do you remember when you said that the music that I was listening to reminded you of a song from when you were a kid? It was a song about tulips… That was Sasha's music I was listening to that night. So that's my surprise! You are getting to meet Sasha for your birthday!" Sam told the perplexed Adam.

"Tulip song?" Liz asked.

"Tiptoe Through the Tulips by Tiny Tim," Adam slurred.

"I didn't know you were a Tiny Tim groupie!" Bobby somehow said with a straight face.

"So glad you could join us, Sasha!" Liz said, trying to sound convincing.

Sasha sat with Sam and Lexy at the far end of the table.

"Is that a girl or a guy?" Adam drunkenly whispered to Liz.

"I'm not sure…" she answered.

"Whatever you do, don't ask Sasha to sing. Trust me on this." Adam warned Bobby and Liz.

"Darn,…I was going to have him or her sing Happy Birthday to you!" Bobby said.

Liz excused herself and moved down to the end of the table where the kids were having a lively conversation. Bobby and Adam both looked hurt that Liz had deserted them. Bobby and Adam just sat there in silence, munching on tortilla chips and salsa.

Eventually Liz made her way back to Adam and Bobby.

"I still have no clue," Liz said.

"Finally after all of these years you admit it," Adam said, thinking he was being funny.

"Sasha's friends are Terry and Pat. In his or her spare time, he or she plays tennis, films documentary films or writes ukulele scores. I could see no discernable Adam's apple," Liz reported.

"Are you saying you failed in this mission, and you need a man to do the job?" Bobby annoyingly asked.

"Too bad you aren't one…" Adam said, thinking yet again in his intoxicated state that he was hilarious.

Sam got up and said, " El Jefe, time for you to open your gifts!"

"Adam, that would be you," Liz pointed out to Adam who was trying to read upside down the nametag that Sam had placed on him.

Liz gave him a white dress shirt with French cuffs. She also gave him cuff links that were blue lapis squares surrounded by sterling silver. She had bought the cufflinks on the Mexico vacation when Adam wasn't paying attention. Adam gave Liz a kiss.

"Gross!!!" Sam and Lexy yelled in unison.

Bobby produced a card containing a gift certificate for a massage.

"Thanks Bobby. I'm sure there's a catch…" Adam mumbled.

"You will have to pay extra for the happy ending…" Bobby told him.

"That's enough!" Liz warned both men. She didn't want to have to explain what a happy ending was to Sam.

"Dad, Lexy and I went to the mall to get you a present, but we didn't see anything that I thought you would like."

"Is that where the outfits came from?" Liz asked rather pointedly.

"We wanted to look festive!" Sam replied.

"Didn't you have enough money for the pants?" Adam asked.

"Dad, it's a dress…"

"Could have fooled me…" he replied.

"I brought this card. I think it's from Grandma and Grandpa Schaeffer," Sam said producing a large white envelope that she had found when she brought the mail in.

"I don't have my reading glasses. I will look at it at home."

Sam decided that wasn't an option, since she was concerned the length of her dress might be talked about again. She ripped the envelope open and started to read in a melodramatic tone. "…to the Love of my Life, Happy Birthday…"

Bobby quickly realized that Adam's parents were not the senders of this card, nor Liz. He realized the inappropriate card was from Mrs. Piggy. He firmly took the card from Sam and said, "Time for the birthday cake!" Liz snatched the card from Bobby's hand and put the card in her purse to give to her attorney, in case she needed it.

"Mom, we can't have any cake cause we are too young for beer!" Sam announced cracking Lexy and Sasha up.

"I need to see some identification, young lady!" Bobby said, trying to help Liz lighten the mood and get the party back on track for Sam's sake.

"We need to sing Happy Birthday!" Lexy announced to the dismay of Adam.

Fortunately at that moment, the door opened and all of the waiters and waitresses in the restaurant came in to sing the restaurant's rendition of Happy Birthday.

"That was the best present, not having Sasha sing," Adam whispered into Liz's ear.

Adam, Liz and Bobby looked at the end of the table to see Sasha lean over to kiss Sam.

"Well, I guess that answers that question…" Liz said.

"Not necessarily…" Bobby replied.

"Seriously Bobby…" Liz scolded him.

Adam looked at Liz and said sarcastically, "Great party, Liz!"

Chapter 18

Natalie high-tailed it to Pamela Tate's downtown law office as soon as she received the disturbing phone call. Natalie decided it wasn't something that she wanted to handle alone, so she called Marilyn as reinforcement on the way. Marilyn said the only important thing left on her agenda for today was to get a bikini wax and that could wait. She could be right there. The truth of the matter was that Marilyn was glad to help. She had felt a little left out when she heard about the party that Nick and Natalie had attended trying to trick Mrs. Piggy.

Natalie hoped that she wouldn't run into Mrs. Piggy on the way to Pamela's private office. Surely not. After all, Tate & Tate was all about appearances. Knowing Pamela as she did, she was sure that Mrs. Piggy would be hidden far from view. She did not fit the image that Tate & Tate would want to project. Pamela probably would put her in the basement, if the building had one.

Natalie parked in the landscaped parking lot adjacent to the historic mansion that was now the home of the law offices of Tate & Tate. If she weren't in such a hurry, she would have enjoyed strolling through the gardens that surrounded the property. Not only did Pamela showcase her impeccable taste restoring the mansion and grounds, but also Tate & Tate had "acquired" it for a bargain basement price. Natalie preferred to not know the details. She walked through a winding path lined with dwarf Indian Hawthorn plants. The plant's pale pink flowers made the already impressive entrance look even more spectacular. At the top of the steps was a huge veranda with white wicker rocking chairs and ferns.

Pamela's secretary was waiting for her as soon as she entered through the leaded glass front door. Natalie thought to herself that this gal had the "Tate & Tate look". She had perfect hair, make-up and clothes. She looked smart. They made pleasant conversation on their way to Pamela's office. Pamela's third floor office was normally off-limits to visitors. Only a private elevator or the mansion's stairwell could access it. Not even Mr. Tate went into Mrs. Tate's office without an invitation. The firm's activities were conducted, for the most part, in the offices of the first and second floor of the building.

Pamela was anxiously awaiting Natalie. She hugged Natalie the moment that she walked off the elevator.

"I know you came straight here, but it seemed to take forever!" Pamela told her, as the two women made their way to a magnificent carved writing desk in the center of the room. Natalie found a seat, opposite Pamela, in one of the two upholstered chairs in front of Pamela's desk.

Her secretary returned to the room quietly bringing in two diet sodas with lime on an antique silver tray and placed them on Pamela's desk. She then closed the two French doors behind her and returned to her desk.

"From what you started to tell me on the phone, it sounds like we may need something stronger," Natalie told Pamela, picking up the diet soda.

Without any warning, Marilyn exited the elevator. It's hard to say who was more startled by Marilyn's sudden appearance—Pamela or her secretary. The only two people who had the passcode for the elevator were Pamela Tate and her trusty secretary. Pamela's hand immediately went under her desk in search of the security panic button when she realized that Natalie was greeting this dark haired stranger with the unusual short, spunky haircut.

"Pamela, this is Marilyn," Natalie said, introducing the two women.

"Natalie tells me that you are a computer forensic expert, but I have a hunch that you are an excellent safecracker also," Pamela said, making reference to the fact that Marilyn somehow cracked the code to get the elevator to the third floor.

Marilyn didn't know what or if she should make something of Pamela's comment. She decided to just help herself to the candy in the crystal candy dish on Pamela's desk instead of dwelling on it.

"I am just going to start from the beginning. Yesterday, my tech person at the firm noticed Mrs. Piggy had been spending a lot of time on Yahoo.com. He has been instructed to alert me if any of the employees are spending personal time on the computer. That is not what they are being paid to do. He knows Mrs. Piggy is of particular interest to me, but he doesn't know why. So, I instructed him to print out her entire search history. Natalie, I called you as soon as I got the report this morning," Pamela stated.

"Thank goodness, you did!"

"So, what was she looking at?" Marilyn wondered.

"Her most researched topic was accidental drowning. She looked at seven different sites, paying particular attention to articles that discussed drowning in home swimming pools," Pamela told the two astonished women.

"Liz has a beautiful pool on the bluff that overlooks the Guadalupe River. She just had it heated, so her family can swim more often," Natalie informed them.

"Liz better make sure she isn't swimming alone," Marilyn added.

"Now that you tell me that she lives on a bluff, this is making more sense. Next, she looked at four sites that discussed falls," Pamela enlightened the women further.

"Is that the only way that she thinks Adam will be with her, by killing his wife? I have seen shit like this on TV," Marilyn told them.

"She tried to specifically find out from what height a hundred pound person would need to fall from to die instantly!" Pamela had to pause after she told them this. The mother of three needed to collect herself.

"Oh my God! It's not Liz she is after, but Sam!" Natalie said, once she realized this.

"I'm wondering at what height a one hundred seventy five pounder would have to fall…" Marilyn asked.

"You haven't seen her. I think it would be more like two hundred pounds!" Natalie corrected Marilyn.

"You have to wonder what kind of person would consider killing a child to be with a man," Pamela said.

"I know the answer to that! A psychopath, that's who!" Marilyn answered.

"There is no man on earth worth killing a child for. There is no man worth leaving a child for. I have never met Adam. Does he give off some kind of Svengali vibe?" Pamela inquired.

"Well…he kind of grows on you after awhile. I wouldn't go out with him now that I've had therapy. He's not my type," Natalie said truthfully.

"Yeah, like a fungus," Marilyn added, in a way that no one was quite sure whether it was intended as a compliment or not. Natalie remembered that Marilyn had said the same thing about Bobby Bain once.

"I'm sure your computer person is top notch, but would you give me access to Mrs. Piggy's computer? I wouldn't want us to miss anything," Marilyn asked, knowing no one in the world was more devious or better at snooping than her.

"No… not at all! In fact, she is being kept 'busy' for the next few hours. I didn't want anyone to run into her here," Pamela told them.

Marilyn and Pamela switched places. Marilyn immediately started typing away on the keyboard. Every once in awhile she would take a deep breath. Finally, Natalie couldn't stand it any longer and asked, "What is it that you are looking for?"

"I'm seeing if she has been corresponding to anyone by e-mail, or if she has been visiting any social network sites," Marilyn explained.

"I wish I had your expertise on the computer," Natalie said, in total awe.

"Me too. I'm a good snoop but I have no choice but to rely on my tech guy. For all I know he might be missing something," Pamela said, finally starting to let her guard down around Marilyn.

"That's because he did! She has been looking for our sweet Sam on Facebook,"

Marilyn announced to the women. Marilyn knew that Mrs. Piggy's next step would be trying to somehow make contact with the teen. This was one of the few times in her life that she wished she would be wrong.

"Did she find Sam's Facebook page?" Natalie asked.

"No, but she sure tried. She tried several variations of Sam's name. Luckily, Liz has me check Sam's account every month when I'm doing the maintenance on her office and home computers. We make sure it's on the most private settings," Marilyn explained.

"I'm going to hire you to do the same for my three kids. You can't be too careful these days," Pamela said.

"Thank goodness she couldn't find Sam. So…where do we proceed from here?" Natalie asked the others.

"I think I should call Bobby. He can notify Officer Becker," Marilyn said.

"What about Liz? I don't want her to think that we are keeping something from her. Do you know how pissed I would be if someone didn't tell me somebody was trying to kill Dirk?" Natalie said.

"I totally agree. I will make sure Liz knows what we have found. I want to double check her computers even though I just checked everything last week," Marilyn told Natalie and Pamela.

"Marilyn, it was really nice to meet you. I'm really sorry about how I acted the first few minutes you were here," Pamela told Marilyn sincerely.

"It's okay. I realize now that I probably scared the crap out of you," Marilyn said, accepting Pamela's apology.

"Something like that. I was serious about having you do some consulting work for me. I could use someone with your special skill set, if you know what I mean," Pamela told Marilyn.

"Here's how to get in touch with me," Marilyn said, handing her a business card. Marilyn's colorful business cards were shaped like a VW bug and had a spikey haired cartoon woman in the driver's seat. On the bottom of the card, it simply had her name, Marilyn, and a phone number. Nothing more and nothing less. Marilyn found it surprising enough that she liked Pamela now that Pamela wasn't trying to act like she was better than her. She especially liked the way that Pamela referred to her talents as being a "special skills set."

"When this is over, all of us girls should get together and do a weekend at Lake Austin Spa. We could even let little Sam come," Pamela said.

"The only problem is that Bobby will want to come!" Natalie said. They all knew this was so true. The thought of Bobby trying to finagle an invite made Marilyn, Pamela and Natalie laugh uncontrollably. They knew he hated missing out on anything.

"If we let Bobby come, then we should invite Nick!" Marilyn said, raising her eyebrows and smiling knowingly.

"Are you kidding me?!? The last thing I would want is for him to see me wandering around in a robe and slippers without my Spanx, no make-up and my hair in a ponytail!!!" Natalie shrieked.

Pamela started laughing so hard that she accidently snorted. This made them all start laughing again.

"Maybe Nick doesn't look good in a robe either!" Marilyn speculated, even though she knew nothing could be further from the truth.

"Just what is in the chocolate you have been eating?" Natalie asks.

"Okay, we all know he's perfect," Marilyn sighed. The other two nodded their heads in agreement.

With that thought the "think tank" adjourned.

No one was the least bit surprised when Marilyn got in the elevator with Natalie and again entered the code to enable the elevator. They both waved good-bye to Pamela as the elevator doors began to close. Pamela walked back to her desk and noticed all of her chocolates were gone. She decided, it was much better to have Marilyn as an ally, rather than an enemy.

When Marilyn reached the parking lot, she decided to wait to put the convertible top down on her bug, so that Bobby would be able to hear every detail. Even so, he found the news so incredible that she still ended up repeating it to him, twice. He agreed to call Officer Becker and then meet her at Liz's office within the hour.

Marilyn tried to put on some music to distract herself from the thoughts of little Sam plummeting off a cliff to her death or found floating lifelessly in her family's pool. After listening to several female country singers blasting out their anthems celebrating womanhood, Marilyn started to wonder what they would do in this situation. She couldn't see Martina McBride, Carrie Underwood or Reba McEntire sitting on their asses doing absolutely nothing! She knew exactly what they would do and decided this might be another one of her "life-altering" decisions.

The rest of her drive was spent carefully formulating her plan. She seriously contemplated whether to include Liz and the others, but ultimately decided that this was something she would need to do alone. Marilyn hadn't always done the right things in her past, but after she earned her degree, she had tried to be on the straight and narrow. Occasionally, she had slipped up.

A few years ago, she had her TV on, trying to fill the silence of her small apartment. The show she had been listening to ended and the following show was a religious show. A young preacher was giving a very passionate sermon. Just as she walked up to change the channel, he started talking about atonement. Atonement, he explained was reconciling your wrongs with God. She didn't even know there was a word for this. Next thing that she knew, she was sitting on the sofa listening to the young man. He explained earnestly it wasn't too late and all one had to do was stop doing the bad stuff, apologize and ask for forgiveness and you would be redeemed. At the time, it seemed like an easy enough solution.

From that day on, she tried to tell the truth. It was easy because she didn't know anyone in New Braunfels, Texas. Until the day she ran into Chris Richards. Chris had been a regular of Marilyn's at Miss Mona's Catty Shack in Las Vegas. Marilyn couldn't make Chris understand that those days were in her past and weren't going to happen again. She had moved on to bigger and better things that weren't going to include his pimply ass. Marilyn thought about picking up her meager belongings and moving, but something unbelievable happened instead. Chris tried contacting a couple of Marilyn's new computer clients to tell them about her previous job experience. He had obviously been following Marilyn.

Fortunately for Marilyn the first client he contacted was Liz. Liz looked Chris right in the eye, as he began telling her all about Marilyn's sordid past in Las Vegas and said nine words—"I don't believe you. Get out of my office!"

Chris tried his luck with Bobby Bain next. Liz had obviously filled Bobby in on the troublemaker. Bobby was ready. He let Chris talk for a moment and then interrupted him with a question. Bobby asked him, "What kind of loser has to pay for sex?" Chris didn't have a good answer. So, Bobby rephrased the question, "You REALLY have to pay someone to have sex with you?" This wasn't quite the response that Chris expected. Chris got up and left Bobby sitting there. Bobby was a little disappointed because he had thought of a lot more questions he wanted to ask Chris. No one was surprised that they never heard from Chris again.

Marilyn was hoping to do something as nice for Liz, as what Liz had done for her years ago. Marilyn knew Liz was no dummy and had probably figured out that most or at least a good majority of what Chris said was true. She felt so fortunate that Liz liked her and wanted to be her friend. She also knew she couldn't blow it and so far never had.

Marilyn pulled into the parking garage for Liz and Bobby's office. There was a New Braunfels police car parked in front and Marilyn assumed that it probably was Officer Becker's. Until recently, the biggest case that Officer Becker had been involved with was arresting a drunk at Wurstfest who tried relieving himself in a vat of boiling oil used to make the Lion's Club funnel cakes. The trial involved Officer Becker having to ID the perp's fried pecker. To add insult to injury, one of the San Antonio newscasters accidently called him Officer Pecker, instead of Becker on the air. To this day, his fellow officers loved teasing him, leaving fried pickles or bottles of cooking oil on his desk. Sooner or later, once he is no longer the most junior officer on the squad, the teasing may subside.

Marilyn marched right into Liz's conference room. Liz was frantically pacing. Bobby and Officer Becker looked concerned. Marilyn quickly filled them in on what had been found on Mrs. Piggy's work computer.

"Hans, what can we do about this?" Liz asked.

"I'm going straight back to the station to talk to the Chief. I will be in touch. Please don't worry Dr. S. We will catch her," Hans said reassuringly, as he left.

"Marilyn, thank goodness you found this out. Can you keep an eye on Sam's accounts? Of course, I will compensate you for the extra time," Liz told her.

"Liz, I've got it. Have you told Sam about any of this?"

"She knows something was making me cry at the drop of a hat. She's pretty perceptive and figured it had to do with Adam. Adam sat her down and explained about Mrs. Piggy lurking around."

"How did she take it?" Marilyn asked.

"She told him, 'Way to go, Dad!' She seemed disturbed that he would do something so thoughtless," Liz answered.

"She does have a point!" Marilyn said, agreeing with Sam.

"Trust me, she isn't the only one with that thought," Liz confided to Marilyn.

"I'm going to head out, unless you need something. I want to set the monitor for Sam's account up immediately," Marilyn explained.

"That would be great. Thanks again, Marilyn. You are a great friend!" Liz said, giving her a huge hug.

Marilyn hurried straight home. She couldn't wait to get on the computer. She knew what needed to be done next.   Marilyn was going to make a hog trap and she knew exactly what the bait would be.

Chapter 19

It was highly unusual for Adam to answer the home phone. Even if he were sitting right next to it, he would often just let it ring and ring, waiting for someone else to answer it for him. His habit annoyed his wife and daughter immensely. He knew the chance that it could be someone calling for him was slim to none -- so why bother, he thought. He didn't want to have to take a message or make small talk. So, it was out of character that Adam answered the phone that day. And of course, it wasn't for him. It was Officer Becker calling for Liz.

"Can I deliver a message to her? This is her husband," Adam asked, even though he did not really want to be an answering service.

"Yes, please. I already tried her cell phone and her office. Could you tell Dr. Schaeffer that the suspect was seen sitting across the street from your daughter's school? Our Officer later observed her following the car your daughter was riding home in," Officer Becker told Adam.

"Well, I hope this means that she has been arrested."

"Unfortunately, we couldn't. It's not illegal to sit across from your daughter's school or to drive behind the car she is riding in," Hans explained apologetically.

"Well, I have a grand idea, maybe next time you can give her a full police escort to our house, so she can get here ahead of my daughter. Then, she can just wait for her here, in the comfort of our lovely home," Adam said sarcastically.

"The officer did follow her. She was given a moving violation for following the other car too closely. We can hope that will be a deterrent in the future. I have personally talked to the campus security and they are on full alert. They will notify us immediately. Today was an unusual circumstance, since the school had a late pep rally. I don't think under normal circumstances the suspect would have been able to make it to the school while your daughter was still there due to her work schedule."

"I am a busy man," Adam told Hans.

"Sir, I just wanted to let you know that we are taking this matter seriously and we will keep you informed as developments occur," Hans said. He suddenly realized Adam was no longer on the line. A show had just come on the television about people living in swamps who survived on varmints. As far as Adam was concerned, that took priority over chit chatting with Officer Becker.

Hans could not believe the nerve of this guy. Hans had to remind himself, he was an officer of the law and it was his job to serve and protect everyone, whether he person- ally liked them or not. He could not believe that this guy just hung up on him. He really needed to let Liz know the rest of the story.   This was a part of the job that he didn't like -- delivering bad news. Hans told himself that he shouldn't take such rude behavior personally. Maybe they just had a bad connection.   He would do the right thing and call Adam back.

"Mr. Schaefer, this is Officer Becker. We must have been disconnected."

"Dr. Schaeffer still is not home," Adam told him. He never acknowledged whether he hung up on the officer or whether it was a bad connection.

"I wanted to let Dr. Schaeffer know one other thing. When the suspect was given the moving violation, she informed the officer that she had a concealed handgun in her purse. She was carrying a TCP 380. In case you don't know, that's a pretty popular gun with the ladies. It's a slim, semi-automatic pistol, but I would venture to say what most women like about it -- is that it's pink. I have even seen some "bedazzle" it with Swarovski crystals," Hans informed Adam.

"So let me guess – it's also not illegal to carry a Barbie-pink gun, sit by my daughter's school, and then follow the car she's riding in?"

"I'm afraid you are correct Mr. Schaeffer."

"Does your Chief know about this?" Adam said, trying to intimidate Hans.

"Yes sir, he does."

"I will give Dr. Schaeffer the message. Good evening," Adam said. He hung up before Hans could reply.

Hans wondered how Adam Schaefer treated his wife. He would bet -- pretty shabbily.

Adam was now even more annoyed than he was before, if that was possible. He was in a no-win situation. If he told Liz what Officer Becker has just revealed to him, then she would give him "that look." "That look," which says "how could you have brought this harm to your family? How could you not have realized the consequences of your actions?" Personally, Adam thought that they were just all overreacting. Especially Bobby Bain. That idiot had gotten motion-activated lights, as bright as airport runway lights, mounted in their oak trees, just because this worthless woman tried looking in their windows one lousy time.   Not to mention the hidden video cameras. Then Bain had the nerve to have the bills sent to him. When he angrily confronted Liz about it, she looked at him like he was crazy for being pissed off. She even told him she was grateful that Bobby had taken care of it so promptly. Didn't she know that he would eventually get to it?

Adam wondered when that moron Bain would just give up. He was always following Liz around like a puppy. Adam had never bought Bobby's story for how he ended up practicing in New Braunfels. Adam was one of the few people, besides Liz, who knew that Bobby's grandfather was none other than Eli Bain of EB Exploration. EB Exploration is one of the country's largest crude oil and natural gas producers. On a bad day, Bobby was worth several hundred million dollars. Adam couldn't believe this when Liz told him. This little tidbit came out when Adam and Liz had their first fight after dating a few months.

His boss's wife, Karen, had introduced Adam to Liz. Adam didn't know that he needed "fixing up" but apparently, Karen decided that he did. It was her mission in life to try and make sure everyone was as happy as she and her husband, Mike.

At this point in Adam's life, he had no problem finding dates. He had a great job, fancy car and enjoyed frequenting the better restaurants and nightclubs in Houston. He rarely felt the need to date any of these women more than a few times. Karen found his dating practices disturbing.

Mike and Karen had been married since their junior year of college. They both had slightly different accounts of how they met. Both of their stories took place at their college chapel and involved singing. This is where the similarities ended. Michael loved embarrassing his wife by coming up with a tale that became lewder and lewder with each telling. Karen would eventually tire of correcting Michael's embellished accounts. She would then start to make up something so obviously ridiculous that no one knew what to believe. Karen once added to Mike's story by saying, "You forgot the part where I had nothing on under my choir robe!"

Adam would have never willingly agreed to let Karen be his matchmaker. Mike wanted to stay happily married to Karen, so on that particular day he threw Adam under the bus.

It seemed a little peculiar to Adam that Mike wanted to discuss business at this girly, mainly vegetarian, restaurant. Adam was really hungry and he wasn't very happy when he had to order quiche for lunch, at Mike's urging. It all made perfect sense when Karen walked in with the tall, thin, gorgeous blonde.

Karen looked quite pleased with herself. The blonde immediately hugged Mike and Mike introduced her to Adam as Liz. Adam decided Liz was probably a model that Karen had met at one of the charity luncheons that she always seemed to be attending.

After a short awkward period, Liz started telling Mike about her recent adventure in Mexico on a medical mission. Adam was shocked to find out she was a surgeon. She had gone to a remote village to help children who had been burnt due to a refinery fire that gotten out of control in their village.

"I didn't know that you spoke Spanish, Liz," Mike remarked.

"Un poquito (a little)," Liz said, with a laugh.

"I think I'm being set up, but Karen said I should ask you about buying gas on your trip," Mike said.

"Okay, but it's pretty embarrassing. We had to stop in this small village for gas. I had read online that tourists had problems at this station, but there were no other options. One of our doctors got out of our van, and asked the service station attendant for two hundred pesos worth of gas. I was sitting in the passenger's front seat of the van, right by the pump. The attendant made such a show of inputting two hundred pesos into the pump. I noticed he had only put one hundred thirty four pesos of gas in when he suddenly pushed a button on the side of the pump and now it read two hundred pesos, instead of one hundred thirty four. I realized he was pulling the scam on us that I had read about! I jumped out of the van and told my friend what he did. Two other attendants then walked over. Surprisingly he put the rest of the gas in our van. As I was standing there, I started getting really mad about him trying to take advantage of us. I decided I was going to say something. The only problem was that I had gotten so mad that I couldn't think of any of the Spanish words that I wanted to say."

"Like what?" Mike wondered.

"I wanted to tell him he wasn't a nice man for trying to take advantage of us."

"That will put him in his place!" Mike said, laughing.

So I stood there and said, "You are a mal (and then there was an extremely long pause) hombre!" I wanted to tell him he wasn't going to get a tip now, but for the life of me I couldn't think of the right words. So I said, "No tipo". Then I told him he was "estupido". Then I quickly got in the van and we drove off."

"Let me guess -- you were probably a foot taller than this guy."

"Easily."

"They are probably still talking about how the giant white woman went loco-calling the attendant a bad man, then telling him that he wasn't getting a tip, because he had acted so stupid," Mike said, while wiping away tears of laughter streaming down his face.

"Everyone else was lovely on the entire trip."

"Good thing, or you might have gotten to see a Mexican jail firsthand!"

The waitress returned to their table with their lunch. She mistakenly thought Liz's steak sandwich was Adam's. She put Adam's quiche in front of Liz.

Liz waited until the waitress was gone and handed Adam his spinach quiche. She leaned over and whispered in his ear," I always heard real men don't eat quiche!"

Adam was at a loss for words because Mike and Karen were sitting there. What he was thinking was that he would really like a steak, some beer and Liz for dessert, but decided to keep this thought to himself. He whispered back, "You would be mistaken."

"What are you lovebirds whispering about?" Mike asked.

"Mike!" Karen reprimanded him.

"Would you like half of my steak sandwich?" Liz asked Adam.

"Only if you will take half of this nutritious quiche," Adam said, hoping he could get rid of part of the egg pie.

"Sounds good," Liz said. Little did they know that this would be the first of many meals that they would share.

When they had both finished their entrees, Liz asked Adam, "Which did you like better?"

"Believe it or not, the quiche! How about you?"

"Definitely the quiche! Glad we switched!" Liz said, with a laugh.

The waitress came back and asked if they wanted any dessert. She told them that they had carrot cake, key lime pie, tiramisu and coconut cream pie. Liz looked perplexed with so many choices.

"I can't decide between the carrot cake and the coconut cream pie. Which is better?" she asked the waitress.

"They are both good," the waitress replied.

"I'm having the same dilemma. Would you be interested in splitting desserts also?" Adam asked Liz.

"That would be perfect," she beamed at him.

In his entire life, Adam had never recalled pleasing a woman so easily.

Karen and Mike passed on having dessert, and excused themselves to look at the knick-knacks in the adjoining boutique. Adam considered asking Liz for her phone number at this point, but had a paralyzing thought -- what if Karen and Mike weren't setting him up? He decided against looking like a fool.

Liz had to return to her studies and had to leave a few moments after Mike and Karen returned to the table.

"That girl is the whole enchilada—brains, looks and funny as hell!" Mike commented as soon as Liz had left the table.

"Doesn't she remind you of a young Grace Kelly?" Karen asked.

"I loved her story about almost getting ripped off buying gas in Mexico!" Mike said.

"You had tears running down your face. I haven't seen you laugh that hard in a long time," Karen told him.

"It was her expressions and hand gestures. Knowing Adam as I do, I bet he will be calling her as soon as we are gone. This is one deal he won't want to let get away," Mike said.

Karen rolled her eyes.

"I didn't ask her for her phone number," Adam informed the two matchmakers.

"What?" they questioned, in unison.

"And to think I've been telling everyone in New York how brilliant you are," Mike said.

Adam who could have easily had a career as a spin-doctor, instead of aspiring CEO, quickly did damage control. "Karen, I can't thank you enough for introducing me to Liz. Honestly, she had to leave so abruptly that it took me off guard. There is nothing I would like more than get to know her better. I'm hoping you can help me with this."

Mike gave him an approving nod.

Karen was beaming. So far, her batting average at matchmaking had been a dismal .000, even though she had been at bat several times. She was actively trying to improve her average, but to no avail. Mike had even gently tried to tell her she might want to put her time and efforts elsewhere. Karen was already jumping the gun thinking what a beautiful bride Liz would be.

"I know exactly how you can impress her. I will plan everything for you," Karen told him.

One of reasons for Adam's success in business at such a young age was his ability to know who to delegate to. He knew from Mike that Karen was a thorough planner. He wouldn't have to do a thing.

Karen called him bright and early the next day at the office.

"Good morning! I just sent you an e-mail," Karen informed him.

"I just opened it. A picture of a sunflower arrangement in a pot tied together at the top with some rope?"

"It's called raffia."

"I thought they were big sunflowers."

"They are."

"I thought you just said they were raffia."

"The bow is made of raffia. They are sunflowers. I have a lot to teach you," Karen teased him.

"I'm lucky that I have you coaching me!" Adam said, trying his best to flatter his boss's wife.

"Thanks! I thought you could have this arrangement sent to her home with a card asking her out. I'll help you with the wording. You will include your phone number and then "Voila!"

"Where am I taking her?"

"You are going to pick her up and take her to a jumping show."

"Jumping?"

"It's a horse thing. She loves horses. She can't wait until she finishes her fellowship, so she can buy a horse of her own. It is a charity horse show. There is a cocktail party prior that you are now invited to.

"My future is in your hands."

Adam was almost as good at taking directions as he was at giving them, so as planned, the first date went exceptionally well.

After a few dates, Adam realized that he would be bored trying to date the kind of girls that he been seeing before. Liz was so refreshingly different from other women. She didn't seem to like it when he spent a lot of money on her. The thing that made her the happiest was when he spent time with her. Other girls were impressed with his job, his car and the restaurants where he took them. None of that fazed her. She liked to eat at hole-in-the-wall dives. Never before had a woman really listened to him. She wanted to know about his family, his childhood friends and how he felt about things that no one had ever asked him about. He felt like he could tell her anything. The only thing he didn't like about her was her friendship with Bobby Bain. Sometimes when he wanted to see her, she would not be available, because she had already made plans with Bobby. Bobby and Liz spent hours together studying, but Adam wanted to spend time with her when she was free. Bobby had persuaded her to help out at the Women's Shelter and it was starting to take time away from their relationship.

The day they got into their first fight, Adam's boss had given a last-minute invitation to him and Liz for dinner with their company's CEO. Adam knew that meant he was likely being considered for a major promotion. He always thought that he would stay single until he was at least 36 or possibly even 38 years old. Since meeting Liz, Adam was rethinking that. His boss and boss's wife loved Liz.

Liz was very excited for Adam when he told her his news. "Adam, I'm not in the least bit surprised by this! You are brilliant. And now everyone is starting to know what I already knew. I can't wait to hear how it goes. Wear your dark charcoal suit, light gray shirt and the tie I bought you for Valentine's Day. You look so amazingly handsome in that!"

"I was thinking you could see how handsome I look in person!"

"I'm sorry, but I'm teaching a GED class at the shelter tonight."

"With that idiot, Bobby Bain, I bet."

"Actually, Bobby is teaching the English and I'm doing the math," Liz answered, ignoring Adam's insult.

"Liz, that guy is never going to amount to anything."

"Adam, he's my friend. Beyond that, he's an anesthesiology fellow, so I think he will be able to support himself."

"He drives around in that stupid Chevette telling everyone, 'it's a 'Vette.' I'm telling you, he's a loser that will never have two nickels to rub together."

"So, is money how you determine if someone is successful?"

"He's always volunteering everywhere. How is he going to make any money doing that? You should volunteer when you already have what you need — your house, your cars, traveled everywhere you want to go, your retirement account and your kids college funds."

"That's an extremely sad perspective."

"It's realistic. We can't all live in your white pony and giant sunflower world, Liz."

"Don't you DARE ever call me that again!"

"I didn't call you a name, I called you Liz."

"It was the way you said it. It wasn't Liz with a soft L, it was Liz with a hard L."

"I just can't believe that you would miss such an important evening to spend it with that dumbass Bobby Bain and a bunch of high school drop-outs."

"You know darn well if I would have had more than six hours notice, I would have been there for you. Bobby is not a loser. Yes, he can be strange, but I like the way he makes a difference, rather than sitting around counting his money."

"What else would he do? It doesn't take long to count a buck and a quarter, Liz!" Adam said, putting extra emphasis on the L.

"You did it again!"

"Liz! Liz! Liz!" Adam said, with each word having more emphasis than the last.

"For your information, Bobby is a MULTI-millionaire. He is Eli Bain's only grandchild. He just likes to make sure people like him for him, not his money."

"Eli Bain? Bain Towers, Bain Communications, Bain Exploration, Bain Banking…"

"One and the same. So Adam, instead of being such a jealous fool, certainly you must realize I'm not after your money. Until this evening, I thought I liked you."

"La-la-Liz," Adam stuttered.

"That's better than Liz with a hard L!" Liz said, with a laugh realizing how silly their argument had become.

"You like me? Because I... I love you," Adam said, for the first time in his life. Usually he told a girl, I THINK I love you, so he couldn't be held accountable.

"Really, cause I love you too, but I must predicate that with I sometimes don't know why," Liz said, being completely honest.

Chapter 20

Bobby was walking down the hall towards his private office when he heard a noise. He stopped a few feet short of his office door to listen more closely. He definitely heard something... a muffled groan...again. He cautiously peered around the corner and saw what looked like a figure moving under his desk. He froze and watched for a few seconds – trying to figure out what was going on. There had never been an intruder in the office before. He chastised himself for spending the time and money to take a concealed handgun course, but not ever using it. What good was it if he was only going to leave his gun in his gun safe at home?? The only thing he could try to do at this point would be catching the intruder off guard. He looked for something – anything – to use as a weapon. He saw a multi-hued Murano glass vase on display close by —one that he brought back from his travels in Italy. He quietly picked it up. Now, he would have a good excuse to return to Europe.

"Jesus Boom!" the voice under Bobby's desk muttered.

There were only two people in the whole wide world that Bobby knew that might say that —one of them was Liz's Dad. The chances of the seventy-something year old man crawling around under the desk were slim to none. The other person was Marilyn. He had forgotten that she was going to be there that evening to work on his computer.

He carefully put down the vase and decided against startling her. He was not sure if he would classify this flashback as PTSD, but he could vividly recall the result of the last time he surprised Marilyn. He narrowly escaped with his life, but the ceiling tiles that she had shot down and landed on top of his head weren't as lucky. That unfortunate incident had not served as a wake-up call for Marilyn, as she still hadn't seen the need to enroll in a concealed handgun course. It didn't stop her from carrying a gun, either. He decided it would be much safer to just peer in and see what she was up to. After all, he paid her by the hour. Maybe she was just sitting in his office shopping online. She was probably doing her Christmas shopping early. He then wondered if he was on her Christmas list.

He carefully angled his body so he could see into the room without her seeing him. The monitor was completely out of view, but fortunately there was a large decorative mirror behind it. He instantly recognized the blue color. Marilyn was on the social network site, Facebook. He found that a bit peculiar since she was supposed to be working on updating his billing system.

He decided to walk briskly in the room and see what her reaction would be. He wouldn't say a word. He would let her wonder whether or not he noticed that she was goofing off on his dime.

"Jesus, you scared me!" Marilyn scowled at him.

"Is that any way to talk to your employer?" Bobby said, as he tried to look over her shoulder to see what she was really working on.

"I am not your employee! If I was an employee you would be paying my taxes, my health insurance and my retirement," Marilyn said, reminding him of her contract status. She clicked on the screen to minimize it. He noticed his billing system popped up in place of the Facebook page.

"You are right. I don't think you realize how much I appreciate your computer skills." He leaned over Marilyn and quietly powered the computer off.

"What are you doing? Is that how you turn the computer off every day? It's no wonder I'm always in here fixing this thing."

"No, but you can always fix it in the morning. Tonight, I'm taking you to dinner. You can't say no because that is what I'm paying you to do tonight. We need to get going or we will miss the sunset."

"You know, just because you are paying me it doesn't mean I will do any activity you want!"

"For God's sake, Marilyn!"

"Where are we going?"

"The Overlook."

"You can't get in at The Overlook without reservations!" Marilyn informed him.

The Overlook was New Braunfels' newest addition to the fine dining restaurant scene. It got its name because it overlooked the Guadalupe River. The restaurant was nestled among century old oak trees high on a ridge overlooking The Preserve's golf course. To say it was popular would be an understatement. It opened two months ago, but rumor had it that the next available reservation was months away.

"I can get us in. I have a connection," Bobby told Marilyn, who had no idea that Bobby actually owned the restaurant. Bobby liked it that way. The only people who knew this well guarded secret were Liz, Adam, and the general manager of the restaurant who had been sworn to secrecy.

"Good thing I dressed up today!" Marilyn said.

Bobby was not sure if she was referencing the upscale dress code or just fishing for a compliment. He was not one to take chances with Marilyn. The stirring that Bobby felt in his loins when he saw Marilyn was not the same kind that they write about in romance novels. It's more of a shrinking feeling – very similar to the effect a man experiences when taking a cold shower.

"You always look fantastic, Marilyn! Let's go, so we don't miss the sunset. This computer thing can wait until another day!"

Bobby made sure that he locked his office door and activated the security alarm before locking the entrance door. He didn't want to take any chances where Marilyn was concerned.

"We can ride together. Why don't you drop your car at your house and I will give you a ride home afterwards?" Bobby proposed.

"Okay, but you aren't spending the night! I want to make that perfectly clear. This is for dinner only." Marilyn referenced Bobby's two ill-fated nights spent at her house.

"Trust me, that is the furthest thing from my mind," Bobby answered honestly.

Bobby followed Marilyn through town to her house. She parked the red bug in her garage. Bobby was truly beginning to wonder if he might have PTSD because he had another flashback. That was the second one today. When Marilyn opened her garage, for a brief moment, he thought he saw his pants hanging from the rafters, again. He blinked and composed himself and they disappeared.

She hopped into his Jaguar and they made their way to the restaurant. Eventually they turned up a narrow tree lined drive with a small sign that could be easily missed. It had an arrow pointing upward that read, 'The Overlook'.

"I feel like we are driving into the sky!" Marilyn told Bobby.

"It looks as if we will make it in time for the sunset."

When they reach the top of the drive Marilyn gasped. "This is the most beautiful restaurant I have ever seen."

"It gets better. Trust me." Bobby said, as he pulled his car up in front of the valet.

"Good evening, Dr. Bain," the valet greeted him by name, as he opened Bobby's car door. Bobby smiled and fished in his pocket for the key fob and handed it to him.

Marilyn walked very slowly into the restaurant, so she could take it all in.

"Dr. Bain, would you like to have a drink on the terrace before dinner?" the maître d' asked.

"We would," Bobby replied.

He seated Bobby and Marilyn where they would have a majestic view of the setting sun and the horizon.

"Good evening ma'am. May I bring you something to drink?" the waiter asked.

"I would like a Cosmo, please."

"Good evening, Dr. Bain. Would you like your usual?"

"Yes, please."

"Everyone here knows you and this place has only been open two months," Marilyn remarked suspiciously.

"Amazing customer service," Bobby answered, without addressing how frequently he has been there.

The waiter brought back Marilyn's Cosmo and Bobby's single malt scotch.

Bobby figured it would be only a matter of seconds before Marilyn revisited the topic of how everyone knew him at The Overlook from a slightly different angle. One thing that he knew about women is that they don't stop until they find out whatever it is they want to know. The only tactic he had in his arsenal was to try and distract Marilyn. "Let's toast to spectacular beauty!" Bobby said while gazing into Marilyn's eyes. Bobby was shocked to see that the toast had at least momentarily flustered her.

"Liz told me that you are dating Renay."

"I was. She dumped me."

"What did you do to her, Bain?"

"I took her to dinner twice, that's what I did."

"You expect me to believe that?"

"Yes, I do."

"I'm confused."

"The first time we went out she had just broken up with her commitment phobic boyfriend of three years. By our second date, he had miraculously got over it and proposed. They are now engaged and have set a wedding date for the Spring."

"Ouch."

"It's okay. She cuts my hair now, so we will probably have a longer relationship that way!" Bobby said, with a small shrug.

"I guess so."

"Are you getting hungry?"

"A little."

Bobby motioned to the waiter who then escorted them back inside the restaurant to their awaiting table.

"What do you recommend, Bobby?"

"Everything I've had is good. I'm going to have the filet mignon with the white cheddar mashed potatoes and the New Braunfels salad."

"New Braunfels salad?"

"Almost everything they serve is grown locally. The goat cheese is from the guy who sells it in the farmer's market. It has greens, tomatoes, cucumbers, radishes, avocadoes, goat cheese and pecans. I like it with the house dressing."

"What is papardelle?"

"It's wide flat pasta. That is what I had last time. It might be one of the best dishes I've ever had -- crab, asparagus, and papardelle in an herb butter sauce. It was delicious!"

The waiter returned with another Cosmo for Marilyn and a single malted scotch for Bobby. A different waiter placed cheese straws on the table and asked them if they were ready to order. Marilyn nodded.

"I will have the crab."

"Excellent choice. Would you like the lobster bisque or a New Braunfels salad?"

Marilyn looked to Bobby for help, since both sounded equally delicious.

"Actually, we would like a cup of the bisque and a salad. I would like the filet mignon."

"Dr. Bain, do you want your steak cooked medium?"

"That would be perfect."

"Ok Bain, how often do you really come here? There is something really fishy going on -- and trust me I WILL figure it out."

The manner in which Marilyn said "Bain" made Bobby have his usual visceral reaction to Marilyn. He might as well have been sitting on a chair made of ice. Lying to Marilyn was never a feasible option. He would have to try to find a way to sidestep the question, so he wouldn't have to answer it directly with an out-and-out lie. It's not that he was ashamed of telling her he owned the place – it just didn't seem to him that she was in a position where she needed to know that.

"I know the owner, but I honestly can't say more due to HIPAA regulations."

This answer seemed to appease her – at least temporarily. Even so – Bobby was eager to change the topic. He was relieved when he saw the lobster bisque and salads arriving. Bobby welcomed the silence while Marilyn tried her fresh salad. He wished the bisque would cool down quickly. He had been craving it since they arrived.

"This is the best soup I've ever had in my life!" Marilyn exclaimed.

"It is delicious."

"Can I ask you a question?"

Bobby thought for a brief millisecond about trying that old joke on Marilyn where the person says, "you just did!" He decided Marilyn probably would not find that as amusing as he did, so he answered, "Sure", instead.

"Why did Liz stay with Adam after this thing with the Pig? She is smart, pretty, funny and can obviously support herself."

"Liz has the ability to see deep inside someone's soul. If she thinks that someone has redeeming qualities then she will be your biggest cheerleader. She did that for you when you first moved here and made your career change."

"That's true," Marilyn said. She was embarrassed that Bobby had referred to her prior profession, but relieved that he didn't seem to dwell on it.

"Anyways, once Liz gets this idea in her head, it's hard to convince her otherwise. Believe me I've tried. I think she can do a lot better than Adam and I'm pretty sure that I'm not the only one of her friends that feels that way. Once she has adopted you into her fold, then she is in your corner."

"What does she do if someone screws up again?"

"Actually Adam, once said it best—Liz will give you 1007 chances, but screw up 1008 times and she is done."

"What chance do you think Adam is on?"

"If I were counting…1007!"

"I'm not sure that you are impartial, Bain."

"Her dog, Butter is a perfect example. I remember the day Butter, her golden retriever showed up as a stray in front of her house. He was about seven weeks old. He was all belly and legs. She picked him up and looked into his eyes and pronounced to him, "You are going to be a great dog some day." I wasn't that convinced. Later that day, I had to take Butter to the vet to have him retrieve the microchip he had eaten off my key to my Corvette. I had to start the car by holding his distended puppy belly up to the ignition. He continued to be a total pain in the ass for about two years. Their backyard looked like a minefield— he dug holes everywhere. He has had four emergency surgeries because he would eat anything to include a Barbie doll head, a lipstick, a rock and my personal favorite--a tampon that he took out of Liz's purse.

When Sam was in grade school, she came home from her Valentine's Day party with all of her Valentine's Day cards in a corrugated brown box to make it easier to carry. She also had a 12 oz. bag of individually wrapped chocolate hearts in the box. Butter decided to eat through the top of the box. He then proceeded to eat the cards because they had those little candy hearts inside. And for dessert, he finished with the individually foil wrapped chocolates. To make matters worse, Butter was already recovering from surgery at that time. Luckily for him, the chocolate hearts that he ate were made of milk chocolate. The vet told us dark chocolate was much more of a potential problem as far as developing pancreatis. In this case, the worst thing that happened to him was that he ended up pooping foil wrappers and Valentine Day cards for a few days. Sam was pretty mad at him though.

Still--no matter what Butter did, Liz would just say, "He is going to be a wonderful dog someday." She just had this great faith. She said that she could see it in his eyes.

And you know what? She was right. After two years which included the four surgeries, multiple vet visits and replacing the grass in their yard twice—he is the best dog ever."

"Maybe you aren't a dog person."

"Maybe not."

"Well, I'm glad she is my friend," Marilyn said.

"Me too. I may have used up a chance or two with her."

"I bet you are the one who has used up 1007 chances."

"Maybe," Bobby said, with a laugh.

The waiter arrived with Marilyn's crab papardelle and Bobby's steak.

Bobby noticed Marilyn eyeing his white cheddar mashed potatoes. He decided to use this as an opportunity to try and make some points with her. "Would you like to try the potatoes?" The words had barely escaped his mouth when she swooped in with her fork.

"They are as good as they sounded."

The waiter returned with croissant-style rolls and honey butter.

"Geez, wouldn't you know that is the only kind of bread I can't refuse," Marilyn moaned.

"How is your crab?"

"Delicious. I've been paid to do a lot of things before, but never to eat!" Marilyn said. She turned beet red realizing Bobby may be thinking that she was referring to her prior profession.

"I hope you are saving room for dessert!" Bobby said smoothly, letting Marilyn's prior comments slide by.

"I wish I had room!"

"Tell you what, we will get yours to go. You can have it for a midnight snack or breakfast."

"Sometimes I can't figure out why you are still single."

"Me neither," Bobby said in agreement and started laughing.

Even though Bobby had started to relax and was having a good time with Marilyn, he still wanted the evening to end soon so he could return to his office and see what she was really up to.

The waiter eventually returned and asked them if they would be having coffee and dessert.

"I have monopolized enough of this beautiful woman's time. Can we have a slice of cheesecake with fresh berries to go?"

"Certainly, Dr. Bain."

"How in the world did you know that I love cheesecake?"

"Who doesn't? Tomorrow morning you can think of it as a cheese danish without the danish and with extra fruit."

"Wow! That's exactly how I would rationalize that!"

"That's scary!" Bobby said out loud, without realizing it. Luckily for Bobby, Marilyn let the comment pass.

The waiter returned with the cheesecake slice in a fancy silver box with a fuchsia ribbon tied into an elegant bow.

"I might actually get up the first time my alarm rings knowing that I'm having cheesecake for breakfast," Marilyn said, while smiling at Bobby.

"Are you ready to go home?"

"But, you didn't pay."

"It's been taken care of."

"You must have saved the owner's life or something."

"I told you I can't talk about it due to HIPAA regulations," Bobby said, wondering if Marilyn even knew what HIPAA stood for. He secretly wondered if she was ever going to drop this subject.

"No, I'm wrong… You didn't save the owner's life. I bet his wife was banging her tennis pro. She went to have her breasts lifted and something happened under anesthesia. When she died he was so grateful that he didn't have to give her and her boy toy half of this restaurant and whatever else they had. So now he lets you eat here whenever you want and for free. "

"Do you REALLY think I would purposely kill someone!?! In case you didn't know, doctors take a sacred oath swearing to practice ethically and honestly. It's called the Hippocratic Oath. I bet that you might have heard of that?"

"I can keep a secret."

"So can I," Bobby said, shaking his head.

"Now, I know why you are single." Marilyn said, in a very matter of fact tone.

Bobby's Jaguar was waiting when they walked out of the restaurant. They listened to jazz music and bantered playfully back and forth until they reach Marilyn's neighborhood. When he put the car in park, Marilyn turned towards him. She raised her eyebrows in a suggestive manner and asked him, "Would you like to come in for some coffee?"

"I would love to, but I have a very early OR time."

"This might be another reason…" Marilyn muttered, referencing Bobby's single status.

Bobby got out of his car and walked around to her side of the car. He gently put his hand on her shoulder as they made their way to her front door.

"I will see you in the morning. Enjoy your cheesecake."

"I will. Thanks again. I actually had a good time," Marilyn admitted

"Me too! Sweet dreams," Bobby said, as he gave her a kiss on her forehead.

Marilyn unlocked her door and entered her house. She rolled her eyes as she closed door. She was not sure if she was relieved or disappointed that Bobby didn't want to come in. She realized that he probably thought she going to toy with his mind again. The thought made her smile.

Chapter 21

Bobby drove straight to his office after he dropped Marilyn off. He tried to push Marilyn's invitation out of his mind. He absolutely dreaded coming into the office building late at night. The parking lot was not well lit and the guard was always asleep at his post, which was not reassuring. Of course, he still didn't have his gun with him. Now that he really thought about it, the only problems he had ever had in the office had both involved Marilyn. He should be reassured knowing that Marilyn was safe at her house, probably dreaming of having cheesecake for breakfast. He hoped that he would be able to figure out what Marilyn was working on earlier this evening. He had called Nick after he dropped off Marilyn. Nick volunteered to come over to help, if he couldn't figure it out.

After unlocking the door and disarming the alarm, Bobby walked back to his private office. He sat down at the computer and waited for it to power back up. While he was waiting, he decided to go recheck the main entrance door to make sure that he had locked it behind him and to reset the security alarm, for good measure. He didn't need any more surprises tonight.

He made his way back down the hall to his office. His computer was now ready for him to log back on it. When he restored the last session, his billing information filled the entire screen just like it had when he had powered it off earlier. As soon as he minimized that screen, the blue Facebook page popped up in its place.

"What the heck!" Bobby thought to himself. A Facebook page for Sam Schaeffer?!? Bobby knew that this couldn't be Sam's real Facebook page. It made him think back on what he knew about Sam's page. He recalled how angry Liz had been, three months ago, when the teen wouldn't accept her Mom's friend request. Liz and Sam battle over Facebook went several rounds:

Round one— Liz tried to friend Sam. Sam rebuffed her mom's gesture. Liz was in total disbelief, especially since she was the person who thought Sam was mature enough to have her own page.

Round two—Several of Sam's friends sent friend requests to Liz. She accepted them because she didn't want to hurt any child's feelings. Sam went ballistic when she saw Liz had written an encouraging note on one of Sam's friend's pages. Liz explained she wrote the post only after reading a melodramatic post the girl had written. Sam yelled at her mom, "Don't write on teenager's pages!" Liz felt like she couldn't win.

Round three—Several of Liz's friends try friending Sam. These family friends had known Sam and had asked about her since she was a baby. They had never missed buying her a single Christmas or a birthday gift. Liz was embarrassed when one of her friends asked if Sam checked her Facebook often because her friend request had gone unanswered. Liz shamed Sam into accepting the grown-ups friend requests. Sam complained EVERY SINGLE TIME they "liked" a picture or wrote "Beautiful!" on one of the pictures that Sam posted of herself, which was pretty often.

Round four—One of Liz's friends informed Liz that Sam was using extremely colorful language on her page. A mortified Liz lectured Sam about this. Sam reluctantly removed the offending posts, but in their place posted something completely unsavory and undeserved about Liz.

Round five—Mother's Day. Sam announced that her present to her mother was that she had FINALLY friended her. Liz decided that she could care less by this point. Liz wondered what Sam did with the money that Adam gave her to buy her a Mother's Day present.

Round six—Sam friended Uncle Bobby, but not after she first tried conning him into a fifty-dollar sign-up fee. The fee was waived when Uncle Bobby blackmailed Sam that he would tell Liz about the special limited offer she had made to him.

Bobby knew that the typical teenager's Facebook page had between eight hundred to a thousand friends, multiple self-portraits and quotes from songs that only they could find meaningful. While the page that Marilyn was looking at had Sam's name on it, it only had twenty-three friends. Sam's real page currently had nine hundred seventy three. The second Facebook page had no actual pictures of Sam. There were pictures, but Bobby didn't recognize any of the kids. Bobby was beyond puzzled.

Liz had told him previously that she had Marilyn check Sam's settings periodically to make sure that Sam kept her page set on the most private settings. When Natalie and Marilyn informed Liz that Pamela's computer guru had found in Mrs. Piggy's computer history ways to cause Sam to fall to her death or to drown, Liz instructed Marilyn to check her page daily for any unusual activity. Liz at no time mentioned anything about two Facebook pages.

Bobby opened a new tab and logged on to his Facebook page. He went to the Friends section and brought up Sam's page. Most of Sam's recent posts involved her part in The Phantom Of The Opera production at her high school. She had several pictures of herself in an elaborate velvet gown. She had one picture where her hair was long with tousled curls. Since watching Sam for Liz, Bobby now knew that hair extensions were responsible for the mass of curls. Bobby closely studied the pictures of her friends. A lot of them he knew, like her best friend, Lexy. It appeared that Lexy had the female lead in the production.

He opened the tab with the dubious Facebook page. There was a picture of Sarah Brightman from the Broadway musical and a few shots of Emily Rossum from the movie adaptation. Bobby recognized no one in her friend section. He noted that Lexy was not pictured as a friend. The pictures looked like Kansas corn-fed kids, not kids with daily access to big city malls.

He contemplated calling Nick to see what his take on this was, but decided not to. He wanted to believe that Marilyn wouldn't be doing anything to put Sam in harm's way, but he was having a hard time coming up with any other scenario. His gut instinct told him that Sam had nothing to do with this second Facebook page. For the life of him, he could not figure out why there would be two Sam Schaeffer Facebook pages.

He spent another hour looking at both pages. Finally he figured, he would sleep on it. One of Bobby's favorite sayings was something his grandfather told him, "Sometimes the best thing to do, is nothing at all." It was a philosophy that didn't work for everybody, but it seemed to work well for his grandfather.

He powered the computer off so he could pull the same page up tomorrow. He locked up, set the alarm and drove home. He knew sleep would probably elude him tonight. He kept wondering if Marilyn was playing on their team, Mrs. Piggy's team or her own team. Maybe, she wasn't even playing the same game, he thought.

The next morning, his alarm rang much too early. He wanted to be sure that he was the first person in the office. He was thankful that Liz wouldn't be in until early afternoon. He wanted to be the one to deal with Marilyn. That should give him plenty of opportunity. He wished he had slept better. Maybe then, his brain would be working on all cylinders. He knew the only way to keep a step ahead of Marilyn would be the element of surprise.

As he drove to work, he kept thinking that his plan should work. If it didn't, then he would enlist Nick's assistance to fix it. He parked his Corvette in his designated spot and walked into the building. Marilyn wasn't here yet. She was probably still devouring her cheesecake. The alarm sounded as soon as he unlocked the door. He was relieved because that meant that he was the first one there.

He turned on the light in his private office and turned on the computer. He made absolutely sure that the questionable Facebook page would be open when Marilyn arrived. He looked out the window down to the parking lot below. No red bug. He decided as long as he was quick, he would make a large pot of coffee for the whole office.

He walked back to his office and looked out of his window again just in time to see Marilyn drive in. He briskly walked back to the kitchen, poured the fresh brewed coffee into two mugs and brought it back to his private office. He also refreshed the Facebook page as soon as he could hear Marilyn greeting the other employees. He was ready.

Marilyn walked in and smiled when she saw Bobby. He handed her the coffee mug.

"Thanks, Bobby!" Marilyn took a sip of the steaming brew.

"I hope you don't mind, but I had one question on what you were working on last night," Bobby told her coolly. He swung the monitor around to show her what it was that he had a question about. It was the Sam Schaeffer Facebook page.

"Oh God!" Marilyn said as she sunk into the chair on the other side of the desk.

"Like I said, I have a question."

"It's not what you think…"

"That's good."

"It's a fake page."

"I realize that."

"That loon was trying to find Sam on Facebook. I thought if I made a fake page then I could keep closer tabs on her. I don't think Pamela's guy is catching everything."

"Does Liz know that you are doing this?"

"No. Please don't tell her."

"I'm not going to promise you anything."

"Please don't be mad at me. I'm only trying to help."

"Could have fooled me."

"Seems to me that you are telling her where Sam is at. Real helpful."

"It's not like that. I'm feeding her erroneous information, except what she could find out by looking at the high school website."

"So you have made contact with her?"

"Yes."

"What name is she using? Heather Smith?"

"How did you know?"

"Because those were the only conversations on the page."

"So, what is your plan?"

"That is the only problem. I don't have one."

"So far it appears that Mrs. Piggy has promised to make Sam's costume look better."

"What if she shows up at their house?"

"She won't."

"Is that why you told her that Sam was on restriction?"

"I need to come up with a foolproof plan."

"Most people don't put the cart in front of the horse."

"I know."

"I want the info on how to log in this page because two people should be monitoring it at all times. What if you were busy eating cheesecake?"

"Does this mean that you aren't mad at me?"

"Not at all."

"Here is the e-mail account and her password. Are you going to tell Liz?"

"Eventually."

"Can you at least tell me ahead of time when you do?"

"Maybe."

"I guess I can't ask for more than that."

"No, you can't. Now, get my billing problem fixed," Bobby said, as he picked up his coffee and let Marilyn alone in the room.

A few hours later, Marilyn knocked on Liz's private office where Bobby was using Liz's computer.

"I have the problem completely fixed. You can use your office and computer now."

"Thanks. You let me know if there is anything else that I need to know."

"You bet I will." Marilyn then walked out, telling the women in the office good-bye as she left.

Bobby walked down the hall to his office. He sat back down in front of his computer. He looked up at his monitor. The blue Facebook page up was no longer up, instead on the monitor, was a photocopy of the deed where he purchased the land for The Overlook. He closed the tab. He opened the next tab, expecting for the Facebook page to come up in its place. Instead, was an e-mail correspondence between Bobby and the restaurant's architect. He closed that tab and went to the last open tab. At this point, he didn't really know what to expect. It was a Word document. He read the message —"I guess I wasn't the only one with a secret!"

Chapter 22

Pamela Tate was counting the days until she could finally fire Mrs. Piggy. She might even use it as an excuse for a party when the time came. Under normal circumstances, Pamela would never allow such a mediocre employee to be part of the Tate & Tate team. So, until she could be fired, Pamela tried to make the best of the current situation by having her supervisor counsel and mentor Mrs. Piggy frequently.

Mrs. Piggy didn't quite seem to comprehend that the point of a counseling session was to let the employee know what areas they needed to improve on, and that then, the employee was supposed to use this feedback to concentrate their efforts in these particular areas. Pamela, remembering hearing how easily Mrs. Piggy had manipulated Adam, had decided that it would be best if her supervisor at Tate & Tate were a woman. She had a feeling Mrs. Piggy was used to sleeping or baking her way out of trouble.

Sure enough, the first time Mrs. Piggy was counseled, she brought her supervisor, Taylor, a Boston cream pie that she had baked. Taylor, who was a health food and exercise enthusiast, seemed completely underwhelmed and unfazed by the gesture. She told Mrs. Piggy that she was sure that it was just a coincidence that she brought the cake in after her dismal evaluation and that under the circumstances, she wouldn't feel right accepting it. Taylor then let her know that she thought the best thing to do with the dessert would be to put it in the firm's break room. This way who ever wanted a piece could help themselves to it. Mrs. Piggy agreed and started to pick up the dessert to take it there.

"No, just leave it there, I'll do it. You have a file to finish by noon," Taylor told her. Little did Mrs. Piggy know that Taylor was about to slice herself a humongous piece of the sponge cake with its vanilla custard filling. Mrs. Piggy had done her own variation of the traditional Boston cream pie and made the ganache on top of the cake with dark chocolate and a hint of cherry.

Taylor's lecture was completely lost on Mrs. Piggy. The next day, she made zesty lemon bars for her co-workers. Their scruples were lower and they readily accepted them. Since Mrs. Piggy had no insight into human nature, it didn't dawn on her that the same co-workers who were eating her lemon bars today would be perfectly capable of throwing her under the bus tomorrow. A red velvet cake, chocolate chunk cookies, Snickerdoodles, a spectacular pumpkin cheesecake with a gingersnap crust and numerous other confections followed the lemon bars. Her co-workers still didn't like her any better or trust her work, but they had no problem devouring the desserts.

Since Mrs. Piggy was hired, Pamela spent more time than she would have liked keeping an eye on her. It was seriously cutting into her shopping and spa time. She had Taylor give her a weekly report about her work. Taylor never asked why Pamela had such a special interest in Mrs. Piggy or why she even allowed someone like her to work there. She knew Pamela wouldn't have her working at Tate & Tate unless she had a darn good reason, but Taylor was having trouble figuring out what it could be.

Pamela continued to carefully review the report that her computer specialist prepared each evening itemizing Mrs. Piggy's computer usage. She hadn't seen anything earth shocking in the report, since the initial discovery of Mrs. Piggy's research on the internet about how far she would have to toss little Sam off the ravine to do her in. Mrs. Piggy's favorite searches remained "falls" and "accidental drowning".

This morning, however, there was something new in the report-- a Pinterest account. Pamela had seen on Facebook where several of her friends moaned about how addicted they had become to this particular site. One of her friends "pinned" the most extraordinary dresses and shoes to her "pinboard" which would then also post to Facebook. Her friend wanted to be sure that she would be ready if Prince Charming proposed to her or she was given a last minute invite to a fabulous charity ball. Pamela was intrigued by the premise of the site, but had not yet visited it because she didn't have any free time to squander away. She knew it would be like baking a cheesecake and somehow convincing yourself that you were only going to have one slice.

Using the login information provided by her computer specialist, Pamela pulled up Mrs. Piggy's "pinboard". The pinboard contained anything that Mrs. Piggy wanted to save for future inspiration.

"Oh no…" Pamela said out loud. She had really hoped that she wasn't going to find anything disturbing. She should have known better. She looked through Mrs. Piggy's pinboard for several minutes and then made a phone call. When she was done with that phone call, she made another call, this time to Natalie.

"Mrs. Piggy has a page on Pinterest!" Pamela blurted out, as soon as Natalie answered the phone.

"Who doesn't? I put my trip ideas, crafts ideas, recipes I might want to try and decorating inspirations on my page. Don't you have one?"

"No, and if I did, it wouldn't look like hers."

"What do you mean by that?"

"It has a whole Spring wedding planned out in excruciating detail. There is a picture of the engagement ring -- a Tiffany cushion-cut diamond surrounded by small round diamonds. My estimate is that it is at least two carats. I guess she couldn't decide on the dress, because there is a picture of two distinctly different Vera Wang wedding gowns. Neither that would look good on her. Next to the wedding dress photo is a picture of the groom in his tux. By the way, the model in the tux, guess whom he resembles? Do I need to go on?"

"Flowers?"

"Pale pink peonies."

"No honeymoon?"

"Honeymoon to Bora Bora complete with a picture of her wedding night negligée. Trust me, that's a picture you don't want to see!"

"Mrs. Piggy must have forgotten two important facts – that she is already married, and so is her imaginary fiancé."

"I will be so glad when the day comes that I can fire her. Considering I'm an attorney who has represented some pretty unsavory types, let me go on record to say she totally creeps me out and I defended some real winners in the early days of my career."

"I guess she is still living in la-la land. No crime in that, unfortunately."

"What concerns me are the invitations. They have a date on them and a groom's name. The wedding is seven months away. She appears to be making her fantasy, her reality."

"I agree. That is unsettling, but…" Natalie said, but was interrupted by an exasperated Pamela.

"Before I called you, I called the store, More Than Just Paper, where the invitations can be ordered from. I pretended to be her. The stupid bitch ORDERED the invitations!!! Two hundred of them, to be exact," Pamela shrieked.

"Oh shit!"

"Exactly!"

"I need to call Liz," Natalie told her.

"I think that would be a good idea. Also, Officer Becker. I will text you the log-in information right now so everyone can see this for themselves."

Chapter 23

Marilyn called The Overlook, and in her most professional voice asked to speak to the banquet manager.

"Good morning, this is Dan. How can I help you?" the banquet manager said when he picked up the line.

"Good morning, Dan. I'm calling from Dr. Bobby Bain's office. I just want to touch base with you before our get together, next Tuesday," Marilyn said.

"Excellent. I was just going to call Dr. Bain and go over some possible menu suggestions with him."

"Actually Dr. Bain is out of the country and unavailable, so I will be your point of contact," Marilyn lied. She gave Dan her name and even her cell phone number, just in case he might have any questions.

"So, am I to call you?" Dan asked, making sure he had fully understood Marilyn correctly. He had always dealt directly with Bobby in the past.

"Yes. Dr. Bain wanted to change the time from eight to six-thirty."

"Six-thirty will be fine. Are we still planning on six guests?"

"Yes and no. At six-thirty, there will be four guests, the other two will arrive at eight."

"So cocktails will start at six thirty and dinner at eight?"

"Please don't repeat this, but poor Dr. Bain is having some major health issues due to his poor dietary habits. He can only have consommé, a garden salad with no dressing, and maybe a small slice of cantaloupe. His friend is trying to encourage him to eat healthier, so he will have the same. None of us want Dr. Bain to be tempted."

"What about the other members of the party?" Dan innocently asked.

"They will eat at six thirty and Dr. Bain really wanted to go all out to impress the other guests. He wanted me to ask if you could fly in some Alaska King Crab legs. Would that be possible?"

"Yes, ma'am. We can fly them in. This is the season. We could even have crab cakes appetizers, our signature salad, Kobe beef filet mignon and Alaska King Crab legs. We have a new potato dish – "Potatoes Provence". It is made with sliced Yucatan Gold potatoes, herbs de Provence, heavy cream, butter and is dotted with goat cheese. It's been a big hit."

"That sounds delicious and the menu sounds perfect. What did you say the dessert was?" Marilyn asked, making sure the most important part of the meal was not forgotten.

"I was thinking dark chocolate soufflé with our homemade caramel ice cream," Dan said.

"That sounds wonderful. Now about Dr. Bain—he might possibly act like he wants the food the others are having, but deep down he knows he can't have it. That's why he is having his guests come early, so he won't be tempted. But between you and me, the man has absolutely no will power when it comes to food. And don't get me started about his exercise program. The man's idea of exercise is lifting a fork, if you know what I mean. I just couldn't live with myself if something happened to him. I'm sure you feel the same way."

"Of course not," Dan answered, hoping he sounded like he cared. Dan thought how he would miss Bobby's generous tips, if something happened to him.

"Could you please make sure that the four ladies are done with their meal and the dishes are cleared by the time Dr. Bain and the other guest arrive? I think that will make it a little easier for Dr. Bain."

"That should be no problem."

"Perfect. We will see you next Tuesday at six thirty. Please, call me if any questions arise."

"I will. Good-bye, Marilyn."

Marilyn hung up the phone and smiled. She then dialed Liz, Natalie and Pamela to let them know that there was a slight change in plans. Bobby originally told the other women that the get together was to thank Pamela for all that she had done so far. The other members were going to invite her to become a member, if she wanted to join. All of the women told Marilyn that the time change would work with their schedules. Marilyn might have told them a teeny-weeny white lie as to the reason for the time change. She was truthful when she said that it was because she had a little surprise for Bobby. None of them questioned the explanation.

On Tuesday night, the four women were all escorted into one of the two private dining rooms at The Overlook. It was filled with Marilyn's favorite flowers, orchids. This was no coincidence.

"Wow!" Natalie said, as soon as she walked into the room. The room had thick white stucco walls and huge arched windows that overlooked the cypress trees and the Guadalupe River below. The windows had very sheer white linen curtains framing the sides. The only color in the room was the floor and the Mediterranean blue table runners on the dining table. The floor was made of broken pieces of Mexican Talavera tiles. All of the patterned tiles pieces were in different shades of blue and white. The effect was dramatic, yet so simplistic.

"This is amazing, I feel like I'm in my favorite place in the world, Santorini,

Greece. It is just like this – white and blue," Pamela said.

"Where is our host?" Liz asked out loud, wondering where Bobby could be.

"He will be here a little later," Marilyn said, giving no further explanation.

"I thought Nick was coming, but the table is only set for four," Natalie said, sounding more than a little disappointed.

"Don't worry, he will be here. He's coming a little later with Bobby. We are going to have a meeting before the boys get here," Marilyn informed them.

"We are having two meetings?" Liz asked, for clarification.

"Yes, it's necessary. Because it has come to my attention that Bobby Bain is trying to take over our club," Marilyn told the women.

"He did kinda force his way in," Natalie said, remembering the night she met him and how he wouldn't take no for an answer when he wanted to join.

"For starters, he wants to rename the club," Marilyn announced, as if it was the most earth shattering news ever.

"I didn't even know it was a real club, or that your club had a name," Pamela informed the ladies.

"It's called The Man Haters Club. Liz's husband, Adam, named it. He thought he was being funny. It was a joke he made to Liz right before Liz went to meet Natalie for a drink. I guess he knew that Natalie and Liz probably talked some smack about him and Tim Moody whenever they got together," Marilyn told Pamela.

"Wait a minute – Bobby joined a women's club, knowing full well, that it was called the Man Haters Club? Now that's kinda different!" Pamela said, wondering what she was getting herself into.

"He thought it would be a good way of meeting women," Natalie told Pamela.

"Are you serious?" Pamela said, beyond astonished.

"You would have to know how Bobby thinks," Liz told Pamela, trying to figure out how to explain how Bobby thinks to Pamela.

"But what about Nick? Isn't he a member of the Man Haters Club too?" Pamela asked.

"Yes!" Natalie and Marilyn answered in unison.

"But he didn't join to meet women, did he?" Pamela asked.

"No. He's Bobby friend," Natalie explained.

"He really misses being in the Army. The Army is very structured compared to the outside world. We are filling a void. He's happy keeping us organized. He made an alert roster, we have official minutes at our meetings and stuff like that," Liz added.

"He better not drug test us or make us do physical training. I'm not a running kind of girl and I have never been able to do push-ups because my boobs get in the way!" Marilyn informed the group.

The waiter appeared and asked the women for their drink orders. Marilyn used this opportunity to ask the women, "Does anyone else want to change the name of the club?"

"Not really," Natalie said.

"I thought it was kinda funny when Adam said it and it became even funnier when Bobby forced his way in," Liz said.

"I'm on your side!" Pamela said.

"How did you find out that Bobby wanted to change the club's name?" Liz asked, even though she knew that it probably had something to do with Marilyn working on Bobby's billing system lately. Marilyn had a few "boundary issues". Liz wouldn't have put it past Marilyn to look at private e-mail communication between Nick and Bobby.

"Just a gut instinct," Marilyn answered, lying effortlessly.

"When are Bobby and Nick arriving?" Natalie asked, obviously more concerned with Nick's arrival than Bobby's.

"They will be here at 8," Marilyn informed the group.

"What are we going to do until they get here?" Liz wondered out loud.

At that particular moment, the waiter walked in with their drink orders. He was followed by two other waiters – one holding a platter of miniature crab cakes and the other their salads.

"We are going to enjoy a wonderful dinner courtesy of Bobby Bain, TRAITOR!" Marilyn declared.

"To the traitor, Bobby Bain… may he wish he never crossed a true Man Haters path," Natalie toasted.

The women all raised their glasses and started laughing.

"Poor Bobby…" Liz chuckled.

"That's right…" Marilyn responded.

"What about Nick?" Pamela asked.

"We could never be mad at Nick. He's too good looking. Plus, it's not his fault that he's Bobby's college friend," Natalie said truthfully.

"I can't believe he is divorced," Pamela said, stating the obvious.

"When we did our stake out together he told me that his now ex-wife, Kim had a boyfriend while they were married. Kim was a stay home mom of their three little girls.

The way he found out was horrible! He had taken off work a little early to surprise her and give her a hand with the girls. Nick said Kim had seemed extra tired lately, so he thought he if he came home early to do something with his daughters, then she could take a nap and recharge her batteries. He and the girls started baking some chocolate chip cookies because they wanted to surprise their Mom with a tea party when she woke up. He said he heard the doorbell and went to answer it. It was a young man with a huge bouquet of flowers. The young man said they were for Kim. Nick said the guy was so young that he thought he was from some delivery service. Nick took out his wallet to tip the kid. The kid then asked him if he was Kim's brother. Nick told him that he wasn't. Then the kid put his hand out to shake, and introduced himself as Kim's boyfriend. Nick told him that was interesting because he was Kim's husband and father of their three girls. Nick said he doesn't remember doing this, but his neighbor told the police he tackled the delivery guy off his porch steps. Then the neighbor said Nick beat the boyfriend with the flowers until there was nothing left but stalks. The racquet woke Kim up and she saw Nick and her boy toy wrestling on the front lawn. Nick said next thing he knew she had jumped on his back and started hitting him, trying to protect her boyfriend. When the police arrived the boyfriend and Kim were both on top of Nick. Natalie told the women that, "Kim hired a cutthroat lawyer who informed the judge that Nick was getting ready to deploy and spun a tale about the flower incident that made it sound like Nick had anger management issues along with a penchant for unpredictable violence."

"Unbelievable! Attorneys like that give us a bad name!" Pamela said.

The women continued to gossip, speculate and thoroughly enjoy their dinner. They some how made room for the dessert. It might have had something with it being chocolate. Marilyn asked the waiter to bring them a new round of drinks at 7:55. The staff had earlier removed all traces of their dinner.

At 8:05, Bobby Bain walked in like he owned the place, which in truth he did. Nick was with him.

"Good evening, girls!" Bobby said, greeting the ladies and not realizing how the endearment grated on their nerves.

"Hi, yourself!" Marilyn answered, so that he would have no doubt.

"Would anyone like anything to eat, my treat?" Bobby asked.

"Thanks Bobby, but I'm not really hungry," Liz answered.

"I have heard some mixed reviews about this place," Marilyn said, knowing that would thoroughly piss Bobby off since he was so proud of the restaurant.

"I can't imagine, I have always had excellent meals here," Bobby told the group, not wanting to let on that he secretly owned the place.

"I saw a cockroach," Marilyn said.

"Really where?" Bobby asked, looking around the absolutely spotless room.

"In the parking lot!" Marilyn finally told an exasperated Bobby.

"I'll just stick with my martini. But thanks anyways, Bobby!" Natalie said.

"Pamela?" Bobby asked.

"No thanks, Bobby. I can't eat this late in the evening," Pamela said truthfully --especially when she was already full of crab cakes, salad, bread, potatoes, filet mignon, crab legs and chocolate soufflé.

"Nick?" Bobby inquired.

"I ate really light today, looking forward to this meal. Plus, I wouldn't want you to eat alone."

The waiter returned and asked Bobby, "May I bring you anything, sir?"

"I would like a single malt scotch and my friend will have a Chimay Ale. We would also like some dinner, please. Surprise us!" Bobby answered, thinking the chef would make Nick and him something amazing.

"Yes, sir!" the waiter said and left the room.

A few minutes later the waiter arrived with a small glass of water with a lemon twist, instead of the single malt scotch that Bobby had ordered. Nick also got a small glass of water and a lemon twist, instead of the imported beer Bobby had ordered for him. The look on Bobby and Nick's face was priceless when the waiter brought in tiny salads without any dressing, the chicken consommé and a sliver of cantaloupe with a pathetic piece of prosciutto wrapped around it. Bobby didn't want to say a word because of Marilyn's previous comments about the restaurant's food being hit or miss.

"This looks delicious!" he loudly proclaimed, trying to sound convincing and trying to make sure Marilyn heard him.

Nick and Bobby finished the paltry amount of food in a few moments. Bobby had been really looking forward to a good steak all day and still was. This was Nick's first time at The Overlook, and he thought to himself that it sure didn't live up to the hype. Nick wouldn't have waited five minutes to come back here, let alone months for a reservation.

"Ladies, I wanted to call this meeting because we are all hoping that Pamela that would join our club," Bobby told the group.

"I would be honored to join," Pamela said.

The women picked up their drinks to toast the newest member of their club. Bobby and Nick looked at each other, and then picked up their water.

Bobby decided this was the opportune time to bring up his agenda. "I thought that since we now have two male members of the club, that we might want to entertain changing the name of the club."

The women just sat there and didn't say anything, even though they were thinking something. Since Bobby was not used to the women being so quiet, he was immediately uncomfortable. The women sensed this and continued to stare at him without any other expression. Finally, he said, "I thought we could call the club something like the Lions Club.

Marilyn fully understood that he meant something similar to the Lions Club, but decided to screw with his mind anyways. "I think that's already taken, Bobby. I think I have bought chocolate bars from the Lions Club or pizza discount coupons," she calmly told him.

"I know that, Marilyn. I meant something similar," Bobby further explained.

"Oh, like the Liar's Club, instead of Lion's Club," Marilyn said, using the opportunity to verbally smack him on the other side of the head.

"I don't like that, I'm afraid people would think we were the liars," Natalie spoke up.

Nick, who had been silent so far this evening, finally spoke trying to steer the conversation back in the direction that Bobby had hoped for, "I think Bobby is trying to say a name like the Tigers Club or the Buffaloes Club."

"I don't know about the other women, but I do not want to be known as a buffalo. Buffaloes have a hump on their back, their hair is known for being unkempt, in fact, I would refer to their do as downright shabby, and they will wallow in mud. I think we should not name our club after any animal that wallows. For the record, I don't want to be a member of the hippo club, or the warthog club either," Pamela said, in her slow Southern drawl.

Bobby and Nick just looked at each other. Bobby's stomach made a loud noise due to his hunger. He looked embarrassed.

"I have an idea. How about the Black Widows Club? No wait, I have it!!! The Praying Mantis Club!!!" Marilyn suggested.

"I like the Praying Mantis Club!" Natalie said, jumping to her feet.

"Woah! Ladies! Did you know that the female Praying Mantis bites the male's head off before sex?" Nick informed the group, thinking that would change their mind.

"Sure we do, that's why it's a great name. Actually, I heard they rip the male's head off. I believe I saw it on TV. It was so cool. They showed a video of the female and this headless male. I loved it! I think they said the females rip the head off to ensure that the male stays hard. Just think rigor mortis, instead of a blue pill. You know sometimes those pills don't work..." Marilyn told Bobby, who had now sat down because he had completely given up forever any hope of changing the club's name.

The waiter returned to the room and handed Bobby the bill. Bobby looked at it and shook his head as if it couldn't be right and handed it back. The waiter whispered something in his ear. Bobby glared at Marilyn. Marilyn smiled broadly back.

"You know The Man Haters Club name is starting to grow on me after all," Bobby said.

"Me too! It's got a nice ring to it," Nick agreed.

"All in favor of keeping the name of the club, The Man Haters Club raise your hands," Liz instructed.

Miraculously all of the hands were up. Bobby and Nick's appeared to go up the highest of them all.

"The Man Haters Club it is!" Marilyn said with great satisfaction.

Chapter 24

"I can't believe that you don't trust me after all we have been through together," Marilyn whined convincingly, when Bobby cornered her in his office. Her eyes darted around the room looking for an escape route from the irate and irrational Bobby Bain.

"Are you serious? I can't believe that you would think that I would," Bobby snarled. His mind raced with disturbing thoughts—the feeding frenzy of the fish pedicure, his 'blind' date with Fernando, almost being shot, Natalie seeing him in the too small pink ruffled robe… He started sweating profusely just thinking about it. The common thread to all of these unfortunate events was Marilyn. He took a deep breath trying to calm down. This woman could push his buttons like no other. Most people have a self-preservation instinct, but not Marilyn.

"Maybe you just mistyped something," Marilyn said, trying to convince Bobby.

"My ass! You have thirty seconds to give me the login and password to the freaking Facebook account," Bobby told her. He took another deep breath. He wondered why people always say to do that. He found he still wanted to wring Marilyn's neck just as badly.

"Stop threatening me. You are making me so nervous I can't think."

"That would be the day…"

"I don't want you answering any of her messages. You don't know how to answer them like a teenage girl would. Kids don't say things like 'groovy', 'far-out' or 'right on' these days, Bobby," Marilyn said, very sarcastically.

"Cool, Marilyn! I forgot how 'with it' you are," Bobby said, mocking her.

"Peace, Bobby!" Marilyn said, showing how she was determined to get her point across.

"I think someone has forgotten that I am the one who watched Sam for a whole week when Liz and Adam were out of the country! What do you feed a vegetarian who won't eat vegetables? What age can a teen get a driver's permit? I bet you don't even know what hair extensions are!" Bobby ranted.

"You would be wrong, my friend," Marilyn said, as she reached up and unclipped a lock of her short dark hair.

"What the heck! You have short hair! I don't get it." Bobby said, perplexed.

"I clip in extensions to make my hair fuller, not longer."

"So, what are you — partially bald?"

"No, I have good hair. The extensions make it great hair."

"Don't they blow off when you are riding around in your convertible?"

"No, I wear a scarf… like Grace Kelly."

Bobby realized, as his brain was processing all of the nuances of hair extensions, that he has been distracted, yet again, by Marilyn. How does she do this? He wouldn't touch a hot stove after being warned repeatedly not to. The consequences were one and the same – a burn.

"Login and password!" he reiterated. He was bound and determined not to be distracted again.

"What length are Sam's extensions? Does she get Renay to dye them to match her hair color?"

"Marilyn, I know you think I'm not very bright, but I could have finished in the top of my class in medical school if I had chosen to. I just didn't personally see that as the most efficient use of my time."

"I'm glad you brought that up. I always wondered who was smarter in school, you or Liz."

"Marilyn!" Bobby shouted. He had forgotten to take a deep calming breath.

"Now I know… it was Liz. Do you think that's why she wouldn't date you?" Marilyn wondered, out loud.

"Marilyn, there is something seriously wrong with you."

"Who are you calling?" Marilyn asked.

"Who do you think? Liz. I need to let her know that you have a fake Facebook account with her minor daughter's name on it.   I just don't know how she is going to take that. Do you think I should try her cell phone or home phone?"

"Okay. Okay," Marilyn said. She sat down at Bobby's computer and started typing. "This is the login and this is the password."

"Now log off. I want to make sure it works this time."

"I didn't even get to look at the page."

"If it works, we can look at it together," Bobby told her.

"Looks like you typed it in RIGHT this time," Marilyn quipped.

Bobby took a deep deliberate breath, and then glared at Marilyn.

"Look! She answered!" Marilyn said, as she pointed at the message on the computer screen.

"Let's see what Mrs. Piggy aka Heather Smith has to say — 'Sam, I would wear the green costume for the play. It will show off your eyes. Your Mom sounds like a bitch. I bet you wish your Mom would just go away. Think how much fun it would be if we lived with our dads only. We could wear what we want to school and never have to clean our rooms. LOL"

"That witch! She is trying to plant a thought in an impressionable teenager's mind to kill her Mom."

"Good thing that she isn't really talking to Sam! Not that I think Sam would murder her Mom," Bobby optimistically said.

"I bet Mr. and Mrs. Menendez thought the same thing." Marilyn wryly said, recalling the Beverly Hills brothers who killed their parents, and then lavishly spent their money.

"What should we answer back?"

"Really... I thought you knew what to write..." Marilyn pointed out.

"Ok, Miss Smarty Pants... How about this? 'Thanks. I had already decided on the green costume also. Most of the time my mom is nice. My dad is actually the idiot.'"

"That would be awesome answer, if you were really Sam. I think you may have forgotten we are dealing with a psychopath. Did you really think that telling Mrs. Piggy that Adam is an idiot is a good idea?" Marilyn questioned.

"Maybe Mrs. Piggy is impressionable..."

"Bobby, for a smart guy, you are clueless about women."

"You might be right."

"I'm sorry can you repeat that? I'm afraid I might have missed something."

"You didn't," Bobby said, not willing to admit defeat again.

"There are actually a lot of nuances to answering one of these messages. This is the kind of job that I was born for," Marilyn bragged.

"So, how would you answer this?"

"First, I would throw a wrench in the equation because teenagers can't stay on task."

"How? But more importantly why?"

"Why? Because if I don't, she is going to know some thirty year old is answering her message."

"Thirty?"

"Yes, once I was thirty."

"Of course." Bobby decided to let this comment alone.

"A real teenager wouldn't be satisfied by Mrs. Piggy's answer. They would want her to boost their self esteem, but then they would take the discussion in a different illogical direction."

"That is true. When I was watching Sam, she did that all the time."

"I would go in a completely different direction than the green costume. I'm going to have fake Sam start writing about wearing an evening gown instead. That is what a real teen would do."

"What about the part about her Mom?"

"I would ignore it. If you ask a teen three questions, they will only answer one."

"True."

"I bet Mrs. Piggy was one of those kids no one liked. She still wants to be the popular kid. I think she believes that the swiftest route to acceptance is to marry Adam."

"I think I get it… We want to keep her the unpopular kid. Fake Sam controls the relationship. That's the way we keep her under control."

"You are smarter than you look, Bain."

"We should take our time answering and be the first to quit messaging."

"Now you are catching on!"

"Let me try again writing the message again."

"Don't send it until I double check it."

"How's this? – 'Heather, I have been thinking maybe I should wear an evening gown, instead of the green costume. My Mom probably has something I could use or I might get my Dad to take me to that costume shop in downtown San Antonio.'"

"Perfect. You are basically sending a message that says Sam doesn't value her opinion about what to wear. It also sends a subtle message that Sam's parents will both help out to get her a great costume. We are forcing Mrs. Piggy to become less subtle in her next message."

"How many days do you think we should wait before answering Mrs. Piggy's reply?" Bobby asked.

"I would wait two days."

"Thanks for your insight, Marilyn. Now I see why you didn't want to give me the password. I could have absolutely botched this whole operation," Bobby lied.

"I'm just wish you would remember that we are on the same team," Marilyn said sincerely.

"I guess I should apologize for scaring you also."

"It would be nice."

"It would be, wouldn't it?" Bobby smirked.

"Funny, Bain."

"Good night, Marilyn."

Marilyn gathered up her belongings. She seemed eager to leave.

"Nite!" Marilyn said and quickly walked out the office door.

Bobby locked the door, so Marilyn could not get back in the office. Even though he wasn't sure that a locked door would stop her. He decided to make sure by waiting until he saw her red bug leave the parking garage.

He walked back to the computer and pulled up the fake Facebook account. He changed the password.

"Touché, Marilyn!" Bobby said to no one, in the empty office.

Chapter 25

"Good morning, Liz!" Bobby enthusiastically greeted her as soon as she walked into the office.

"You seem very chipper this morning," Liz observed.

"I suppose I am."

"Does that have anything to do with you and Marilyn being here last night?" Liz teased.

"How did you know we were here?"

"Adam and I saw the lights on when we drove by the office building on the way to dinner. I was afraid I had left them on, so I asked him to pull into the parking lot and then I saw Marilyn's Bug and your Corvette were here. So… is that why you are in such a good mood?"

"Possibly."

"Bobby, why do you always have to be so cryptic?"

"Because it bugs you…or maybe because I am a man of mystery…" Bobby rambled.

"You get no argument from me. You are a mystery…"

"Where did you and Adam go for dinner last night?"

"Gruene Door."

"I should have guessed." Bobby said, making fun of how Liz would eat at the same place over and over until she was sick of it.

"But it's good!" Liz replied.

"I know, but a little variety is nice."

"Bobby, I'm not going to get into one of those weird discussions with you where everything has to have a sexual overtone."

"You just did," Bobby countered.

"Marilyn added those big curly eyelashes to her Volkswagen bug's headlights. Did you see them?" Liz said changing the subject and the tone of the discussion.

"No. I stayed here for a little bit after she left," Bobby explained.

"She kinda looks like her car and you better not repeat that I said that!" Liz warned Bobby.

"Is that better than when people look like their dog?" Bobby wondered seriously.

"Have you seen her dog?" Liz inquired.

"Yes, she does resemble him in a way. He has spiky hair like she has -- only her hair is black and the dog's is white. They have the same temperament, too. Her dog acts like a cat in a dog costume."

"What kind is it?"

"A Westie. She got it through some rescue. She thought it would cheer her up."

"Poor Marilyn…" Liz thought out loud.

"My ass!"

"What is it with you two? One minute you guys are hanging out and the next minute you are at each other's throat."

"I actually think we spend more time at each other's throats."

"I think you guys could be great friends. She's not dating anyone and neither are you."

"I have standards…"

"Really? Since when?" Liz laughed.

"It just sounded good when I said that," Bobby said, with a sheepish grin.

"I have been meaning to ask you something. You told me that you would tell me if you saw Mrs. Piggy on any of the surveillance tapes. Have you seen her lately?"

"I'm glad you mentioned that because I wanted to talk to you about that. The security company hasn't seen anything suspicious. I monitor it on my phone and it has been quiet. I do think the camera by the backdoor should be moved just a bit to get a wider angle. I just didn't want to do it when Sam was home. I don't want to upset her."

"Sam has been uncharacteristically quiet about the whole subject, which usually means that it is bothering her more than she is letting on."

"Unfortunately, I agree with you, Liz."

"Do you want to go over there now? Sam is at school and Adam is working from home today."

"No thanks. He would probably kick the ladder out from under me if given the opportunity. He is still griping that I charged all of those motion lights and surveillance cameras to his account. I would prefer to do it when no one is home."

"I don't know if it counts for anything, but I appreciate what you did. I sleep better knowing that those lights and cameras are there. We both know the real reason why Adam is upset."

"Do you know every stinking time he walks in front of the one of the cameras he puts his hand up and gives it 'the bird'?" Bobby tattled.

"Does that really surprise you?"

"Not really. I just wish he would stop mooning the camera. I already know he's an ass."

"Are you serious?"

"Yes, the image is burned into my retina, unfortunately."

"I will talk to him. I think it's just his way of dealing with the embarrassment."

"I don't think that's it…"

"I just remembered Adam is flying to Houston early tomorrow morning, but coming back in the late evening." Liz said, ignoring Bobby's comment.

"What about Sam?"

"We have a hair appointment with Renay immediately after school. Would that work?"

"Sure, I think we should finish in the O.R. at about three. That should give me plenty of time to get the camera adjusted and make sure it is working properly." Bobby told her.

"Sounds like a plan."

"It sure does…"

Chapter 26

Bobby was a little early, so he looked for his phone and began to examine it while waiting for Renay at The Overlook. Marilyn had agreed to not divulge his secret that he was the owner of the fine dining establishment. He didn't know how much that little favor would cost him – but he knew it wouldn't come cheap. He realized that he spent way too much of his free time contemplating ways of getting even with her, but deep down he knew he was no match for her wits. He may have the degrees and the book knowledge, but she was light years ahead of him in street smarts and survival skills.

Bobby checked the app on his phone that showed him the surveillance cameras at Liz's house. All was quiet on the western front. And the northern, the eastern, and southern fronts as well. Butter and Fritz were lazily sunning themselves on the back terrace. He didn't tell Liz, but he had saved every single image of Adam "shooting the bird" and his scrawny hairy ass mooning the camera. Adam will one day wish he hadn't acted so childishly. Bobby intended to embarrass the hotshot businessman at a later date. It's not a question of if -- just a question of when and how. Of course, he had to make sure he didn't anger or embarrass Liz and Sam in the process.

The Overlook was really hopping. It had become quite the place with the locals and the tourists. *Texas Monthly* gave the restaurant its highest rating. He could expand the restaurant, since he owned the adjacent land, but he thought some of the mystique was how hard it was to get into the place. Reservations were now being taken for two months from today.

Bobby hadn't even hesitated when Liz had asked him if she could use the restaurant for Renay's wedding shower. He smiled when he thought about the irony of it. After all, he had been dating her when her ex-boyfriend proposed. He was always the groomsman, never the groom.

Renay's fiancé seemed like a nice enough fellow. He had just gotten scared thinking about mortgages, kids and saving for retirement. Who wouldn't? Renay was able to forgive him because within two weeks of leaving her, he admitted to being the biggest idiot in the world. He then proposed marriage, sealing the deal with a beautiful ring that had belonged to his Grandmother.

Bobby had enjoyed his two weeks of consoling the beautiful hairdresser, and he liked the spiffy, longer hairdo she created for him. He teased Renay that the new "do" took at least two years off of his age. If you asked Liz, she would say that it was his teenage-like behavior, not the new "do" that made him seem child-like.

Bobby deep down knew Renay was too young for him, but it helped heal the wounds from his last brief girlfriend, Sandy. He met Sandy through this ridiculous organization that Liz had practically forced him to join. The organization was called, "It's Just Pie" and it was a fundraiser for a wildlife rescue group. For his $500 donation, they would arrange up to three "pie" dates at their wildlife rescue sanctuary. If a couple liked each other after getting to know one another over pie, then they could stroll through the safe parts of the refuge observing the animals. Bobby thought it didn't seem any more desperate than what he had been doing thus far to find a mate, so he sent them a check.

He was stood up on his very first date. Since everyone at the rescue knew why he was there, he was uncomfortable beyond belief when his date didn't appear. He sat at the bistro table, silently cursing Liz for getting him into such an awkward and embarrassing predicament. When he tired of the workers snickering behind his back, he decided to walk outside to see the animals, just in case his date was running late.

Bobby walked up to a cage containing a little brown Rhesus monkey. His plaque said his name was Timmy and he had come to the sanctuary two years ago from a research facility that closed. Bobby started to talk soothingly to the little fellow. Apparently the monkey didn't like what Bobby was saying or the manner in which he said it. A moment later, he found himself in the middle of a one-way poo-slinging contest with the little monkey clearly being the winner. Bobby left in a huff, vowing to never return for his other dates.

Liz tried her best to maintain her composure when he told her about the date that didn't occur the next morning, which was difficult when she imagined Bobby covered in monkey poo. She calmly reassured him that everything happens for a reason and she had a feeling that his second date would go better. He reluctantly scheduled the second date.

Bobby couldn't believe his luck. Sandy, his date, was early and waiting for him. She reminded him a lot of Liz because she was tall, blonde, and vivacious. She was easy to talk to, and the time flew by. She was even in the medical field - a surgical nurse.

Bobby told Sandy about his disastrous first date. He even felt comfortable enough to tell her about the poo-flinging monkey. Sandy insisted on seeing the monkey that flung the poo at Bobby. The little monkey was as taken with Sandy as Bobby was and instead of flinging poo, immediately began to pleasure himself to both their amusement.

They exchanged phone numbers, and before he had pulled his Jaguar out of the parking lot she sent him a picture of Timmy masturbating with the title of "Our First Date". Finally, he thought - someone he could see himself falling for. He boldly asked her out for dinner the next night. She accepted. And she asked him out for the night after that. On their third date she received a phone call and told him that she was sorry, but she had to take it and excused herself from their table at dinner. She seemed a little sad when she returned to the table, but never discussed the call with Bobby.

He found that he wanted to know everything about her. Sandy told him that her parents were killed in an automobile accident when she was seven, and she had no brothers or sisters. Her grandparents had stepped in to raise her and they were now gone. It broke his heart to think that she had no family.

They went to a winery, to a film festival, took an Italian cooking class, went antique shopping, and visited the zoo. Sandy was the type of girl that he could take to his favorite hole-in-the–wall Mexican restaurant, or to the theater to see a touring Broadway play. She introduced him to Greek food, putt-putt golf, and karaoke. He introduced her to Texas barbeque, sumo wrestling, and Alison Krauss. Everything was perfect and Bobby had never been happier.

In fact, Bobby couldn't help but think that Sandy could be "the one". He decided to let her in on one of his deepest and darkest secrets. A secret that he had only shared with Liz. Even though Bobby was a successful anesthesiologist, what he really wanted to do was own restaurants. He didn't think that Sandy was dating him because he was a doctor, but he would soon know.

He called her and told her to wear jeans and sneakers on their date. When he pulled into her driveway to pick her up she was already waiting outside. "I couldn't wait to see you!" she said, as she jumped into his convertible before he could even get out to open her door. She threw her arms around his neck and gave him a long kiss before asking, "Where are we going?"

"Patience is a virtue," was all Bobby said and he took her hand. She playfully socked him in the arm and then nested back in the Corvette seat.

They drove down some back roads until they arrived at an abandoned brick and concrete building that partially extended over the Guadalupe River.

"Was that for generating electricity?" Sandy asked.

"Originally it was a grist mill to grind grains, then it was converted by the next owner to also be a cotton gin, and later using the hydroelectric generating capabilities, started to supply the citizens of New Braunfels with electricity somewhere in the early 1900's."

"Fascinating! I think there is someone in there, because I see a light."

Bobby pointed to the absence of power lines to the building. "Are you sure you aren't seeing a reflection?"

"No, it's a light. Look, it flickers. I hope some kids haven't lit it on fire."

"Stay here and I'll go check it out!"

"No, I'm going with you!"

Together they briskly walked up the grassy bank to the old brick building. When they reached the top of the stairs, Sandy pointed to the cut chain that held a lock on the massive metal doors.

Sandy whispered, "I hear music."

Bobby stuck his head close to the opening in the door and said, "I believe it's Alison Krauss." Then he swung the door the rest of the way open.

Sandy started to laugh and said, "Bobby Bain!"

She walked into what had been the Engine Room. The ancient wooden floor had been swept and Bobby had scattered pale pink rose petals everywhere. There was a small bistro table placed to maximize the view, with a linen tablecloth that reached all the way to the floor. The giant windows that overlooked the dam had votive candles in clear glass holders on the windowsills. The flames seemed to dance slowly in the reflection of the leaded glass windows and the rushing water below.

Bobby had also strategically placed a small wicker loveseat, with a Shabby Chic comforter on the back, so they could enjoy the amazing view of the water rushing over the dam.

He led Sandy to the loveseat and motioned for her to sit down. Then he went and brought back a chilled bottle of Pinot Grigio from the vineyards that they had visited in Fredericksburg one Saturday. They sat there enjoying the wine, each other, and the view.

They danced to Alison Krauss. Bobby kept teasing Sandy that she was leading. She teased him back that it was hard to move when he was holding her so close. "I'm just trying to polish my belt buckle," Bobby replied.

"Bobby, that's what cowboys say when they have on a big Western buckle, not a regular buckle!"

A gentle rain could be heard on the tin roof. Bobby led Sandy to the bistro table where they dined on croissants, chicken salad with grapes and toasted pecans, and artisan cheeses. Then Bobby brought out a box with the Two Tarts Bakery label on it. "Your favorite dessert!" he said.

Sandy got up and sat on Bobby's lap. "No, that's my second favorite!" she announced and started kissing him slowly and deliberately.

Bobby started to breathe deep breaths in between Sandy's intoxicating kisses. The rain seemed to be beat on the roof harder and faster, mirroring the intensity of their kisses.

"I still can't get used to Texas storms," Sandy told Bobby.

"I'm sure it will blow over soon. This building has been here over a century, so I'm not too worried about it going anywhere."

Sandy then went back to her side of the table and opened the box, smiling knowingly. She took the chocolate covered macaroon out of box and slowly raised it to her mouth. Bobby took a deeper breath. She took a small bite and slowly closed her eyes.

Then she took a deep breath. "That is sinful," she announced.

"You will get no argument from me," Bobby agreed.

"Here, have some," Sandy said.

Bobby noticed she wasn't trying to hand him the macaroon.

"Too late!" Sandy said, and ate the other half of the macaroon.

Bobby had never wanted a woman more in his life than he did at this moment. This was the first time in his life that he wasn't dating someone with the sole intent of getting in her pants. It was the oddest feeling – being so sexually attracted to someone and not fully acting on it.

Sandy got up and walked to the windows that faced the bank. "The water is over the bank, we can't get back to the car!" Sandy told him.

Bobby didn't know at this point how Sandy was going to take this turn of events.

She took the two chair cushions and placed them next to each other on the floor in front of the big windows that overlooked the dam. She then placed the comforter from the loveseat on the floor and announced, "Home sweet home!"

Bobby took the Allison Krauss CD out and replaced it with a Teddy Pendergrass one.

"I guess it's a good thing we have another bottle of wine," Bobby said, as he opened the second bottle. Sandy picked up the glasses and took them over to the comforter.

The lightning appeared much closer and started to light up the room.

"I'm going to blow out the candles. We may need them later," Sandy told Bobby.

They both returned to the oversize comforter and removed their sneakers.

"Bobby, who owns this place?" Sandy wondered.

"I actually do," Bobby told her.

"So, you weren't REALLY putting me in harm's way when we walked in here? You were just trying to scare me so I would cling to you closer, like this." Sandy pushed Bobby back into the cushion and started to kiss him in a way that rendered him unable to think clearly.

"Something like that," Bobby said, and now pushed her back into the cushions. He lowered his body on top of her and she could feel how badly he desired her. He started to kiss her until she was the one breathing deeper. He reached up and unbuttoned the top button on her blouse. She took her leg and crossed her lower leg over his and put her hand under his shirt.

"Oh my God!" Sandy said and pushed Bobby to the side.

"What's wrong?" Bobby cried.

"You HAVE to make this place into a restaurant!"

He looked at her and pulled her close and looked her straight in the eyes and said, "Sandy, I'm in love with you."

"Thank goodness!" Sandy said, and unbuttoned all of the buttons of his shirt. "You won't be needing this."

"Then I guess you won't be needing yours." Normally Bobby would want to close the deal before his date changed her mind, but tonight he wanted to take his time and savor every moment. He continued to kiss her and began to kiss her the way he wanted to make love to her. She started to moan. He stopped and offered her some wine.

"I can't believe you are teasing me this way," Sandy said. She grabbed the wine glass and took a large drink. Then she removed Bobby's shirt and started to push him back to undo his belt, but he stopped her.

"I love this song," Bobby said and stopped kissing Sandy. "Close the Door" by Teddy Pendergrass was now playing. He just sat there listening to it.

Sandy started to slowly unbutton her shirt. Bobby looked at the pale pink lacy bra that barely contained her breasts. She tossed the shirt to the side.

Teddy's "Turn Off the Lights" began to play. "Bain, you are not playing fair."

"Don't you like Teddy?" He asked as he put his finger on her lip and started moving it down her neck. His hand then went behind her back and he unsnapped her bra.

"I like Teddy, but I love you."

The storm and their passion continued to increase in frequency and intensity until there was no more. The two lovers awoke with the sun beaming through the windows. Bobby looked out the window to see the water had receded, but he carried Sandy to the car so she wouldn't get muddy. The whole way back on the drive to Sandy's house, they held hands and made plans for the restaurant they were going to open.

Later that day she left him a message when he was in the O.R.—"Bobby, something hasn't gone as I had hoped. Wish I could explain. Will hope to explain it to you, someday."

He never heard from her again. It had been the best 3 months of his life.

He called her work and found out that she quit with no notice. Her house was vacant. He hired a private investigator that finally surmised that she must have been in the Federal Witness Protection Program, because she had disappeared without a trace. He advised Bobby it was best not to pursue the matter any further. Bobby wondered if he would ever find out the truth.

Liz couldn't even cheer him up. She suggested that he could go talk to Adam's therapist, Mr. Miller. She confided to Bobby that she had also started seeing Mr. Miller and found it very beneficial.

Bobby eventually agreed.

Mr. Miller didn't look the way that Bobby expected--he was about six foot two.

"So… what is a good-looking guy like you doing in a place like this?" Mr. Miller asked Bobby when he met him.

Bobby slowly went over every excruciating detail that he thought might shed some light on his situation.

Mr. Miller finally told him, "Bobby, it is perfectly normal to be down. Everyone deals with things in different ways, so I can't tell you how long you are going to feel this way. Though my rule of thumb is - don't be down longer than you dated her. So, you told me you spent three months with her. I think if you still feel this horrible in two and a half months, then you probably need to see me again."

Bobby muttered, "Thank goodness we weren't together seventeen years."

"E-x-a-c-t-l-y!" Mr. Miller's voice boomed.

"I kinda thought from what Liz told me about you that you were going to say something more profound. I was hoping to start feeling better today."

Mr. Miller took a small yellow lined pad out and drew a picture. It looked like a girl with long hair and a smiling face. He then looked up from his drawing and asked Bobby, "Do you go to church?"

"On occasion," Bobby answered truthfully. On occasion Bobby set foot in a church for a wedding or funeral, but Mr. Miller hadn't been that specific, so Bobby didn't consider it a lie.

Mr. Miller then drew a round pig on the same page and a pearl necklace. "Matthew 7:6. Don't cast your pearls before swine."

Bobby looked more than perplexed.

"You gave this girl your best. You gave her pearls. But you didn't even know if the pig's real name was Sandy, or not!" Mr. Miller voice boomed again, and he carefully ripped the picture of the girl, the pig and the pearls out of the tablet and handed it to Bobby.

"Geez, I never thought of it that way. I did give her my best, and you are right I don't even know her real name," Bobby said.

"Maybe it was Petunia," Mr. Miller said cracking himself up by referencing Porky Pig's girlfriend.

Liz was glad when Bobby appeared to be back to his peculiar ways within a week of seeing Mr. Miller. He was still sad, but it no longer seemed like it wouldn't get better. Bobby wished Renay would hurry up. He didn't like having this much time to think on his hands.

"Bobby!" Renay said, for the second time.

Bobby jumped. He was relieved she had finally arrived.

"Man, you were in a land far, far away…" Renay teased him.

He laughed. One of the waiters came over and Renay ordered some basil strawberry lemonade from the bar. The basil was grown on the grounds of the restaurant.

"So, are you becoming a bridezilla?" Bobby teased.

"Are you sure you want to hear this?"

"Renay, we only went out for two weeks. You deflected my advances like an experienced fencer," Bobby told her, sincerely.

"I did manage to get the screen door between you and me on our last date. Didn't I?" she teased.

"I knew from our first date, I didn't stand a chance with you. I just wanted you to feel guilty, so you would cut my hair better."

"Well, it worked."

"I know! I have never received so many compliments on my hair."

"Oh my goodness, can you believe Liz was able to book this place for my wedding shower?"

"Wow!" Bobby said, feigning surprise. He had immediately suggested that Liz use the restaurant when Liz told him she wanted to throw Renay a shower.

"They aren't usually open for lunch, but we are having a luncheon. I'm super excited."

"I'm sure Liz will make it very special."

"We just figured out the menu."

"I bet basil strawberry lemonade is on that menu," Bobby guessed.

"Is it that obvious? I love the stuff. I tried making it at home, but it wasn't as good."

"It's just lemons, Poteet strawberries, Tito's vodka and fresh basil according to the description on the menu."

"But what makes it a little bubbly?"

"I think you are right, there must be an ingredient missing. I think it might be a splash of Seven-up. Why don't we ask?"

"Do you think they would tell us?" Renay speculated.

"There is only one way to find out?" Bobby told her. He waved the waiter over.

"My dining companion has a food allergy. Could you find out if there are any additional ingredients in the lemonade besides what are listed on the menu?" Bobby asked with great authority.

"Why didn't I think of that?" Renay wondered.

The waiter returned. "Sierra Mist, sir. Anything else?"

"Thank you so much. I don't believe we have any other questions," Bobby told him.

"I'm going to try that food allergy thing next time I need to know something," Renay said hoping she would remember that little white lie.

"Did you bring Sam's hair extensions?" Bobby asked, changing the subject.

"I sure did!" Renay said, as she slid a clear plastic container containing the long blond extensions toward Bobby.

"It looks like someone was scalped. Sam told me that a lot of the hair comes from India. Is that true?"

"A good majority of it does."

"Where is this from Sweden?" Bobby asked seriously.

"Most of the hair comes from Asia, India or Eastern Europe. If I had to guess, I would say this is from Eastern Europe since it's blond. The label said it was virgin hair."

"What does it matter if it comes from a virgin?" Bobby asked.

"It's just better quality hair!"

"Is that why it's so expensive? Virgins are hard to come by."

Renay suddenly realizes that she and Bobby are having two different conversations. She started laughing and had a hard time stopping.

"Bobby, virgin hair means it's never been dyed or permed."

"Geez…" Bobby mutters.

"I put the clips in that Sam likes, so it's ready to go."

"How do you clip them in?" Bobby asked.

"Don't worry, Sam knows. They are just like her other extensions."

"No, I'm just curious."

"It's easy. There is an instruction page on the back of the packet."

"That's good."

"When are you going to give them to her? I hope I don't accidently say something."

"You won't!" Bobby assured her.

"You are going to stay Sam's favorite uncle with this present," Renay assured him.

"So, have you set a date for the wedding?"

"Yes, you will be getting a save the date card soon. You can bring a date," Renay informed him.

"I can't, she is getting married that day."

Renay smiled sweetly at Bobby, and they both burst out laughing.

Chapter 27

Bobby parked his maroon Toyota Tundra across the street from Liz's house. He chose to drive the truck today because no one would recognize it. He very seldom used it. He preferred the Jag or the Corvette on most days. He decided this time it would be easier to go incognito.

On the way over, he had double-checked with Liz to make sure Adam was still out of town for the day and that she and Sam were still going to Renay's to have their hair done. Liz assured him that he could safely reposition the camera without Adam's "help. She told him she would call if there were any changes in their plans. She thanked him again for doing this when Sam wouldn't be around to be reminded of what Adam had done. He thought it was best that Liz didn't have any advance warning of what he was really up to. He wasn't sure she would understand. This was strictly a need-to-know operation and she really didn't need to know. Of course, Liz might think otherwise.

Butter and Fritz were watching his every move from their vantage point on the front porch. Dogs always seemed to like Bobby, and vice versa. Butter's tail started to wag harder and faster the closer that Bobby got to the front gate. He entered the code to open the gate, and was then officially greeted by the canine ambassadors. This greeting included being jumped on by both dogs and having his crotch smelled by Butter. Which made Bobby think -- thank heavens people didn't walk up and smell each other's crotches. Fritz was constantly underfoot --trying to stand everywhere that Bobby was trying to walk. They appeared attention-starved, but Bobby knew otherwise.

Butter insisted on showing Bobby his new tug toy that he was quite proud of. His tail thumped loudly against everything that it came in contact with. Bobby put down the sports bag that he was carrying so he could pet the lonely animals.

"Okay, we can play tug-of-war, but only for a minute," he told the overly enthusiastic golden retriever.

Bobby picked up the end of the toy that Butter offered him and quickly found he was no match for the smelly hound. Butter was a seasoned pro with many hours of tug-of-war behind him. Butter would zig when Bobby would zag. When all else failed, Butter would just assume a new position by clamping his large mouth over Bobby's hands, slobbering all over Bobby. Bobby decided he had more than enough and conceded to the determined pup. "You won, Butter. Now go away," Bobby eventually had to tell the dog.

Bobby glanced over towards his sports bag just as Fritz had decided it was time to mark it as his own. The entire front of the bag was dripping in urine. And this wasn't just any run-of-the-mill type of dog urine -- this was Fritz's piss. How could such a small dog pee so much? He picked up the water hose and rinsed the putrid stuff off the bag.

Thank goodness, the bag was zippered shut and waterproof.

"Seriously Fritz, I'm a male also, and I don't see the need to pee on everything I see," Bobby explained to the attentive, small white terrier. Fritz yapped something incoherent, but apparently enthusiastic back to Bobby.

"Time to get to work," Bobby told the pups as they continued to follow him to the side of the garage. Fritz had enough with the mention of the word "work" and decided to lie down and sun himself instead.

The garage door opened as soon as Bobby entered the five-digit pass code. Every single entrance was now guarded by at least one additional security measure thanks to Bobby. He noticed Adam's new gleaming Audi was sitting in the garage. For a moment, he forgot that Liz had dropped Adam off at the airport. He really wasn't in the mood for Adam or any of his non-sensical BS. Not today, or any day.

He easily found a six-foot aluminum ladder sitting in the corner of the meticulously neat garage. He then carried and placed it in front of the misaligned camera. He cautiously climbed the rungs of the ladder keeping a watchful eye out for Butter the whole time. Butter and his tail were just an accident waiting to happen. Bobby pulled out his phone so he could look at the surveillance app. He wanted to verify the new alignment. He made one more small adjustment to the camera -- and then it was perfect. He checked his phone one last time. The alignment was just as he wanted.

He climbed down from the ladder only to be greeted by his two furry supervisors. Bobby decided they all deserved a treat. He unlocked the door to Liz's house, and they all went in for a small reward for a job well done. Both dogs immediately went in, sat in front of, and stared at the small cookie jar shaped like a dog's head that contained their bacon flavored dog biscuits. As Bobby lifted the top of the container, Fritz started to sit up and beg. This trick assured that he got the first biscuit. Butter was a tad more patient, but then swallowed his biscuit whole, without even tasting it.

After he let the dogs back out, Bobby walked over to the liquor cabinet and poured himself a drink. All that Adam had left was some inexpensive whiskey that he kept in a Waterford decanter. Cheap bastard, you aren't fooling anyone, he thought to himself. It was rotgut compared to what he was used to -- but it would have to do for now. He made sure that he washed the glass, dried it and returned it to its proper place. No need for anyone to know.

Now, he was ready. He picked up his bag and walked into the guest bathroom. It was time... he proceeded to empty the contents of the sports bag on the counter — a change of clothes, disposable surgical gloves and his new unregistered gun. He was surprised how easy it was to get an unregistered firearm. It just took a little know how and a lot of cash in small bills.

He wondered how long this matter would take. He surmised there was no real way of telling. It didn't matter. He wasn't going to turn back at this point. He planned on staying until the problem was history. He never thought he would be doing such a thing, but all that really mattered was the final outcome. He was sick and tired of seeing his friend Liz live such a life. This had been going on for far too long, and it was time to put finally put a stop to it -- once and for all! So he changed into the other clothes, put on the gloves, picked up his gun and went outside to wait for his "guest" to arrive. Boy, would they be surprised. Liz might not forgive him right away or maybe ever, but hopefully she would eventually see this was for her and Sam's own good.

And he waited.

Chapter 28

"What do you mean that I canceled the order? I did no such thing! Why in the world would I do that? I want to talk to whoever is in charge!" Mrs. Piggy hollered into her home phone.

A few moments later, a supervisor was on the phone with her. "Hello. How can I be of assistance?" the supervisor asked, ever so politely.

"I was just told by that other lady that my wedding invitations were canceled. Now, what are you going to do about this?" Mrs. Piggy demanded.

"I will need to look into this and I will call you right back. Is this a good number?" the operator asked.

"Yes, but WHEN are you going to call me back?"

"It should only be a few minutes."

"It better be. My fiancé is not going to be very happy about this."

"I promise it will just be a few minutes," the supervisor sincerely told her.

Exactly eight minutes later, the supervisor called Mrs. Piggy back. "Our records indicate that you are the one who canceled your order. They were canceled five days after they were placed."

"You people are screw-ups!!!" Mrs. Piggy screamed.

"Ma'am?" the supervisor inquired.

"WHAT?"

"To cancel an order, you must answer two security questions that only you know the answers to. Our records indicate that you answered both of these questions correctly."

"That's bullshit!"

"Ma'am you canceled the order on the Internet. We have a copy I can e-mail to you. You entered the password that you created AND answered the two security questions correctly. I don't know how you could say we made an error."

"What were the two questions?"

"What is your favorite thing about your fiancé?"

"And?"

"You answered: his money."

"No, I meant what was the second question?"

"Oh… It was -- where did you fiancé propose to you at? You answered: none of your business. I don't see how someone could have answered these questions and had them match what you input when you first placed your order," the supervisor pointed out.

"I DID NOT cancel my order! What am I supposed to tell my fiancé?" Mrs. Piggy asked.

"Would you like me to call him and explain the dilemma to him?" the supervisor asked.

"You better not!" Mrs. Piggy said.

"I could let him know what options there are. You could re-order with a rush, or pick a simpler design," the supervisor suggested

"No, he doesn't know!" Mrs. Piggy shrieked.

"Of course, he doesn't---You just found out a few minutes ago," the supervisor said sympathetically. The supervisor had no idea that what Mrs. Piggy had just let slip was that her fiancé had no clue he was getting married. Nor did he know that he was divorcing his wife to marry this delusional woman.

"Can you just reorder them with a rush?" Mrs. Piggy inquired.

"We can, but there will be an additional charge," the supervisor informed her.

"I can't afford that!" Mrs. Piggy moaned, obviously forgetting that she had just told the helpful supervisor that she liked her fiancé's money.

"Tell you what, I'll waive the additional charge," the supervisor said, just wanting to get off the phone with the whack-job.

"So, when should I expect them?"

"They should arrive by the end of next week. Is there anything else I can do for you?"

"No," Mrs. Piggy said and abruptly hung up.

Little did she know that canceling the wedding invitations was actually Pamela's brilliant idea. Her computer guy provided her with the order information, password and answers to the security questions. He even logged her on to Mrs. Piggy's computer, so that the order would be canceled from her own computer. Pamela only wished that she could see Mrs. Piggy's face when she found out the order had been canceled.

Mrs. Piggy just sat there and started to second-guess herself. Had she canceled the wedding invitations??? She had been really mad at Adam shortly after she ordered them. She knew that when he fired her he said that they could no longer be in touch… but she missed him so much! He had even sent her an e-mail that read, "I want to make this perfectly clear – do not have any contact with me of any form." She was sure he didn't mean it. Why would he not want to be with her?

She wondered what he saw in Liz anyway. It really pissed her off that everyone liked Liz. Everyone acted like Liz was perfect. She got sick of the others in the office talking about how kind Liz was, how naturally beautiful she was, how much Sam looked like Liz, and what a good doctor she was. Mrs. Piggy told herself that she could have been a doctor, if they didn't expect you to make all A's. She told herself she was a damn good office worker - Adam didn't yell at her as often as he did when she was first hired. She also concluded that being tall and beautiful was completely over-rated.

She remembered why she had gotten so mad at Adam. That day, she had decided to throw caution to the wind and call Adam at work. She dialed his work phone number and was told by his new male secretary that Mr. Schaeffer wasn't available. She was parked across the street from his office and could clearly see his car in his reserved parking place. She was so upset that she then dialed his cell number. A number she had only used twice the entire two years that she worked for him. Both had been for business emergencies.

"Adam Schaeffer," he answered in the deep voice that she knew so well.

"Adam, it's me. I just needed to hear your voice. I've been so depressed. This separation has been so hard," she blurted out.

"You need to leave me alone. Liz almost left me because of what you did!" Adam sternly said.

"But I miss your handsome face," Mrs. Piggy whined.

"I can understand that. I guess I am the handsomest boss you have ever had," Adam decided.

"And also the funniest. You know, I'm the only one who ever got your jokes," Mrs. Piggy naively told him, not realizing she was actually insulting him.

"That's true."

"Your new secretary is a man?"

"Liz is pretty steamed."

"Do you like him?"

"He's all right."

"I've really missed you."

"I'm working on a merger that will be talked about for years," Adam boasted completely oblivious to Mrs. Piggy's feelings.

"There is no one smarter than you, Adam. I bet you will make a lot of money from that."

"Of course, I want to buy a vacation home for my family."

"Oh…"

"This company, under my leadership, has been growing exponentially."

"Do you miss me, Adam?"

"I miss those little muffins that you used to bring in. Where did you buy those at?"

"I didn't buy them. I would bake them especially for you."

"They weren't bad. They were almost as good as what you can buy in a bakery."

"I could bring you some tomorrow."

"I will be out of town tomorrow," Adam told her somehow forgetting the inappropriateness of his and Mrs. Piggy's behavior. Not to mention the danger of the situation, and above all how he should be thanking his lucky stars that Liz had allowed him to return home.

"I need to take a call," Adam told her, bored now that she was no longer complimenting him.

"I have been so depressed since I stopped working for you!"

"Maybe there is a self-help book that you could read," Adam suggested, hoping that she would stop whining and return to telling him how great he was.

"I don't think there is one for my specific problem," Mrs. Piggy said not realizing how true and pathetic of a statement that she had just made.

"Gotta go," Adam said, forgetting to tell Mrs. Piggy to leave him and his family alone. He didn't wait for her to answer and just hung up on her. Of course, he wouldn't mention the conversation to Liz. She would want to call the police or something equally dramatic.

Mrs. Piggy couldn't believe he had just hung up on her! She wanted to tell him how much she loved him, and especially start telling him about the wedding. What if he wasn't free that day? He had to make sure he was divorced by then. Once Sam was out of the way, he wouldn't have any excuses for not divorcing Liz.

She started replaying the conversation in her mind. What in the world did he mean when he said he was going to buy a vacation home for his family? He was probably talking in a secret code. Someday soon they both would be laughing about how she forgot what the code word for vacation home was.

She had just read that morning in a woman's magazine that one of the most common mistakes that women make in a relationship is overanalyzing what their partner says. She didn't want to mess this up. She wouldn't think about what Adam said, how he said it, or that he hadn't contacted her. She needed to just stick to her plan. That reminded her that she needed to check the Facebook account.

She walked over to her computer and turned it on. The little brat seemed to take forever to respond to her messages. There hadn't been a message for the past two days. She saw there were two new e-mails. Both were from the wedding invitation store. The first message was a copy of the order that had been canceled. The second was where the invitations were being reordered with a rush. Thank goodness the supervisor had left off the rush charge. She had been having problems making ends meet. She was still surprised Adam hadn't offered to help her out with her rent. It wasn't like he couldn't afford it…

She was surprised to see she had a personal message on Facebook. It was about time, she thought to herself.

She read the message and then reread it — "I'm sick of trying to figure out what to wear to the play. Why don't you come over today to my house and help me decide? We can swim afterwards. I'm not allowed to swim alone and my Dad is out of town and my Mom will be at the hairdresser. My address is 12 Preserve Ridge in The Preserves. Just message me back, yes or no. Hopefully yes! Your friend, Sam."

Mrs. Piggy smiled.

She walked out into her garage and picked up a screwdriver. She then proceeded to unscrew the license plate from the front of her car. She then replaced it with one that she had taken from the mall. She wished she could have gotten both plates, but the mall security camera precluded this. The security at The Preserve would only write down the front plate anyway.

She calmly went back into the house and put her gun in her purse. She then went back to the computer and sent Sam a message – "See ya soon! I will bring some cup-cakes."

She went to the freezer and took out the cupcakes that she had so carefully baked. She had outdone herself - devils food with Flexeril/Phenergan butter cream frosting. She had sampled a teaspoon of the frosting and slept like a baby until morning. She could only imagine the effect they would have on the skinny brat.

Chapter 29

Bobby realized he couldn't change his mind after he read the message that Mrs. Piggy had sent to Sam. If he chickened out now, Mrs. Piggy would probably ambush Liz and Sam when they returned home from their hair appointment. He couldn't have that. He did momentarily dream up an alternative plan. What if he invited Sam and Liz out for a late dinner, so that way Mrs. Piggy would ambush an unsuspecting Adam when he returned from his business trip, instead? As much as he disliked Adam, he decided he better stick to his original plan.

If he was successful, Liz might look at him as her knight-in-shining-armor, instead of as her "brother" or her pathetic, pesky friend. He knew he could not afford to fail. He could already see the headlines in the news – "Cross-dressing doc killed by lunatic." Bobby unconsciously flung the long blonde hair extensions from in front of his shoulder to his back, as he waited.

He had practiced putting the extensions in and out by following a tutorial he had thankfully found on the Internet late last night. The teenage girl on the video explained everything nice and slow. She showed the viewer how to clip the extension in, where to place them and what products you could use with them. Luckily, his hair was just long enough to hide the clips. He thought if one squinted their eyes just right that he somewhat resembled one of those fancy underwear models with their long flowing blonde mane.

Bobby thought to himself how warm it was standing on the terrace overlooking the river. At first, he thought it was probably due to the Kevlar vest or maybe the long emerald-green velvet cloak that he wore over it. But, he had to be honest with himself - it was his nerves. This was something that he hadn't counted on- after all, he was known to have "nerves of steel" in the OR. He would have normally said he was sweating like a pig, but today he didn't like the sound of that.

He looked over the railing at the turbulent rushing water below. The river had risen dramatically due to the recent heavy rains. That would be his luck he thought-- to pass out due to the heat while he waited, and plunge into the swollen river below. It would probably take days for the authorities to identify his body, that is, if they ever found it. The hair extensions and cloak would be ripped from his body within minutes of entering the turbulent water. At least no one would think he was a cross-dresser when they recovered his body. The headlines would now read instead – "Love-sick doc leaps to his death." This wasn't the kind of epitaph he was hoping for and quickly moved into a shaded area of the terrace overlook to wait.

The time seemed to just stand still as he waited. He restlessly kept shifting his weight from one foot to the other foot, and then right back, again and again. He wasn't sure if he had been standing on the terrace for two minutes or two hours. The longer he waited, the more he second-guessed the effectiveness of his plan. He should have at least told Nick what he was up to. Nick could have followed the pig and sent him a text so he would know whether she was on foot or driving over. Bobby realized he could have been waiting inside Liz's house in air-conditioned comfort until Mrs. Piggy was closer, if he would have just involved Nick in his scheme.

Earlier that afternoon, he realized that he had completely forgotten to inform the subdivision gate guards that the Schaeffer family was expecting a guest that afternoon named "Heather". Right after he notified the guards, he thought to himself that Nick would have never made such a rookie mistake. But he didn't want to involve Nick or anyone else, just in case the plan didn't work. The truth of the matter was that Bobby wanted to be the one and only hero in Liz's eyes. He could see the headlines – "Brave doctor captures dangerous stalker." The story would hopefully include accounts from his colleagues on what a brilliant doctor he was, how no one was the least bit surprised that Dr. Bobby Bain had thought of such a brilliant plan and how scads of scantily clad women were now camping out in front of his house in hopes of seeing a glimpse of the attractive anesthesiologist. They would probably ask him to consult on a made-for-TV movie. He would bring Liz along if Oprah asked him for an interview. Liz has always felt a kinship with Oprah because they both had golden retrievers.

He was snapped back to reality when he suddenly felt the urgency to pee. He realized he forgot to "take a whiz" earlier when he was still in the house - a huge tactical error on his part! The more he tried not to think about it, the more he did. Now, he had two options – to go back inside and use the half bath right inside the door or to simply relieve himself off the terrace right where he was standing. He would rather go back to the air-conditioned comfort of Liz's house. The bathroom also had close proximity to Adam's liquor cabinet.

The problem with that option was he wanted Mrs. Piggy to think he was Sam. He could only do that if kept his back to her. He surely knew he didn't look like an under-wear model from the front. From behind, the hair extensions were spot on and the cloak concealed what he liked to think of as his "muscular physique", though others might not have agreed with that assessment. Deep down, Bobby knew Mrs. Piggy would not be able to resist shoving him off the terrace to his death.

So, the second option it was. He knew he needed to hurry. Mrs. Piggy would be mighty suspicious if she saw Sam "taking a leak" off of the terrace balcony.

Bobby couldn't believe it. Now, that he decided to go, he found that he couldn't. He remembering studying this in med school. It was called paruresis, or as most people would refer to it —"shy bladder". Bobby had heard the lab talk about it when someone was not able to produce a sample for a drug test. It had never ever happened to Bobby before today. He was beyond relieved when a few moments later he was finally able to "go". Hopefully, nothing else would go wrong…

Chapter 30

"How are my two most favorite and beautiful clients?" Renay cheerfully greeted Liz and Sam, as soon as they walked into the hair salon for their scheduled appointments.

"Hi Miss Renay! Do you want some ice cream? I'm going to get some next door while you cut my Mom's hair," Sam said, as she ran to her hairdresser and gave her a huge hug.

"I would love some, but I'm going to pass because I have to fit into my wedding dress!"

"I was wondering… do you need a flower girl?" Sam asked, hopefully. For some unknown reason, Sam had always wanted to be a flower girl. When she was younger, she would often offer her services as a flower girl to the most casual acquaintances. But to her dismay, no one ever took her up on the offer.

"Honey, that is really nice of you to volunteer, but Renay probably has someone in her family in mind," Liz tried to gently tell the teen, and at the same time, let Renay know it was okay for Sam to not be in her wedding.

"Actually, your Mom is right. I do have someone in mind. Let me show you the picture of her dress and how she will wear her hair," Renay said, as she walked with the two over to her station.

Renay pulled out a book that was titled, "Our Wedding". The cover had wide abstract hot pink and white stripes. In the middle of the cover, was a cute cartoon of a bride with a huge list in her hand that curled down around her feet. The bride had a pencil tucked behind her ear, over the veil. Over the bride's head, were many cartoon bubbles that showed her dreaming of a tiered wedding cake, an island honeymoon, a sparkly ring, her wedding dress, and a bouquet of flowers. When she opened it up, it had pockets for the bride to put clippings from magazines. It was also divided by tabs into sections. Renay opened the book to the tab that said bridal party.   She turned to the picture of the flower girl.

"Wow! That is the prettiest flower girl dress I have ever seen," Sam said, trying her best to hide her disappointment that she was not going to be the one wearing it.

"Wait till you see her hair. My flower girl has long blonde hair just like this," Renay said, as she turned to the next clipping.

Sam looked at the page and immediately started to scream and jump up and down excitedly. Then she started to hug Renay so hard, that she almost picked her up.

"Look, Mom!" Sam said as she pointed to the page that showed a young girl with beautiful blonde cascading curls just like Sam's. On top of the page, she had written Sam Schaeffer as flower girl.

"Liz, I should have probably run this past you," Renay said, apologetically.

"Are you kidding me? If you only knew how long Sam has wanted to be a flower girl…"

"Okay, now I'm not going to have ice cream either. I need to be able to fit into my dress," Sam announced.

"You know what, I just changed my mind. I do want ice cream after all," Renay said, not wanting to be the cause of Sam's totally unnecessary diet.

"Then, I will too," Sam said, changing her mind right back.

"What kind do you want? I'm going to have the chocolate covered bubble gum flavor. Lexy says it's really good. And did you know that she ended up swallowing a piece of the gum on accident? Mom, did they ever teach you in medical school what happens when you swallow gum?"

"If they did, I don't remember."

"I bet Uncle Bobby remembers," Sam said, matter-of-factly.

"I bet he would," Liz said. Liz admired the way Bobby handled Sam's out-of-the-ordinary questions over the years. The questions started when Sam was about four. Her favorite question back then was asking how every animal had sex, very much to Liz's embarrassment and bewilderment. "Uncle Bobby, how do dolphins have sex? Uncle Bobby, how do turtles have sex?" and so on, were the usual type of questions she would ask the second that she saw him.

At first, Adam and Liz would look helpless when Sam would pose another "sex" question to Bobby. The adults could not figure out why Sam would only want Bobby to answer her, and why in the world this topic fascinated her. Then Adam began to egg Sam on by saying something like, "Wow, that's a good question, Sam! Bobby, how DO goldfish have sex? I have always wondered the same thing." Bobby would patiently start every answer with the very same beginning: "Once upon a time there was a boy turtle (or whatever creature Sam happened to be curious about at the time) who loved a girl turtle so much that they decided to get married. After they were married for awhile they realized that they had too much love left over, so they decided to have sex to get a baby turtle to give their extra love to, and then they all lived happily ever after."

Years later, when Sam was close to seven, she informed Liz, Adam and Bobby that she found out in school you didn't have to be married to have sex. She couldn't contain her excitement over this discovery. She couldn't wait to let Uncle Bobby know. Adam tried to seize the opportunity to belittle Bobby, but Liz shot him a piercing look that made him reconsider. Bobby, without delay, told Sam it was still a good idea to be married, or you could end up getting things that you didn't ask for. Bobby seemed to see the cogs turning in Sam's head as she asked, "The turtles would get a baby goldfish instead of a baby turtle?" Bobby said, "It could be worse - you could end up with a baby snake, or even a baby crocodile." Sam then declared that she wasn't going to ever have sex because she wanted neither a crocodile nor kids. She then innocently asked Bobby how she could get a golden retriever puppy because that was what she really wanted. At this point, the wide-eyed adults just looked at each other without saying another word…

Liz had full confidence that Bobby could handle such a mundane question as what happened to gum if you swallow it.

"Sam, can you bring me an ice cream also? I think we have a lot to celebrate," Liz said.

"I'll get you the chocolate covered bubble gum also!" Sam told her Mom enthusiastically.

"Could you make mine coconut instead?" Liz asked.

"I'll let you have a taste of mine if you want," Sam sweetly offered.

"Thanks honey!" Liz answered, hoping that Sam would later forget her offer.

"Miss Renay, what kind would you like?" Sam asked.

"I would like the chocolate covered strawberry."

"I think I will get that instead," Sam told them.

"Then you don't have to worry if you accidently swallow the gum!" Liz pointed out.

"Mom, you aren't fooling me, I know you would rather have some chocolate covered strawberry, than chocolate covered gum!"

"I guess I can't fool you…"

"Nope. Not like when I was little. Mom, remember how I would hand you my cone if it were going to drip and ask you to 'fix it'? You would eat half of it and hand it back. Boy, I was really dumb when I was little."

"Those were the good old days," Liz said, with a laugh.

"Now you have to work a lot harder to fool me!" Sam informed her Mom.

"That's the truth…I thought you were going to get us some ice cream," Liz pointed out.

"I'm just waiting for the money."

Liz handed Sam some money, and off she went.

Liz turned to Renay and said," I can't thank you enough for including her in your wedding. Do you realize for the first time EVER she didn't ask for her hair to be dyed?"

"I feel so bad for you when Sam is pestering you. I don't think Sam realizes what all you are going through with Adam and the Liz wanna-be. I meant to tell you Adam stopped by the other day and wanted to buy you a present. He wanted to get you shampoo. I hope you don't mind that I sent him down the street to the new florist instead."

"So, you are saying I should thank you for the beautiful bromeliad arrangement that he brought home?"

"Maybe..." Renay said, with a knowing smile.

"He is really trying to be nicer and more considerate. Last year for my birthday he bought me a steam mop because I commented that would be nice to have..."

"Is this what I have to look forward to once I'm married?" Renay wondered out loud.

"I hope not!" Liz said, with a laugh.

"I think you are being over analytical after what happened. I think you are constantly worried that you are missing some sign of trouble."

"You might be right. My first instinct when he brought the bromeliad home was that something was wrong. I started wondering why he was buying me flowers. Unfortunately, I was right."

"What???" Renay asked incredulously.

"My intuition told me to look at his cell phone, and sure enough she had called him that very morning."

"But he told you, right?"

"Not until he was completely backed into a corner with nowhere to go."

"I'm sorry, Liz."

"I'm trying to be patient."

"When will she realize that he is married? I'm telling you, she gives me the creeps!" Renay said, as she had an involuntary shudder.

"You aren't the only one who feels that way."

"When is Bobby going to give Sam the new hair extensions?" Renay asked, changing the subject as only women can.

"What extensions?" Liz asked.

"He bought Sam some hair extensions as a present. It isn't her birthday, is it?"

"No, that was three months ago. He always asks me before he buys her something expensive."

"He even had me put the clips in, even though I told him that Sam likes to sew them in herself. He said he wanted her to be able to wear them right away."

"How long ago was this?"

"I gave them to him two days ago."

"That isn't like Bobby to not tell me."

"Let's go ahead and get your hair shampooed. It looks fantastic by the way. No rats chewing on the ends…" Renay said, referencing Mrs. Piggy's rat-chewed hair.

"I can't believe you just said that!"

Liz sat down in the chair in front of the shampoo bowl. She put her head back in the basin and then suddenly jumped up and said, "I have to go! Tell Sam I will be back for her. I have to go home!"

Renay did not even have a chance to say a word. Liz was gone…

Chapter 31

Sam walked back into the hair salon carefully balancing the three ice cream containers. She handed Renay the container with the chocolate covered strawberry ice cream and a small plastic spoon.

"Your Mom had to run home, so I guess you are going to have to eat her ice cream also," Renay told her.

"Yuck, no way… She got coconut!.."

"And what is the matter with coconut?" Renay wondered.

"Come on, Renay! Look at those pieces of coconut. They look and taste like toenails clippings!.."

"Sam! Anyways, how do you know that?" Renay teased her.

"My Mom gets so mad every time I say that. Especially if we have company."

"I can understand that…"

"Why don't you eat it, Renay?"

"I can't. I don't have your metabolism. I guess we can put it in the freezer in the break room."

"Did she say when she was coming back?"

"She did say she would be back for you," Renay reassured Sam.

My Mom has been saying all week that she needs a haircut, so it's kinda weird that she left," Sam explained.

"I'm sure she wouldn't have left if she didn't have to. I'll get her scheduled right back in to cut her hair, don't worry."

"My Mom would NEVER leave ice cream or pie, trust me."

"What are you trying to say, Sam?"

"I think I need to go home right now." Sam said, unable to keep her voice from shaking.

"Do you want me to call your Dad?" Renay asked.

"No, he's out of town until tonight."

"If your Mom isn't back by the time I'm done with your hair, then we will call her and I can even take you home," Renay tried to reassure Sam.

Sam was staring at Liz's melting ice cream when she looked up and said, "Renay, I think we need to go right now."

"Okay, let's go then," Renay said, now wondering if the teen could be right. Renay grabbed her purse out of the bottom drawer of her station, and turned to Sam and said, "Let's go!" They hurriedly left the salon.

Sam looked relieved and told Renay, "I can drive your car, if you want, since you don't know the way to my house. It will be lot faster."

"Okay," Renay said, not knowing the teen still did not have a driver's license or even a learner's permit. Renay handed Sam her keys. Sam pushed the button on Renay's key fob twice and unlocked all the doors. They quickly got in the older white Altima and fastened their seatbelts. Sam started the car and they squealed out of the parking lot. The car bottomed out as Sam pulled out of the salon into the street.

"Oops!" was all Sam could say.

Sam accelerated through a yellow light, just as it turned red.

"It was yellow!" Sam declared.

Renay realized that she was getting nauseous, and they hadn't even driven a full block yet. Once again, the car slid as they made the next turn too quickly.

"How long have you had your license?" Renay finally inquired.

Sam didn't answer the hairdresser. Instead, she reached over and cranked up the volume on the Katy Perry song that was on the radio. She loudly started to sing along -- something about kissing a girl and liking it...

The next few blocks were driven without a single word being spoken. Sam had slowed down for the next few turns, but Renay remained nauseous. Renay started to wish she hadn't just cleaned her car out- the only thing she could find in case that she had to barf were some tall leather boots that she had paid way too much for. In addition, the watermelon air freshener that she had recently hung on the mirror didn't quite help her queasiness either.

"Our entrance is right ahead. Are you okay, Renay?"

"I think the ice cream didn't agree with me."

"My Mom tries to tell me that my driving makes her sick," Sam said, thinking that such thing was impossible.

"I can't imagine!" Renay answered, trying to convince the teen that actually she found that thought ludicrous. It wasn't that long ago that Renay herself had learned to drive. Sam's driving unquestionably reminded her how her own parents acted like they were having a heart attack when she was behind the wheel. She tried to convince herself that Sam was doing better now that she was getting used to her car.

Sam moved the car into the right lane without looking as they approached the guardhouse at the Preserve.

"Don't you need to slow down?" Renay yelled over the music.

"No, the gate opens when you live here. You should see how fast my Dad drives through here. My Mom drives slow and waves at the guards. They wave back, and that makes her happy. She is kinda weird that way."

Unfortunately, Sam was used to driving through that lane in her family's cars that were programmed to automatically open the gate - a detail she had evidently missed. As expected, the arm remained down as they crashed through it.

"Oops!" the teen said again.

Renay picked up her boot now thinking she was going to need it. Sam actually slowed down on the next turn.

"There's my house!" she shouted as they again bottomed out as they swung into the driveway.

"Uncle Bobby is here! Renay, stay here!"

Sam put the car into park before it stopped. The car's transmission made a sickening grinding sound. She left the car running and the door open as she ran full speed towards her backyard where the family's dogs were barking ferociously.

Renay sat stunned in the passenger seat and found herself unable to move. She wanted to get out, but her hands were shaking and her legs were way too wobbly. As she sat there, a brand new silver Maserati zoomed in the driveway and stopped. A woman jumped out of the car and ran to the side of the house. Renay remembered Liz introducing her as Natalie during a party that Liz had thrown. Not even two minutes later, a cherry-red Volkswagen bug convertible parked behind the Maserati. A woman with short, spiky, dark hair sprinted towards the backyard. Renay closed her eyes while she took a couple deep breaths to compose herself. When she did this, she thought she could hear a police siren. But then again, she couldn't be sure because her heart was pounding so loudly she could hear it in her own ears. She opened her eyes to see what looked like Liz racing around the corner of the house heading in the direction of Natalie and the spiky haired woman.

Renay could hear the police sirens now getting closer and louder. She hoped they wouldn't be too late.

Chapter 32

Bobby thought nothing could have been worse than just standing there in Liz's backyard and having to take a leak, but boy…had he been wrong. His bladder might be empty now, but he was still finding it difficult to stand still and wait for Mrs. Piggy to try and push him over the ravine. He wanted to do a multitude of other things which included: just leaving, checking his phone (that had inconveniently been vibrating like crazy in his shorts' front pocket under the cloak), get another drink or two, or just turn around and see where in the hell the swine was. But he knew better. The plan was in action and he couldn't just leave. It was his plan -- good, bad, or otherwise. He knew the multitude of phone messages that he was receiving had to be from Marilyn. He had already checked his phone when he went to the bathroom. Another drink would be a grand idea, but Mrs. Piggy would probably come just as he went inside. And no matter how bad he wanted to, he simply could not turn around. He needed to keep his back to her. He could pull this off, as long as he didn't prematurely turn around.

He had positioned himself very carefully. He made sure that he couldn't easily go over the rail into the ravine. Mrs. Piggy had assumed that Sam weighed about ninety pounds according to the information that Pamela had provided. Bobby weighed closer to one hundred ninety, but his figure was well disguised under the cloak. It would be no easy feat for a woman as short as Mrs. Piggy to push Bobby Bain, dressed up as Sam, into the ravine.

Mrs. Piggy was also counting on the element of surprise. Bobby just needed to stay focused and listen for any sound that indicated that she had arrived. He sure hoped that Fritz and Butter would give him some kind of warning – a bark, a growl, or even the thumping of their tails.

God, how he wished his phone would stop vibrating! It was very distracting. Marilyn was averaging a call every five minutes. He needed to be concentrating on listening for Mrs. Piggy's arrival. He surmised that Marilyn was more than just a little hot at being duped by him on Sam's fake Facebook page. Marilyn seemed to be the type of woman to hold a grudge. He broke out in a cold sweat upon thinking of the time that she mentioned the Portuguese Nut Cracker. He started to regret not including her on his plan also. He realized it was far better to have Marilyn as an ally than as an enemy.

Immediately after, he had the most disturbing thought –what if Mrs. Piggy didn't try to push him into the ravine? What if she had a different plan? Maybe she was going to shoot Sam and then dump her body over the railing… Why hadn't he thought about that? He had a Kevlar vest under the cloak, but he had no protection if she decided to cap him in the head! And then his thoughts changed again, why was he second-guessing himself now? He was so damn cocky before, thinking how brilliant his plan was. Now she would probably calmly walk up to him from behind while he was sweating his ass off and kill him mafia-execution-style. Then he would lie there in a pool of his own blood, piss and feces. She would return home and everyone would wonder who killed Bobby Bain and why in the world was he dressed up as Goldilocks or perhaps Little Green Riding Hood. That would certainly be how he would be immortalized – as the guy who thought it was a green hooded cloak, instead of red.

Finally, he started to calm down. Of course, she would just try to fling him over the side of the ravine – a gun would make too much noise in the suburbs. Plus, it could be traced back to her. Officer Becker already knew that she had a gun registered in her name.

He heard the dogs move. He could hear their dog tags slowly jingling as they lazily made their way toward the front of the house. Damn, that was where the dogs always waited for Liz, in the front of the house. Had he ever seen the dogs in the backyard? Not unless there was food or swimming involved. He would have no warning if Mrs. Piggy entered by the side. If he had told Liz about his plan, she would have pointed out that Butter and Fritz's weren't exactly sentry dogs. They had naps to take and sunbathing to do.

Realizing the dogs were no longer in the backyard made him feel very vulnerable. He started to doubt if Liz would ever forgive him. She had forgiven him for several stupid stunts over the years. Only once before did he ever think she wouldn't ever forgive him. That was the night before her wedding – the night he stupidly crossed the line and told Liz how he felt about her and that idiot, Adam.

He thought he'd just heard the gate open. He was tempted to turn, but he didn't. He positioned himself like he had learned to in the one lousy year that he played football in junior high. He would be impossible to knock off balance.

Just when he was beginning to think he had imagined the noise he felt the tremendous shove. He quickly moved to the right and spun around. Mrs. Piggy crashed into the short rod iron fence in front of him. She was immediately back on her feet and trying to push him over the fence. This time they locked eyes.

"You're a dude!!!" Mrs. Piggy exclaimed.

Bobby reached under the cloak for his holster. He brought the gun out and leveled the gun at her chest and said, "I believe you are trespassing…"

For a brief second, Bobby thought of shoving her fat ass into the ravine. But he quickly came to his senses, while thinking about prison cuisine and communal showers!

"Get your hands over your head, you, PIG!" Bobby ordered.

Mrs. Piggy did as commanded. It looked like a scene you would see on a TV cop show.

Convinced that she was unarmed, Bobby told her to stand in front of him with her hands holding both sides of the rail. Bobby reached in his other pocket for the handcuffs. He hoped they were strong. He had been in a hurry to get them and didn't have time to buy them at the military surplus store all the way across town. Instead, he bought them at the adult sex-toy shop right off of the interstate. He assumed they would be sturdy enough. However, Bobby didn't really have any experience with handcuffs, one-way or the other.

He went to move towards Mrs. Piggy to cuff her, but soon found he couldn't move. The damn hair extensions had tangled around one of the iron tiki torches that lined the patio. Not accustomed to having long blonde hair, Bobby hadn't realized that when he jumped to the side, his hair would become a huge jumbled mess that would momentarily immobilize him. Mrs. Piggy seized the moment and pulled a small pink gun out of her bra.

"You didn't think of looking there did you? Drop your gun, Rapunzel!" the swine exclaimed.

Bobby reluctantly let his gun drop to the ground.

"Now, give me your handcuffs."

Bobby was much more reluctant to give those up. No one was going to find Bobby Bain with hands cuffed behind his back, with his hair stuck to a tiki torch and wearing women's clothes. He ran as fast as he could into the house. Half of his hair was left behind. Mrs. Piggy was in hot pursuit. Butter and Fritz had heard the ruckus and ran into the house also. They didn't want to miss anything that might be fun.

Chapter 33

Bobby sprinted faster than he ever remembered, running toward the unlocked door of Liz's house. He was trying to beat Mrs. Piggy to the house so he could shut the door and lock it behind him, but she was right on his heels. As soon as he made it through the door, he decided to take cover behind Liz's enormous kitchen island. Unfortunately, right before he made it behind the island, he tripped over the green velvet cloak that he was wearing. His head hit the travertine marble floor with a loud thunk and Bobby went limp. He was out cold.

Mrs. Piggy was concerned that he might be setting another trap. She cautiously walked up to the seemingly unconscious body and gave him a little prod with her foot. No response. It was then that she decided there was only one truly foolproof way to make sure he wasn't playing possum. Mrs. Piggy then kicked him really hard -- in the nuts. There was still no reaction. She was now absolutely convinced that he was out for the count. No man could ever be that good of an actor.

She studied his face carefully and realized it was Dr. Bobby Bain, Liz's close friend. She vividly recalled that Adam didn't care much for Liz's long-time partner and friend. After her brief encounter with Dr. Bain this afternoon, she decided she wasn't that fond of him either.

She calmly walked over to the kitchen sink. She used one of the dishtowels to begin removing her fingerprints from Bobby's gun. At the same time, she kept her eye on Bobby sprawled out on the floor, motionless. Disposing of Bobby was going to be easier than she had thought.

Meanwhile, Butter didn't know what to make of Bobby lying on the floor. Usually, Bobby was sneaking him morsels of food. Butter was probably thinking that Bobby was too far away from the refrigerator to be doing him or Fritz any good. Butter started to lick at Bobby's face, and then began to paw and nudge at him. Mrs. Piggy didn't care for this. She picked up a wet kitchen sponge from the sink and threw it at the massive dog. The wet sponge hit the dog squarely on the shoulder. Butter's attention was now diverted to a potential game of fetch with Mrs. Piggy. The dog picked up the dripping sponge in his enormous mouth and came running toward her, at full speed.

"Shoo! Shoo! Go away!!! I mean it, I freaking hate dogs!!!" Mrs. Piggy screamed as she danced and darted around trying to get out of the path of the playful one hundred plus pound retriever.

It was too late, because Butter zeroed in on the dishtowel that Mrs. Piggy was wiping the pistol down with. He lunged for the towel believing Mrs. Piggy now wanted to play a game of tug-of-war, instead of fetch.

Since Butter showed up at the Schaeffer's house for the first time, Adam had little use for the dog except to torment him. Every evening when Adam pulled his car in the garage, he would find Butter waiting for him with an old ripped up towel waiting to play. Adam and Butter would play a few rounds of tug-of-war. Adam would start to play dirty and flick the poor dog in the nose trying to get him to relinquish his death grip on the towel. Butter would let go for a second, but his next grip was always right where Adam was holding the towel. The pain would force Adam to let go, and Butter would run out in the yard with the towel, victorious until the next evening. The end was always the same - Adam would retreat into the house with his hands and suit sleeve completely covered in dog slobber, bitching about what a stupid and useless dog Butter was.

What Mrs. Piggy did not know was that Butter was going to win this game at any cost. Fritz, not wanting to be left out of the fun, started to growl and bite at Mrs. Piggy's ankles, flanking her from the right and then the left. Fritz was wagging his stubby tail the whole time. Butter and the pig continued to fight over the towel, until Butter seized an opportunity and ripped the dish towel-wrapped-gun from Mrs. Piggy's hands. Butter ran out the open door into the yard. He taunted her with his prize by laying it down in the yard in front of him. He bowed down with his butt high in the air, tail wagging back and forth as if to say, "Come take it, I dare you."

Meanwhile, Bobby started to moan. Mrs. Piggy decided he was easier to deal with unconscious, so she picked up the closest thing at hand, a flour canister from the kitchen counter, to bust over Bobby's head. Fritz was not making it easy for Mrs. Piggy to accomplish that. He was gnawing on her ankles like they were a juicy turkey leg. He had never really played this game with a human before, only with Butter, but it was always fun.

"Go away, you little bastard!" Mrs. Piggy yelled at the persistent terrier. He let up for a second, and Mrs. Piggy kicked him for all she was worth. He yelped and retreated.

"Don't you kick MY dog!" Sam yelled as she suddenly ran into the kitchen.

By now, Bobby had already risen to his knees and was trying to use the island to pull himself up with one hand, while grabbing his aching crotch with the other. Mrs. Piggy then went ahead and raised the canister above her head to finish Bobby off. Liz had fallen in love with the simple Country French ribbed glass canisters with their silver lids while on a vacation in France. This one was labeled "Farine", which was flour in French. Sam knew how mad Liz was going to be that this weird woman was trying to kill someone in her kitchen, and that she would be really mad if the canister got broken.

"Don't you hurt that lady!" Sam said, not recognizing that the woozy "woman" was her Uncle Bobby, dressed as her.

"It's you that I'm going to hurt, you little brat!" Mrs. Piggy shrieked. Mrs. Piggy put the canister down for a second and then reached between her droopy breasts, and retrieved her pink revolver. She aimed it at Sam's head.

Fearlessly, Sam picked up the only thing she could find – a large loaf of French bread, and hurled it at Mrs. Piggy. Mrs. Piggy realized it was only a loaf of bread and kept her steady aim on the teen. The bread bounced off of Mrs. Piggy's flabby left arm and knocked over a bottle of extra virgin olive oil, where it shattered on the floor.

"Guess you won't be making it to your Dad's and my wedding, will ya?!" Mrs. Piggy taunted Sam.

"You are CRAZY! My Dad would NEVER marry you!" Sam shouted back defiantly.

Mrs. Piggy slapped Bobby's hand off the island and then kicked Bobby squarely in the middle of the back, knocking him back to the floor. She momentarily put the pink revolver on the island and once again raised Liz's heavy glass canister over her head, to ensure Bobby was no longer in the picture.

Suddenly, there was a huge explosion. The flour container shattered into thousands of pieces and a giant cloud of fine white dust lingered above the pig. If no one knew Mrs. Piggy personally, they would have said that she looked almost angelic standing there, surrounded by a cloud of fine white powder. Except that angels don't have urine streaming down their legs, forming a large puddle underneath them. The explosion had been a gunshot and it was quickly followed by another one. The pink revolver spun right off of the granite island. It landed with a thud in the far corner of the kitchen. Everyone looked in the direction where the shots had just come from. They were stunned to see Natalie holding the gun. When she realized they were all looking at her, she calmly blew on the end of her Colt .45 Commander, like a scene from a spaghetti Western, and without more ado tucked it back into her oversized Prada tote. Now, everyone in the room really knew the reason that Natalie always carried such a large handbag.

Bobby had somehow managed to pull himself up and was standing behind Mrs. Piggy with a fry pan poised above her head. Bobby wasn't sure whether he was standing due to his sheer determination, or just trying to avoid another kick to his groin. As soon as Mrs. Piggy started to make a break for it, he promptly stopped her with a fry pan to the back of her head.

"Damn!!!" Sam said out loud.

"Samantha! Stop your cursing!" Liz said, as she rushed into the kitchen.

"Mom! Where have you been?" Sam said, as she ran to her Mom to embrace her.

Marilyn was now in the kitchen also. She walked over with a grin on her face, and picked up the fry pan and hit Mrs. Piggy one more time, squarely in the face as the pig was struggling to get up. Marilyn ended up chipping a couple of Mrs. Piggy's front teeth.

"I've always wanted to do something like that!" Marilyn excitedly announced to the stunned group.

As Mrs. Piggy was lying on the floor, Fritz walked over and lifted his leg on her. Marilyn helped unclip the hair extensions out of Bobby's hair. Sam was very confused now that she realized the "woman" was actually her Uncle Bobby. Sam thought to herself that this for sure explained why Uncle Bobby never married! Marilyn then wrapped the blond extensions in the now tattered and soiled green cloak. She walked out the open door to the terrace, picked up the remaining extensions, and threw everything over the railing into the rushing Guadalupe River below. They would never be seen again, much to Bobby's relief. She also brought back the handcuffs that she found outside. Bobby took them from Marilyn and struggled with trying to get them on Mrs. Piggy's wrists.

"Here, let me help you. There is a little trick to that," Marilyn advised him.

Bobby just looked at her funny.

"It's not what you think! I saw it on a cop show on television," Marilyn said, unsuccessfully trying to convince Bobby.

"No one move!" Officer Becker yelled as he entered the room with another officer.

"Everything is okay, Hans. She is over here and we have her handcuffed," Bobby told him.

"What is that?" Officer Becker asked pointing to the goo from the floor that Mrs. Piggy was now lying in as he approached her.

"Flour, extra virgin olive oil, bread, urine and blood, I believe," Natalie said analyzing the mess.

"Great..." Officer Becker said imagining the smell that this would make in the police car.

"Do you have to put her in your car like that? Who cleans your police car when someone pees or vomits in it anyway?" Sam asked as only a teenager would or could.

"I guess we could rinse her out in the yard. Is that okay Dr. Schaeffer?" Hans asked recalling how he could still smell vomit in his squad car from the piss poor cleaning job done two weeks earlier. Normally, the newest officers were on DUI duty. Hans had stopped a kid for an expired license tag and noticed the open fifth of whiskey in the front seat beside him. He had no choice, but to give him a Breathalyzer test. When he failed, he arrested him for a DUI. The scared kid upchucked immediately when Hans put the cruiser into drive to take him to the station, and Hans had smelled the foul odor ever since.

"Why don't you use the master bath shower? I think you will need hot water to dissolve the oil and it's large enough that the officers can stand in there with her." Liz said rationally.

"Are you sure? We can transport her just like she is," Hans said wondering how Liz could remain so calm and rational. Then, he remembered she was a doctor and also had a lot of practice managing chaos simply by being married to her husband.

"No, it's fine. Do what you need to do." Liz said reassuring Hans.

"What the hell is going on here?" Adam said as he stormed into the room.

"Dad! I thought you were coming back tonight after I was asleep!" Sam said.

"I caught an earlier flight," Adam said, looking like he wished he wouldn't have changed his plans.

Adam went pale when Officer Becker pulled Mrs. Piggy to her feet.

"Adam!" Mrs. Piggy exclaimed in a tone that implied she thought he was there to rescue her.

All eyes were turned towards Adam. If it were possible, Adam got even paler. His face dropped, and he looked completely uncomfortable in his own skin. Liz looked over at him and realized she had never seen that side of him before. He usually seemed so confident and strong, but now he no longer had any resemblance to such an image.

"What is she doing here?" Adam meekly asked.

Mrs. Piggy looked astonished that he would talk about her in that manner. She thought to herself it was as if he didn't care.

"She was here to kill YOUR daughter, and I suppose anyone else who got in her way." Bobby tersely answered.

"Oh…" was all that Adam could say.

"Yes, Liz and Sam are both PHYSICALLY unharmed," Bobby sarcastically said realizing that Adam hadn't even approached either one, nor asked them if they were okay. Bobby made sure that he emphasized "physically" because he could only imagine what the TRUE damage was.

Officer Becker could be heard reading Mrs. Piggy her Miranda rights. Then, he turned Mrs. Piggy over to two female officers that had arrived. The two officers didn't look very sympathetic to Mrs. Piggy's predicament.

Bobby grabbed the bottle of shampoo from the kitchen desk that Liz had been holding for Officer Becker to pick up as evidence. He removed the post-it note that Liz had scribbled "Officer Becker" on, dropped the note on the floor, and handed it to the unsuspecting female officers.

Liz found herself instinctively wanting to speak up, but ended up saying absolutely nothing.

Bobby followed Liz into the laundry room, and she gave him some old towels. He walked back into the kitchen and handed the towels to Hans himself, so that Liz wouldn't have to see Mrs. Piggy again. This whole time Adam remained frozen in the very same spot.

Suddenly, Sam said to everyone, "Where's Renay?"

"Oh no!" Liz said losing her composure at the thought that maybe Mrs. Piggy could have hurt Renay.

"I'm right here! I was waiting outside just like Sam told me to. Just when I decided I was going in, the police arrived and told me to stay in the car. Officer Becker just told me I could come in. Is everyone okay?"

"Everyone except his fiancée!" Bobby said while glaring at Adam.

"Fiancée?!?" Renay gasped.

"Well... That's what the psycho bitch thought she was. She idiotically thought Sam was the reason why Adam wouldn't leave Liz, and she decided to come here to kill her!" Marilyn said, summing up the hellacious last hour.

"How did you all know to get here?" Renay asked wondering how in the world so many people and the police could all possibly know to show up at just the right time and place. She had no sooner asked this question when she realized that this probably had something to do with Bobby wanting the blond hair extensions.

"I called Natalie and Officer Becker on my way over," Liz explained.

"But you left before us. How is it that we beat you here?!" Renay said, trying to logistically figure that out.

"Mom won't ever talk on her phone and drive. I bet she pulled over to call them. Plus, we took the shortcut! Remember?" Sam proudly announced.

"When I got to our subdivision, the police were everywhere. They said some lunatic driver had just crashed through the resident's gate. The driver didn't even slow down. Apparently, they just plowed through the gate!" Liz started to explain.

"Oops," Sam said quietly.

Liz didn't hear Sam, and continued, "It took forever to get through the other gate. They were not letting anyone in the subdivision. Marilyn was right behind me. Thank goodness, Marilyn knew one of the police officers and he let us go right through."

Marilyn didn't let on how she knew the police officer or in what capacity. She especially didn't volunteer that she already knew Bobby and Mrs. Piggy were at Liz's.

The reality of the situation started to hit Renay and she began to tear up. She thought of her smashed up white Altima that she had always taken such good care of. She had never missed an oil change. Not that it mattered one bit now. She knew she would get a bill for the smashed up gate and maybe even a bill for the police being dispatched. With all of these unforeseen expenses, she could not help but to see her dream wedding going up in smoke.

"Mom, I'm the one who smashed through the gate!" Sam confessed when she saw Renay crying quietly.

"But you don't drive!" Liz said.

"I actually did pretty good until I forgot that Renay's car didn't have a sensor for the gate. Didn't I, Renay?" Sam said, fishing for compliments on her driving prowess.

Renay didn't have to answer because Officer Becker walked back in and asked Renay if she wanted assistance getting her car towed to the body shop.

"Oops!" Sam said again. Not only did her eyes get wider, but her skin began to pale, just like Adam's.

"Renay, Adam and I will make this right. You have my word. We will get you a rental car until we can get this straightened out. Won't we, Adam?" Liz said.

Adam didn't answer. He was still pondering how a little inappropriate attention like texts, phone calls and secret meetings from someone he wasn't married to ended up endangering his wife, daughter, his family's friends, and then embarrassing himself in front of the whole community. He should have listened to Liz when she told him simply--that it wasn't an appropriate relationship if he had to hide it. He had foolishly thought what Liz didn't know wouldn't hurt her. Mrs. Piggy saw his weakness and exploited it for the whole world to see.

He looked over at Officer Becker who had donned gloves to put the pink pistol in a sealed bag reserved for evidence. Adam was starting to shake, thinking of the irony of the color of the gun. It was the same color as the Barbie Corvette that he had surprised Sam with when she was little. How she loved that car! He had to really watch her because she tried driving it to the mall one time. Now, the color would probably invoke memories of this idiotic woman trying to kill her, rather than all of the fun she had as a child. He wondered why he was so self-destructive.

Everyone stopped talking when they heard the door opening from the master bedroom. Mrs. Piggy came out with her head down like a common criminal and a towel wrapped like a turban on her head. Her hands were handcuffed behind her. One of the female cops was in front of her and the other one was behind her. They all stopped in front of Officer Becker. He removed the towel. Mrs. Piggy was completely bald—like a billiard ball!

"What the fuck?" Sam said first.

"Samantha! I have had it with your language today," Liz said like it was an ordinary day, instead of the one that they had just all endured.

"Sorry Liz, but I'm with Sam on this one. What the fuck?" Marilyn said.

"Was she wearing a wig before?" Natalie asked.

"I think there was something in that shampoo," the younger of the two female cops said.

"I want to make damn sure I don't use that brand!" Natalie added.

"It's what we sell at work. I recognize the bottle," Renay said looking worried all over again.

"Oh darn! I bet I grabbed the wrong bottle. Liz, where did you have that bottle of tainted shampoo that Mrs. Piggy left at the house?" Bobby asked feigning innocence.

"It was in the kitchen. It was labeled 'for Officer Becker'," Liz replied.

"My mistake. Yep, here is the post-it note on the floor with Officer Becker's name on it. It's only hair… It will grow back before you know it. In two or three years, no one will ever know that you were ever as bald as a baby's ass," Bobby said unsympathetically.

"I'll take it from here," Officer Becker told the two officers while trying to maintain his professional composure. He turned Mrs. Piggy in the direction of the door.

"Hold up just a minute!" the previously silent and shocked Liz said.

Mrs. Piggy lowered her head even further as if trying to make herself invisible to Liz and the police. Officer Becker held Mrs. Piggy's arm so she could go no further and turned her towards Liz.

"I just wanted to make sure that you understand one thing before they lock you away, and that is you are NEVER going to have my family. You had a great family of your own and you foolishly discarded it for a man who could care less about you. Now, you have nothing for your efforts but a bald head, and hopefully, some jail time. Anyway, you picked the wrong member of the family to try and latch onto. He's not the one responsible for all the things that that you wanted. That would have been me and you ARE NOT MY TYPE!" Liz said and turned and walked away towards Sam and her friends.

"Mom, who is going to clean up this mess?" Sam asked, breaking the deadly silence.

"Your father," Liz said, making everyone wonder if she was referring to the disaster in the kitchen or the disaster he had created for his family.

Chapter 34

Liz was such a light sleeper that she was almost always the first one to wake up in her household. Prior to the Mrs. Piggy situation, Liz would usually wake up thinking about simple, mundane things -- like what kind of breakfast tacos to make her family. If she lingered in bed, it was just long enough to plan her day. Sadly, because of all the stress and trouble she had been through, breakfast had been the last thing on Liz's mind lately. However, this morning knowing that Mrs. Piggy had been arrested last night and her family was safe for a change, she could allow herself the luxury of lingering in bed.

Adam had his back to Liz. This seemed to be somehow prophetic and par for the course. Narcissistic Adam seemed to have turned his back on Liz (and their marriage) both literally and figuratively throughout this entire mess.

Adam, much to Liz's chagrin, possessed the uncanny ability to fall asleep at the drop of a hat -- as if he didn't have a care in the world -- and stay asleep forever. He didn't know the meaning of the word "insomnia." Sam took after her dad. She seemed to have inherited this particular gene from Adam. Liz certainly contributed to her overall genetic engineering, but this obviously dominant trait was an unexpected result.

Liz, unfortunately, was an entirely different story. Lately, she tossed and turned the entire night worrying about this, that, and the other -- usually drifting off about an hour before the God-forsaken alarm clock went off. This dichotomy in sleeping habits left the normally calm, rational, and even-tempered Liz pissed off beyond all belief. In addition, Adam had the obnoxious and totally disrespectful habit of falling asleep just as Liz would try engaging him in meaningful and important spousal bedtime conversation -- as evidenced by his loud roof-rattling snoring. Previously, Liz might have just accepted this. But not now, the Mrs. Piggy incident had forever changed Liz. Before, if she were upset about something, she would quietly cry herself to sleep, being careful to not disturb Adam. But now, she wanted revenge. She had mastered the art of wiggling around in the bed just enough to keep Adam from falling into a deep restful sleep pattern -- but not enough to actually wake him. She had figured that if she was going to lose sleep, then so should the people who were responsible for this whole hopeless mess. If Liz could have figured out a way to keep Mrs. Piggy from falling asleep, she would definitely considered that, too.

When Liz finally got out of bed, she was shocked to see that it was already 9:32. She felt very different this morning. She walked into the bathroom and decided to take a look. She took a long look in the mirror. It was not her imagination-- she did look different. The anxious look was gone, and so were the dark circles under her eyes. They had been there for so long that Liz was beginning to worry that they were there to stay. She wouldn't miss them... not one bit.

She thought about how much her life had changed in the last few months. She was not just thinking about the lack of sleep. How many hours had she worried? How many times had she cried? How many times did someone point out to her that she had one brown shoe on, and a black shoe on the other foot? It was embarrassing. She never knew if she should just tell them that she was under tremendous stress, or just let them think she was nuts. Of course, now it looked as if this was going to be all over the news, so the reason for her stress would no longer be a secret. Hopefully, the hoopla would die down quickly.

She couldn't wait to get into her shower. It had been a long time since she had taken a long, hot leisurely shower. She should probably be grossed out that the police rinsed Mrs. Piggy off in this very same shower, but for some reason she could care less. She was grateful that they had cleaned up the clumps of Mrs. Piggy's "Liz-colored hair" from her shower floor. The only reminder of anything happening the night before was the bottle of the tainted shampoo that the police left behind.

She still couldn't believe that she never said a word when Bobby handed the officer the bottle of shampoo that Liz knew contained hair remover. That little voice inside of her that previously had always told her to do the right thing became eerily quiet last night.

She wondered if she should make an appointment with Mr. Miller to ask him why she didn't say anything. Was there a good reason? She would leave it to Mr. Miller to figure out why, and she vowed she would never worry about it again.

She was aware that Bobby knew exactly what he was doing when he handed the police the bottle of hair remover that Mrs. Piggy had sent. She also knew Bobby had zero remorse that Mrs. Piggy was bald. She could hear him saying something like: "that swine gave up that right when she decided to kill Sam." Of course, Bobby was absolutely right. The more Liz thought about it, Mrs. Piggy gave up her rights when she went after her husband. Liz started to imagine herself jumping on Mrs. Piggy's back when she would come over to stalk Adam. Liz could also see herself with horse clippers in her hand, clipping a reverse Mohawk into Mrs. Piggy's rat chewed hair.

Liz could not imagine what kind of person would walk away from their husband, break up her marriage, and then try to destroy another family in the process. Liz just knew she was glad that she had no doubt that she could NEVER be that kind of person.

Suddenly, Adam walked past Liz in the bathroom. Without a word, he smacked her on her rear. Liz decided to keep quiet, but made a mental note to mention that to Mr. Miller when she saw him next. She knew that Mr. Miller's effective communication session was completely lost on Adam. It wouldn't be the first session where Adam would need a "do over".

Liz was actually shocked that Adam was even up while she was still there. Liz was almost always the first person up in the household. Adam had really dark circles under his eyes and his hair was matted. This immediately prompted Liz to ask him, "Did you sleep okay last night?"

"No, I listened to your snoring ALL NIGHT!" Adam said, somehow ignoring the fact that his creepy ex-employee entered their house last night to kill their daughter and anyone else who got in her way, and the police hauled her away in handcuffs.

Liz didn't really see a reason to apologize for finally sleeping through the night after three months of being on edge. So, she simply didn't.

"The police want me to come by today to make a formal statement," Liz told him.

"Have fun," was all Adam could say.

The old Liz would have started to cry. She would have thought Adam didn't really mean that. She would have told him again, and he would have reluctantly gone. He would have made her drive. He would have been on his phone the whole time. Now, Liz is starting to have an epiphany—she has been carrying this family like a piano on her back. She then decided things were going to be very different when she returned home today. She shouldn't have to get all her emotional support from her friends anymore.

"Bobby is going to pick me up in a bit and take me to the police station so we can make our statements. Don't use the shampoo on the shower floor. I'll give you a call when I am done," Liz told Adam.

Adam mumbled something incoherent about her calling him later when she was ready for some of the "good stuff." This was his customary manner in which he would refer to sex. Sex has forever been Adam's favorite topic to talk about. She realized having his ex-paramour try to kill his daughter the day before would not change a thing.

Liz heard Butter and Fritz starting to bark. For a moment, she became anxious. But then she remembered that Mrs. Piggy was behind bars and that she could relax. She could hear Bobby talking to them now. Butter readily answered with a very enthusiastic bark. Liz knew that particular bark and knew that food was most definitely involved. Fritz was usually the more talkative of the two, unless there was chow involved and then Butter's shyness disappeared.

"Bobby Bain, what are you feeding my dogs?" Liz yelled out the breakfast room door.

"How did you know?" Bobby replied.

"Why do you continue to think that you can hide anything from me?" Liz marveled.

"That's a damn good question, Liz!"

"So…what are you feeding my soon-to-be overweight dogs?"

"I thought they might enjoy some barbacoa tacos. Come on Liz, it's their reward for last night" he explained.

"Remind me not to kiss them today," Liz stated emphatically. While Liz loved Mexican food to the point that she could eat it for three meals a day, seven days a week, she did draw the line at eating barbacoa (beef cheeks), lengua (tongue), tripas (pork tripe) or menudo (beef tripe stew). It was a waste of anyone's time to tell her how tasty these dishes are. Her mind was made up.

"They screwed up the order in the drive thru. Those bastards! I think they gave you lengua."

"Do you really think today is a good day to screw with me, Bain?"

"Umm… I guess not."

"I need to bring Fritz's rabies vaccination records with us to the station."

"Why?" Bobby asked.

"As you know Fritz peed all over Mrs. Piggy. I wonder how a little guy like him can hold so much pee! Well, before that, she reported that he was gnawing on her ankle like it was a juicy bone. They want to make sure he has his shots," Liz informed him.

"If I would have known that I would have gotten him another taco, or maybe a bowl of menudo," Bobby said, unable to resist teasing Liz one more time.

"The police ran tests on the chocolate cupcakes that Marilyn found in the backyard on the patio table."

"And?"

"Drug-laced!"

"I'm not surprised. Mrs. Piggy was bound and determined to get rid of Sam one-way or the other, wasn't she? Thank goodness, she is locked up and can't hurt either one of you."

Right about that time, Bobby and Liz heard Adam carrying on in the bathroom. "Liiizzz!!!!" Adam yelled.

Liz ran into the bedroom. Bobby followed to see what all the commotion was about.

Adam was now standing there, in the bedroom, dripping water everywhere. He was holding a towel around his torso, and his hair looked like a dog with a bad case of mange. Only a few, sparse clumps of his normally coiffed hair remained. It was obvious Adam had once again tuned out Liz at a most inopportune time and used the tainted shampoo she had just warned him about.

"Why didn't you tell me? You did this on purpose!" Adam said, not taking any responsibility.

"Adam, there is a word for men who act like you. It's called ALONE! I think if I were you I would remember that…"

Bobby had already backed out of the bedroom. He didn't want to make the situation any worse by laughing in Adam's face. Liz joined Bobby in the hall.

"Does this mean we will be having a Man Haters Club meeting later today?" Bobby asked.

"Huh? Why would you say that?" Liz asked.

"You and Natalie originally said the club meets whenever a man irritates us. Well, I don't know about you, but Adam just irritated the hell outta me!" Bobby said, unable to keep a straight face.

Aknowledgements

Like many people, I always wanted to write a book, but I never could think of anything to write about. Most authors want to write a great literary work that will stand the test of time and while that would have been wonderful, it wasn't my motivation. I only wanted one thing and that was to make you laugh out loud. Enough that you would be embarrassed if someone was sitting next to you or especially if you were alone at home. I wanted you to remember silly things from the book that would crack you up later when you thought about it. I truly want to thank everyone who helped me achieve the dream of being an author. So, thank you to everyone who encouraged, discouraged, asked to be a character in the book, gave me feedback and caught all of my horrible grammatical mistakes because all of those things made it better.

A HUGE THANKS to the team at Next Big Step Publishing Company.

Martha Singleton, my editor – There is no one I would rather work with on this project. You are the whole enchilada!

Greg Singleton whose business and legal advice has been invaluable. I believe this makes you the sour cream and the guacamole!

Looking forward to more projects!

To Rick Barganier – Thank you for starting this project with me and being my lifelong friend and irritant. Marilyn and Bobby wouldn't exist without you.

To Cody Vance for capturing it all in one illustration – the absurdness and fun of this book! I am so grateful that you drew the cover for me. You made the project real with that one simple gesture.

To Chaz and Suzie Reilly – Thanks for doing the hard job of the first "edit" and "critique" of the book. Glad you two paid more attention to grammar in school than I did!

Last, but not least, my family:

To my mom, Jan Leader for discouraging me in the most hilarious ways that I morphed into encouragement. For the record, my mother did not teach nor condone the cussing, sex or drinking in this book. I love you!♥

To Alex, my daughter – You are my world! ♥

To Dave, my darling husband – thanks for ALWAYS making my dreams come true and making them even BIGGER than I dare. ♥♥

About the author

Lisa Leader always knew that she would become a writer someday, when the timing was right.

When an elementary school teacher first posed the question of what she wanted to be when she grew up, Lisa replied that she was going to be a doctor, a writer, a teacher, and a horse trainer.

The teacher advised her that women couldn't be doctors, but she could work for one – and that a person could only have one job.

Today, Lisa is a successful eye doctor, and while she does not train horses, she enjoys riding her two horses, and writing as time permits. She is currently working on her second novel in the Bobby Bain series.

She is most proud of being a mother to her daughter Alexandra, who followed her into the health care profession. Lisa lives on the outskirts of San Antonio with her husband David, and her dogs, horses, and perhaps a cat (or twenty).

What's next for Bobby Bain ?

"They say a way to a man's heart is through his stomach. I'm going to weave a bowl out of bacon. I'm going to fill it with farm fresh scrambled eggs. I'm going to make him a buttermilk biscuit and have fresh squeezed orange juice for him," Marilyn announced.

"Wow! That sounds delicious. The Donut Ho has been advertising something just like it. You will have to tell me how you weave that bacon into a basket, because my family would love that," Liz remarked. The Donut Ho was a New Braunfels institution. Texas is known for hellacious thunderstorms with huge raindrops and gusting winds. One of these winds took the "le" off of the "Hole" part of the sign, so the "Donut Hole" became the "Donut Ho." The donut shop's popularity surged immediately. The owners printed up some cute t-shirts with the "le" hanging off the sign and the rest was history.

"Crap!"

"What? Oh, he can't have the biscuit on his new diet."

"No, that's not it. Do you think Bobby knows the Ho is making those? I didn't think it was common knowledge."

"You can still make it!" Liz encouraged Marilyn.

"I wasn't going to really make it, I was just going to buy it at the Ho and put it on my own plates. I was going to save time that way because it takes me a little longer than it used to to look fabulous," Marilyn explained.

"I could be wrong, but I think Bobby would value honesty in a future partner."

"Really? I was thinking bacon and a really nice push-up bra."